WHAT NOW

JAMEY MOODY

What Now

Edited: Kat Jackson

If you'd like to stay updated on future releases, you can visit my website or sign up for my mailing list here: www.jameymoodyauthor.com.

I'd love to hear from you! Email me at jameymoodyauthor@gmail.com.

As an independent publisher, reviews are greatly appreciated.

❀ Created with Vellum

CONTENTS

Also by Jamey Moody   v

Chapter 1   1
Chapter 2   10
Chapter 3   19
Chapter 4   28
Chapter 5   37
Chapter 6   47
Chapter 7   57
Chapter 8   68
Chapter 9   78
Chapter 10   86
Chapter 11   94
Chapter 12   103
Chapter 13   112
Chapter 14   122
Chapter 15   130
Chapter 16   138
Chapter 17   148
Chapter 18   156
Chapter 19   164
Chapter 20   173
Chapter 21   182
Chapter 22   191
Chapter 23   198
Chapter 24   206
Chapter 25   216
Chapter 26   224
Chapter 27   232
Chapter 28   240
Chapter 29   248
Chapter 30   256

Chapter 31   266
Chapter 32   276
Chapter 33   284
Chapter 34   294
Chapter 35   300

Fifteen Years Later   307
About the Author   311
Also by Jamey Moody   313
The Woman at the Top of the Stairs   315
Chapter 1   321

ALSO BY JAMEY MOODY

Live This Love

The Your Way Series:

* Finding Home

*Finding Family

*Finding Forever

The Lovers Landing Series

*Where Secrets Are Safe

*No More Secrets

*And The Truth Is ...

*Instead Of Happy

*It Takes A Miracle

One Little Yes

The Great Christmas Tree Mystery

Who I Believe

The Woman at the Top of the Stairs

The Woman Who Climbed A Mountain

The Woman I Found In Me

With One Look

*available as an audiobook

"**M**an, I wish I had a cigarette," Lissa muttered as she got out of her car and walked across the street. *Where did that come from*, she wondered. She walked into the bank trying to figure out why, all of a sudden, she wanted a cigarette. It had been over twenty-five years since she'd lit her last smoke.

She smiled to herself as the reason why became clear in her mind.

"Can I help you?"

Lissa had stopped in front of a woman's desk that was in an open area of the lobby. The sign in front of her simply read Accounts. "I hope so," Lissa replied with a pleasant smile. She looked down at the nameplate on the woman's desk. "Maise, I need to close an account and open a new account."

The woman returned her smile and looked over her shoulder at the offices that formed an L-shape in her area. Lissa figured Maise was the receptionist/assistant/traffic director for this part of the bank.

There were only two main sections of the bank and they

were separated by the counter where tellers were waiting on customers. In a small town, a bank this size offered customer assistance on one side and the other side usually housed the executives that oversaw operations. It had been so long since Lissa had actually come inside the bank that she began to think she was on the wrong side.

"If you'll have a seat." Maise indicated the couch and chairs immediately behind her which were arranged into a makeshift waiting area. "All our account managers are helping customers at the moment. I'll see if I can find someone else to help you."

"Thanks," Lissa said with another smile. She sat down on the end of the couch and let her gaze wander through the offices. The front wall of each office was glass, so anyone in the bank could see what was happening. Each occupant, whether they were an account specialist or something else, did indeed have a customer sitting across the desk from them.

She sat back and let out a deep breath. It wasn't like she was in a hurry. Her thoughts went back to a few minutes ago. The reason she'd thought about smoking a cigarette was because of her brother. That's the reason she was here in the first place. A sad smile played at the corners of her mouth and she was surprised when tears began to sting the back of her eyes.

"Good morning. How can I help you?"

Lissa sat up and quickly blinked before the tears spilled from her eyes.

"I'm sorry, I didn't mean to startle you," the woman said.

Lissa looked up into warm blue eyes that were full of concern. They belonged to a woman who was obviously younger than Lissa, but she stood with an air of authority about her.

"It's okay." Lissa quickly rose to her feet. "I'm waiting for assistance. They're all busy." She smiled and waved her hand at the offices around them.

"I'm not. Come with me," the woman offered and led them through the lobby, past the tellers and over to the other side of the bank. Her dark brown hair swayed just below her shoulders with each step she took. Lissa fell in step behind her and hurried to keep up.

They walked into the president's office and the woman paused at the chairs in front of the desk. She stuck out her hand and smiled. "I'm Addison Henry. Have a seat."

Lissa took the woman's hand and felt the same warmth from earlier when she'd looked into her eyes. "I'm Lissa Morgan."

Addison nodded and went around the large desk and sat down.

"I can wait for someone else," Lissa explained. "You're the president of the bank. I'm sure you have other things to be doing."

Addison smiled. "Every customer is important. What is it you needed help with? Don't you think the president should be able to handle each job at the bank?"

"Hmm," Lissa mused. "I don't doubt your abilities, but I'm guessing it's been a while since you opened a new account."

"Is that why you're here?" Addison gave Lissa a pleasant look.

"I'm here to close an account *and* open a new one."

"Okay. I think I can handle that," Addison said confidently. She turned to her computer and started tapping the keyboard.

Lissa watched her with an amused smile. For someone who gave off such a commanding vibe, there was also an aura of kindness emanating from Addison Henry. Lissa wanted to concentrate on anything other than the reason she was here and Addison was a welcome distraction.

"Could I have the name or number of the account you want to close?" Addison looked at her with a friendly smile.

"Yes." She recited the account number. "It's my brother's account. He died," Lissa stated.

Addison's gaze immediately found Lissa's eyes. "Oh no." She gave her a compassionate look. "That explains why you had such a sad look on your face. I'm so sorry, Lissa."

Lissa smiled. "Thank you. I was thinking about him when all of a sudden there you were."

"I didn't mean to sneak up on you."

Lissa sighed. "Honestly, I was remembering how much he smoked. It's actually what killed him. But the funny thing is..."

Addison raised her brows and waited.

Lissa looked into her eyes and couldn't believe the bank president was not only helping her manage her accounts, but she was also listening to her.

"The funny thing is that when I stepped into the bank I had such a craving for a cigarette. I couldn't understand it since I gave up smoking more than twenty-five years ago. But while I was waiting, it occurred to me that I was thinking of Peter—that's my brother—and he couldn't give them up, like I did." Lissa shrugged. She wasn't sure why she'd shared that story with this woman whom she'd just met. Surely, it had to be the grief.

Addison smiled. "I'm glad you quit."

Lissa chuckled. "You don't even know me."

"Sure I do. You're one of my bank patrons and I'm guessing you've been with this bank for a long time."

Lissa nodded.

"Then I'd like to get to know you better. You want to close your brother's account and what is it you'd like to open?"

"My sister, younger brother, and I have formed a partnership with our family estate. We want to open a bank account in the partnership's name," Lissa explained.

"Okay. What's the partnership name?"

"Uh, MFP," Lissa mumbled.

"MFP?"

"Yeah." Lissa looked down at her hands. "The P stands for partnership."

Addison tilted her head. "And the MF?"

Lissa shrugged. "It's a m-f-ing partnership."

A burst of laughter passed Addison's lips. "Seriously?"

"Yep. The Morgan Family Partnership, but that's not what we call it," Lissa said with a playful smile.

Addison chuckled. "I think I like your family. I have to admit," Addison said softly as she leaned across the desk, "I've never opened an account for a m-f-ing partnership."

Laughter bubbled out of Lissa and it felt so good. "You asked."

Addison joined her laughter. "Indeed I did." She turned back to her keyboard and began to type. "There is a Calista Morgan who can access your brother's account."

"That would be me."

"Calista," Addison repeated the name. "That's unique and beautiful."

Lissa watched her lips as she said her name and liked the way it sounded. *What are you doing?* She chided herself. *The frigging president of the bank is helping you and you're ogling her lips.*

"Uh, my dad named me. It means most beautiful. He said I was the prettiest little thing he'd ever seen."

"Aw, how nice is that!" Addison stopped typing and met Lissa's eyes.

"I'm not sure he felt that way when I hit my teenage years." Lissa chuckled.

Addison chuckled and looked back at her computer.

"I have the documentation to close the account," Lissa said. She slid the papers across the desk to Addison and she picked them up and studied them for a moment.

"Do you want the remaining money in the account in a check or cash?" Addison asked.

"Can you transfer it into the new account?"

"Sure, we can do that." Addison continued to type. She hit a button and the printer on the table behind her desk began to spit out papers. "I'll need your signature and that will close the account."

Lissa signed the paper that Addison handed her and waited as she went back to her computer.

"I need your sister and brother's names for the new account."

"My sister is Marielle Morgan Cooper and my brother is Ben Morgan. I have copies of their driver's licenses." Lissa gave Addison the papers.

"You are prepared." Addison smiled.

"Oh, I've been trying to get this done for a few weeks. I think I finally have all the documentation the bank needs."

"Your sister uses her maiden name as her middle name?"

"Yeah, my parents thought when my sister and I got married we could use our last name as a maiden name so they didn't give us middle names. It worked for my sister, but I've never been married, so it didn't work out like they planned for me."

"Hmm." Addison furrowed her brow. "I'm not married

either and I haven't ever really thought about it. A lot of women use their maiden names as middle names now." Addison went back to her computer and continued to type. "Almost finished."

Lissa shook her head. "I still can't get over the bank president taking care of this for me."

Addison smiled as she clicked her mouse to print the new account paperwork. She turned to Lissa. "I don't get to interact with customers as much as I'd like, so I'm happy to do it."

"Well, you're very good at it and easy to talk to. I can't believe I've been telling you all this."

Addison tilted her head. "I noticed several accounts with Morgan as the last name. I take it you're from here and your family banks here too."

Lissa nodded. "Our family business is Morgan Milling. I haven't always lived here. I came back a few years ago to help out. I'm kind of stuck here now."

"Morgan Milling, is that livestock feed and such?"

Lissa smiled. "That's right. We actually make some of the feed and wholesale others."

"You make feed?"

Lissa chuckled. "No. I leave that to my brother. I take care of the business end of things."

"How interesting. I'm a city girl. Would you give me a tour sometime?"

"I'd be happy to." Lissa smiled and narrowed her eyes. "I have a question for you. Why would a city girl who's not married come to a small town like Brazos Falls, Texas?"

Addison stared at Lissa.

"The people who move here are usually young families that want a small town vibe to raise their kids or they come here to retire. Oh wait, I know."

Addison's expression brightened. "Go ahead."

Lissa leaned back in her chair and studied Addison. "I think you are a star in the financial world and this is just a stop on your way to the top. Eventually, you'll be the CEO of the holding company that owns not only this bank but many others."

Addison chuckled. "From your mouth to the board of the holding company."

"Well, I have a feeling we're lucky to have you here."

"I hope so."

Lissa stood up. "I've taken up enough of your time. Are we finished?"

"If you'll get your brother and sister to sign these forms, they will be able to sign checks and link the business account to their personal accounts."

"Thank you, Addison. It was a pleasure meeting you."

"Do you come in the bank very often?" Addison asked as they walked to the door.

"I use the drive thru or the mobile banking app, but maybe I'll come in more often."

"You'd better come by and say hello then." Addison gently placed her hand on Lissa's forearm.

"Calista Morgan," a woman said as Lissa and Addison stood outside Addison's doorway. "I haven't seen you in forever."

"Hi Karen."

"I was sorry to hear about Peter," Karen replied, holding a stack of file folders to her chest.

"Thanks. I forgot you don't work in the drive-thru any longer. It's nice to see you." Lissa turned to Addison and smiled. "I'd better get back to the mill. Thank you again for helping me."

"I'll be calling you for that tour." Addison returned her smile.

"I hope you do."

Lissa walked away with a smile on her face. Addison Henry would be an asset to this small town. She had certainly made this day a lot better for Lissa.

2

Addison walked back into her office with a smile on her face. She loved working with customers and considered them her people. Her goal was for every person who trusted her bank with their hard-earned money to know that she was available to help them in any way she could. She hoped Lissa Morgan would come by again and see that she meant what she'd said.

Her phone buzzed on her desk with an incoming call that brought her out of her satisfying moment. She could tell from the ring pattern that it was an outside call not from within the bank.

"Addison Henry, how can I help you?" she answered.

"Could you lend me some money?"

A big smile immediately settled on Addison's face. "Do you have any collateral?"

"How about my good name?"

"Um, let's see, I don't think you paid me back from the last time I lent you money on your good name."

"What? I thought my wife paid you back."

Addison chuckled. "Rachel did pay me back, Suzanne, but it was *your* loan."

Suzanne Scott had been Addison's best friend since she'd graduated from college. They'd met when Addison moved to Dallas and started her career in finance. She was not only Addison's closest friend, she was also like family since Addison didn't get to see hers often enough.

"Why are you calling me on the bank line?"

"I didn't think you'd pick up if you knew it was me," Suzanne said. "It is during business hours."

"What? I answer when you call, even if it is during bank hours."

"I'm calling to see how things are going. I don't know why you think moving to a small town is going to further your career faster." Suzanne loudly sighed.

"Because I'm the boss, Suzanne. That's why it was a good move. By the way, I miss you, too."

"Who said anything about missing you?" Suzanne protested.

Addison chuckled. "I've got everything unpacked and I have a good grasp on the situation here and can see some areas where I can make things better."

"I'm not surprised, my financial genius of a friend."

"When are you and Rachel coming out for a visit?"

"Oh, I don't know if I'm ready for small-town Americana. When are you coming home?"

"This is my home now, Suzanne."

"Yeah, yeah. How long is this going to take? When will you be promoted back to Dallas?"

"Come visit and I can show you around. It's not a bad little town."

"Do those people know how lucky they are to have you?"

Addison smiled. "Just this morning I opened an account

for a very nice woman and she was quite surprised the bank president was helping her. So yeah, I think they know they're lucky. At least she seemed to appreciate it."

"Why wouldn't she! Most bank presidents don't open accounts; they're busy doing all the big bank things that presidents do. Have you made any friends?"

"Not yet. I've only been here less than a month. But I've met a lot of nice people."

"Don't get any ideas that you'll find a better best friend than me. I'm yours for life. The people you meet will simply be acquaintances since you're not going to be there long."

Addison shook her head. Suzanne had been upset about this move from the beginning. "I could never find a better friend than you. Why would you even say that!"

"Because you moved!"

"It's not like we see each other every day."

"I know that, but we did stuff together most weekends. Rachel misses you because now she has to do those things with me."

Addison couldn't keep the laughter from bubbling out of her. "Rachel was with us most weekends!"

"Okay, okay. We'll come visit soon."

"Thanks for checking on me, Suz."

"Wait, maybe you'll find you a handsome rancher or better yet, perhaps it's time you find out why women are the answer to everything."

"I know what you're going to say. I should go on a date with a woman, but I've told you, Suzanne, I don't have time to date and I'm not into women."

"You don't know that," Suzanne said.

"Oh, I know, what if I find a handsome rancher who happens to be a woman?" Addison teased.

"Have you met someone? Are you holding out on me?"

"No!" Addison suddenly thought about Lissa Morgan. She wasn't a rancher, but she did supply feed.

"Hey, are you still there?"

"Yep, but I've gotta go to do bank things. Come visit," Addison insisted.

"I love you, Addy," Suzanne said.

"Love you, too."

Addison hung the phone up and wondered what Lissa Morgan did for fun. Maybe it was time she made a friend or two.

Lissa walked into the feed store and smiled at her brother who was behind the counter.

"Hey, have you met the new bank president?"

"Yeah, I've met her," Ben said.

"She helped me close Peter's account and open the new one for the partnership. She's really nice."

"You weren't flirting with the bank president, were you?"

"Oh yeah, Ben. That's what I do. I flirt with women while they're helping me with my dead brother's estate," Lissa said as her voice got louder.

"Okay, okay," Ben said, holding up his hands. Then he chuckled. "What am I talking about anyway? When was the last time you actually went on a date?"

Lissa gave him a menacing look. "The dating pool in this town is non-existent for me. You know that."

"New people are moving into town all the time."

"Yeah, I was just telling Addison that the folks that move here are either young and raising a family or retirees. I'm a lesbian living in paradise," Lissa deadpanned, walking towards her office.

Ben followed her and leaned on the doorframe. "What I should've said is that you never know when someone will come to town."

Lissa looked up at her brother and smiled. "I don't need a girlfriend or a partner to have a good life."

"I know that. It's just...you're an incredible person and someone would be lucky to have you as their partner."

"Thanks?" Her brother wasn't one for sentimentality so this was a little out of character.

"Uh, they want us to sponsor the Fall Fest Fun Run and 5K," Ben said.

Lissa nodded, thankful for the change in subject. "Okay."

"Someone came by from the Chamber of Commerce and said they'd sent you an email."

"All right. I'll look at how much it will cost us."

"Maybe we could get the family involved," Ben commented.

Surprised, Lissa looked at her brother. "You're going to run?"

"Not me," Ben scoffed. "Maybe the boys or Marielle. Besides, you don't have to run."

"That's true. Maybe I'll walk it. Do you want me to ask Leo and Joe?"

"They might do it if you ask. What about Max? He might do it if you get Marielle on board."

Lissa chuckled. "If Marielle can get Max to put his video game controller down he might do it."

"That Max," Ben said, shaking his head. "I love my nephew even if he beats me every time we play."

"Well, that's not saying much, brother. I beat you!" The front door opened and a customer walked inside. "You know it's true. Now go sell feed and leave this to me."

Ben laughed and went back to his job.

Lissa turned to her computer and opened her email. Sure enough there was an email with the different levels of sponsorship available for the Fall Fest. She noticed the list at the bottom of the page of sponsors that had already committed. A smile crossed her face when she saw the Brazos Falls National Bank near the top.

* * *

Lissa turned the corner and continued her walk up the street. After signing up to sponsor the Fall Fest, she'd decided to participate in the 5K, but she was walking it. Her nephews and sister had agreed to join her, along with her sister-in-law, Kara. There would be a combination of runners and walkers in the Morgan family.

When she neared the end of the block she noticed a familiar face arranging flower pots on the front porch of a small bungalow.

"That looks nice," Lissa said loudly from the curb.

Addison looked up from her project and smiled. "Hey there," she replied. "How are you?"

Lissa walked up the sidewalk. "I was out for a walk. I didn't realize you lived here."

Addison waited for her to reach the porch. "I haven't been here long. Do you live around here?"

Lissa nodded. "I live right around the corner. You can probably see my backyard from yours."

Addison smiled. "Do you have a dog? I hear a dog barking down the way when I sit on my back porch."

"No, but I have a cat."

"Oh, so you're a cat person."

"Uh, both. I love animals," Lissa admitted. "I'm out

walking to get ready for the Fall Fest 5K. I saw the bank is sponsoring it."

"We are. I've noticed in the short time I've been here that the bank sponsors almost everything."

Lissa chuckled. "That's life in a small town." She tilted her head. "Hey, why don't you join me? You're not a runner, are you?"

"No," Addison scoffed. "I do enjoy yoga though."

"I don't run anymore, but I thought it would be fun to walk the 5K."

"That does sound like fun, I think. I mean, I'm going to be there anyway." Addison shrugged. "It's a good opportunity to get involved in the community."

"Right." Lissa nodded. "The bank president has to be seen and active in the town."

"Something like that." Addison met Lissa's eyes and smiled. "Can I run in and change my shoes?"

"Sure."

Addison grinned and hurried into the house.

Lissa grabbed a broom that was leaned up against the house and swept off the fallen leaves from the plants.

"Thank you," Addison said, coming back out the front door.

"These mums are beautiful. I love the color they add to your front porch." She handed Addison the broom and looked at the front of the house. "You've really made this place cute."

"Thanks. It needed some curb appeal. We'll see how long I can keep these plants alive." Addison chuckled.

They walked out to the street and continued along in companionable silence.

"Do you walk every evening?" Addison asked after they'd walked a little ways.

"It depends on when I get home from work, but I'll walk more now since the 5K is coming up. You're welcome to join me."

Addison looked over at her and smiled. "I'd like that. Have you been back to the bank since I opened your accounts?"

"No." Lissa chuckled.

"I thought about calling you the other day for that tour of your mill," Addison commented.

Lissa looked over at her. "You did? You weren't just telling me that to be nice?"

"No. I really do want to see it. For a city girl like me, that's something new."

"Oh wow. I hope you're not expecting too much."

"I'll just have to come see."

"Okay. I'm going to hold you to that."

Addison grinned. "So is this Fall Fest thing a big deal?"

"It's a way for the stores on the town square to get people out to shop and it's something for the whole community. Even if they don't want to participate in the 5K there will be other activities for kids and families."

"What about your family? Are they running?"

"My nephews are running. My sister and sister-in-law will probably be walking."

"Your whole family lives here?"

"Yeah, my brother has two boys. Leo is eighteen and Joe is fifteen. My sister is divorced and moved back a few years ago. Her daughter, Blythe, is off at college and her son Max is sixteen."

"I imagine you are their favorite aunt," Addison said with a smile.

Lissa chuckled. "They come to me when they're in trouble with their folks or need a friendly ear." Lissa studied

Addison for a moment then asked, "Did you know anyone when you moved here?"

"Nope. It was a little daunting, but I have friends not too far away in Dallas."

"Well, you know me now. If you need anything, I'm right around the corner and you know where I work."

Addison smiled at Lissa. "Thanks, I appreciate that."

"Do you want to do this 5K or are you just being nice?"

"What do you mean? You're the one being nice, including me and all."

"Okay, just checking. Then, shall we do this again tomorrow?"

"I'm in." Addison grinned at Lissa.

3

Addison had walked with Lissa several times last week and had an idea for their walk tomorrow. She was reaching for her phone when she heard a knock on her open office door.

"Hey Prez, are you busy?" Lissa said with a smile.

"Hey, I was just about to call you. Come in." Addison came around her desk and sat in the chair next to Lissa. "I know we can't walk tonight because of my meeting, but I was thinking that I could come to the mill tomorrow near closing time and you could give me that tour."

Lissa's face lit up. "That would be great."

"I was also thinking that I'd bring my clothes with me and we could change and walk around that area. I haven't been in that part of town much."

"What a great idea." Lissa chuckled. "I don't imagine you'd have a reason to be in that part of town. Let's see, we're on the edge of town, just off Main Street. We're near the cemetery, and what else?"

Addison laughed. "I know where you are." She tilted her

head as her mouth curved into a smile. "What brings you to the bank today?"

"I came to make a deposit and decided to forego the motor bank and come inside for a change."

"I'm glad you did. You know, you could do that more often," Addison suggested. "It's a good way to get a few extra steps in for the 5K."

Lissa chuckled. "And to say hi to a certain bank president."

"As long as you're in the bank." Addison shrugged amused. "I'd be hurt if you didn't come by."

"I'd never want to do that."

Addison caught Lissa's gaze and neither of them said anything for a moment.

"Okay," Lissa said, getting up. "I'll see you tomorrow for your tour and our walk."

"Can't wait."

Addison walked back behind her desk and sat down. She didn't take her eyes off Lissa until she'd left the lobby.

"Excuse me." Karen stepped in Addison's doorway. "Do you have a minute?"

"Sure. Come on in."

"I don't know if you know this, but Lissa is a lesbian," Karen stated.

"Okay..." Addison's brows knitted together.

"It's just that I saw you two walking the other day and thought you should know."

"Uh huh." Addison paused, then realization hit her. "Oh, I get it. If I'm seen with Lissa, other people will think I'm gay?"

"Well..." Karen sputtered.

"I thought you and Lissa were friends," Addison said.

"We are, but I'm married and we've known each other forever."

Addison stared at Karen, not sure what to make of her statement. "Uh, well, it doesn't matter who is gay, Karen. A friend is a friend."

"Right, right."

"And we treat everyone the same," Addison added.

"Of course we do," Karen said, obviously feeling the awkwardness she'd caused in the room. "I thought you should know."

Addison watched her leave and could feel the anger rise to her cheeks. She knew Karen was a gossip and hoped that would shut her down in the future. Addison wasn't naive and knew she couldn't change a person like Karen, but she could certainly make sure she didn't do that in her bank.

She reached for her phone and called Suzanne.

"Hey, what's wrong?"

"Can't I call my best friend?" Addison scoffed.

"Yes, but it's business hours. Are you okay?"

"I'm fine. I called to tell you and Rachel to plan on coming to visit the weekend after next. We're having this thing called Fall Fest and it will be a good way for you to see this small town."

"Okay, sounds fun. Now, what's the matter?"

"Oh, I have a gossip in the bank and she shared a little tidbit about my new friend. I didn't appreciate it."

"Is this Lissa, the woman you're walking with?"

"Good guess."

"It's not a guess, Addison." Suzanne chuckled. "She's the only friend you've made so far, or at least the only one you talk about."

Addison thought back to her conversations with

Suzanne and she wasn't wrong. She did talk about her walks with Lissa.

"So what did she say about her?"

"Oh, she just thought I should know that she's a lesbian."

"Oh dear God. Did she think she was going to rub off on you?" Suzanne laughed.

"Probably. It was the way she said it."

"Fuck her. We lesbians are good friends to have."

Addison laughed. "Don't I know it."

"Sorry, Addy."

"It's okay. I hope she realizes there's no place for gossip in my bank."

"Hell yeah! You go, President Henry!"

"The funny thing is that she and Lissa are supposed to be friends."

"Trust me, she's not Lissa's friend."

Addison sat back in her chair. "Yeah, I think you're right. Once you meet Lissa you'll understand why it made me angry. You're going to love her."

"She's got to be okay if you like her. I know how cautious you are."

"Yeah, yeah. You've only told me that a million times. I'd better get back to work. I'm really looking forward to seeing you and Rachel."

"Us too. Love you, bud."

"Love you, too." Addison smiled. Suzanne was right. Addison didn't mean to be cautious, but she worked a lot and that didn't always go along with making new friends.

* * *

When Addison walked into the mill office, Lissa looked up and quickly got up from her desk.

"Hi," Addison said as Lissa approached.

"Hi. Oh good, you brought your clothes in with you." Lissa nodded at Addison's bag in her hand. "You should change before the tour. It's dusty in the back and I'd hate for you to get that beautiful suit dirty."

Addison looked down at her skirt and heels then back at Lissa's appreciative stare. She smiled and raised her eyebrows.

"You can change in my office." Lissa ushered Addison inside and closed the door.

Addison quickly changed into her leggings, shirt, and walking shoes. She took a moment to look around Lissa's office and noticed a picture on her desk. Lissa had a big smile on her face and four young people were surrounding her with matching smiles.

She opened the door so Lissa would know she'd changed and waited for her to come back inside. "That's a great picture," Addison commented.

Lissa looked at the picture and smiled. "That's my niece and nephews. I try to get them together every summer for a picture."

"Nice tan," Addison said with a grin.

"We love the lake."

"Oh that's right. I hear there are two lakes nearby."

Lissa nodded.

"Do you have a place at one of them?"

"Oh, no. There are several places with public access and I have a friend who doesn't live here, but has a cabin. They let me use it whenever I want. I'll have to take you out there when the weather warms up. I mean, if you'd like to."

"I'd love it. I grew up near water." A dreamy smile

crossed Addison's face and she added, "Being near the water makes me happy and gives me peace. It's the place that gives me calm when I'm stressed or having a hard time with something."

"I know what you mean." Lissa smiled. After a moment she said, "Okay, let's start this tour. Obviously, this is the storefront, but through here is where we make and store the feed."

Lissa took her back to an area where machinery whirred and men were busy working.

"They take the raw materials: wheat, cottonseed hulls, and other ingredients and mix it together. Then it goes in here where it is compressed and made into long tubes. It goes from there through a cutter that snips it into these smaller cubes."

"Wow, I had no idea," Addison said over the noise of the machinery.

"Then it goes into this tank. Watch as that lever allows the cubes to fill the waiting sack. Once it's full, the top is sewed shut and it travels along that conveyor belt where it can be stacked on pallets," Lissa explained.

"That's amazing," Addison said, awed.

"Let's go this way, it's much quieter." Lissa led them out of the production area back towards the office. She stopped before they got back to the office door. "This is the dock. People can back their vehicles up and have their feed loaded. Over here"—Lissa pointed to stacks of feed on the other side of the large area—"is where the different varieties of feed are stored for folks that drive up. There's cattle feed, horse feed, and deer feed in these rows."

"So a rancher pulls up, backs in, then goes inside to order what they want?"

"That's right. Then Ben or the dock hand will load their order and away they go."

Addison nodded and followed Lissa into the part of the building that led to the warehouse. It was a long corridor, large enough for a forklift to travel down to deposit the pallets of feed in their designated rows.

Lissa stopped before entering the warehouse. "This area is used for storage and seasonal items, but it also happens to be where the cats like to hang out."

At the sound of Lissa's voice, a half dozen cats ran out from behind sacks of feed and empty pallets.

"Look at them all! They're adorable!" Addison exclaimed. She looked over at Lissa and could see the delight on her face.

"Ben teases me that they only come to the sound of my voice because they think they're going to get fed."

"That's right. Lissa thinks they see her, but actually she looks like a big sack of cat food to them," Ben said, laughing as he walked up to them. "Hi, Addison. We met when you first got to town."

"I met a lot of people that first week, but I remember you. We were both waiting for take-out at the Mexican food restaurant. How are you, Ben?"

"It's nice to see you. I hope my sister isn't boring you."

"Not at all. This is fascinating."

"Do you need a cat? We have more than enough," he said, giving Lissa a look.

Addison laughed.

"You know I don't feed these cats," Lissa said.

"Right," he replied with a smirk. "Lissa knows this business better than I do, so if you have any questions, she's the authority." Ben turned to Lissa. "I'll lock the front if you'll get the door in the back."

"Thanks." Lissa nodded.

"It was nice to see you again, Addison."

"You too, Ben."

After he'd walked away Lissa quietly said, "Ben and I have an ongoing feud about the cats. He doesn't like me to feed them because he wants them to eat the rats and varmints that come along with a feed business."

"But?"

Lissa shrugged. "How can I not give them treats? It's like having pets at work."

"Don't you have a cat at home?"

"Yeah, she came from here. Do you see that gray one there? That's her brother."

"Do you have names for them?"

"Yes, but they don't answer to them." Lissa chuckled. "I call that gray one Dart because he doesn't walk; he darts around everywhere he goes. That black calico is Star. Do you see how she's dark all over, but right between her eyes is a light tan patch that looks like a star?"

Addison gasped. "It does."

"That big orange one is Tom because—"

"He's the tomcat."

"That's right." Lissa chuckled.

Addison was oddly delighted at Lissa's satisfied look.

"Let's go this way." Lissa led them through a large space where pallets of feed were lined up on each side of the aisle. "This is cattle feed and over there is horse feed," she said, indicating different rows of feed.

They walked into a larger back area where there was more feed and stacks of minerals and other nutrients for the animals.

"One more thing," Lissa said, stopping them at a large

sliding door and looking over to another large building that was open on one side.

"Do you see those big piles of grain?"

Addison nodded. "What are those huge spider-looking arms going into that large vat?"

"We don't just make cubes. Some ranchers like to feed a loose blend. Those spider arms take the ingredients up into that large mixer. The different feeds have their own recipe. Ben cringes when I use that term, but that's really what it is."

"Oh, I think I get it. The different raw materials are mixed together for different rations for the animals."

"That's right! Then we have a truck that the mixed feed is loaded on and delivered to the ranch feeders. Does that make sense?"

"It does. Wow, this is really interesting. I didn't know what to expect."

Lissa began to slide the huge door closed.

Addison noticed a pin in a hook on the facing of the door and reached to remove it. When Lissa slid the door closed, she pushed the latch over the hook and Addison put the pin through to lock it, but not before she brushed her fingers over Lissa's hand.

Their eyes met and neither said anything or moved.

4

"Thanks," Lissa said as Addison pulled her hand away.

They started the long walk back to the front of the store and Addison looked over at Lissa. "Hey, I wanted to tell you that I don't think Karen is your friend."

"Uh oh. What did she do?"

"After you left my office yesterday she made a point of telling me that you're gay," Addison said gently.

Lissa scoffed. "You mean she didn't tell you that day you helped me with our accounts? Karen loves to be in everyone's business. She doesn't realize how harmful the things she says can be."

"She said she'd seen us out walking together and thought I should know."

"Oh." Lissa stopped. "Hey, is it a problem for you to be seen walking with me?"

"No!" Addison exclaimed. "You're my friend. I wouldn't have said anything, but I thought you should know what Karen is saying about you."

"I don't want to cause a problem with your job, Addison."

"What? You're not."

"I haven't had a girlfriend since I moved back to help with the business, so I don't know how the town would react to that. My folks are both gone now, but I'm kind of stuck here."

"You know, you said you were stuck here the first time we met. How so?"

"Well, at my age, it might be hard to move away and find a job. Ben needs me, but, to be honest with you, I miss gay friends."

"I'm sorry it's like that for you. It shouldn't be!" Addison was becoming angry.

Lissa gave her a curious look, but they began to walk again.

Addison was a little surprised at her own reaction, but figured it was because her best friend was gay and Lissa was a new friend being treated unfairly.

"Please promise me you'll tell me if anyone treats you differently at the bank. I won't stand for it, Lissa. I hate gossip, but especially when it's about good people."

Lissa stopped at the door to the storefront and smiled over at her. "I'm good people? You haven't known me that long."

Addison noticed all the noise from the machinery was gone and it was eerily quiet. Everyone must have left for the day. "You know, I was talking to my best friend today and she reminded me how cautious I am when making new friends. You must be all right or we wouldn't be friends."

Addison stared into Lissa's eyes and thought what a beautiful light brown color they were. Her dark blonde hair was streaked with a few strands of gray that made it shine in the dim light and the combination of her eyes and hair gave Addison such a feeling of warmth.

"You are good people," Addison stated. "And no one messes with my people."

Lissa smiled and nodded. "I'm glad I'm your people."

Addison grinned. "Come on, let's go walk and forget about what assholes some people can be."

* * *

Lissa quickly changed into her walking clothes and as they left the mill she turned to Addison. "I'm so glad I came into the bank that day."

Addison gave her a broad smile. "I am too. I didn't realize how much I needed a friend. Plus, all these walks have improved my yoga."

Lissa chuckled. "Maybe I'll try yoga with you when the 5K is done."

"Please do. I look forward to our talks."

"I do, too." Lissa looked over at Addison and smiled.

As they walked along, Lissa thought back to their earlier conversation. She'd felt her heart fall into her stomach when Addison told her what Karen had said, but then it rebounded and filled with relief when Addison defended their friendship. And then she'd felt something else when Addison vowed that no one messed with her people and Lissa was included.

"Uh, Lissa. Are we walking into a cemetery?" Addison asked, bringing Lissa out of her head.

Lissa chuckled. "It's one of the best places to walk. There's no traffic and the streets are good. Some of the names on these markers are interesting."

"Okay, if you say so," Addison said, following along.

They walked along and Lissa pointed out some of the founding families' graves at the beginning of the cemetery. As they walked towards the back of the expanse, the graves were newer.

"I'm having trouble with something you said earlier this evening," Addison said after they'd turned and started back to the front of the cemetery.

"What's that?"

"You said you were stuck here because of your age. You don't think you could get a job someplace else? I'm thirty-five, Lissa. You're not that much older than me."

"Thirty-five, huh." Lissa smiled at Addison then looked ahead. "I'm forty-nine, Addison. That's kind of old to be starting over somewhere new."

Addison eyed Lissa as they walked. "Forty-nine? I'd have never guessed, but then, Karen looks so much older than you."

Lissa chuckled. "Good genes."

"I think it's a good heart."

"What?"

"Yeah, you're the kind of person who wants to help people, not harm them. Maybe it shows."

"Huh? That's an interesting theory. Could it be healthy eating and exercise, too?"

Addison laughed. "That might have a little to do with it. Speaking of healthy eating. I'm getting hungry. Did I see a food truck on the corner when I drove up the street to the mill?"

"Yes. They make the best gorditas and tortas."

"You'll have to explain to me what that is. I'm thinking it's Mexican food, but..."

Lissa chuckled. "We could order on the way to our cars. By the time we get back our food will be ready."

"That sounds perfect. Now what's a tor-what?"

"A torta," Lissa pronounced the word slowly. "It's like a Mexican sandwich. They take the meat you choose and add on cheese and other goodies and put it between thick slices of bread."

"Ooohh, that sounds good. What was the other thing you said?"

"Gorditas. They are sort of like tacos, but instead of a tortilla it's a flat corn pocket. They put the meat and other extras inside the flap. I love them and this truck makes the best ones in town, in my humble opinion."

"I'll have to take your word for it because I'm going for the torta. I didn't have much lunch today and now I'm starving."

They walked up to the food truck and placed their orders. Lissa explained to the cook that they were going to walk the short distance to the mill to get their cars.

"Wow, you really are hungry."

"Why do you say that?"

"Because you're practically running."

Addison laughed. "Do I need to slow down, old lady?"

Lissa threw her head back and laughed. "I'll show you who's old." Lissa grabbed Addison around the waist and tickled her. When she bent over to laugh, Lissa hurried past her and got to the cars first.

Addison walked up still laughing. "No fair!" she panted. "How did you know I was ticklish?"

"I didn't. I took a chance." Lissa grinned. "Sometimes the wisdom of age pays off," she said in a somber voice.

Addison looked at her and they both burst out laughing.

They got in their cars and drove down the block to the food truck. Sure enough, their food was ready.

"Follow me to my house. I have beer that would go

perfectly with your torta," Lissa told Addison, handing her a sack of food.

"That does sound good. Lead the way."

The smile Addison gave Lissa made something flutter in her stomach. She quickly got back in her car and drove towards home, making sure Addison was behind her. As she looked in the rearview mirror and saw Addison's lights, she took a deep breath. So much for being old and wise. The idea that Addison thought of her as a friend made Lissa's somewhat lonely, closed heart suddenly open up. "Slow down," she said to her reflection in the rear view mirror. "She's your friend and that's all you need."

Lissa looked ahead and hoped she wasn't lying to herself.

Addison pulled in behind Lissa and got out of her car. "This smells heavenly. I can't take it much longer. I almost opened it on the way to your house."

Lissa laughed. "Come on in."

They walked through the living room to the kitchen and set their sacks of food on the table. Lissa got each of them a beer and was about to make a toast when a cat came hurrying down the hallway into the kitchen screaming, "Meow!"

"Hey there," Addison said, bending down to look into the cat's eyes. "Who are you?"

The cat stared back at her and must have decided she was okay because it began to rub against Addison's legs and purr.

Lissa took in the spectacle as it played out in front of her. "I can't believe it," she said quietly.

Addison dropped her hand down to pet the cat between its ears. "Can't believe what?"

"She is never friendly when she meets someone new."

"What's your name, sweet princess?" The cat continued to purr and closed her eyes and basked in the pleasure of Addison's head rubs.

"Her name is Callie," Lissa said with a smile, still marveling at the cat's gentleness with Addison.

"Callie the calico," Addison commented.

"That's kind of how she got her name. When I discovered her and her brother as kittens in the back of the mill, I called her Callie to try to get her to come to me."

"Oh, so you named her after yourself," Addison teased.

Lissa visibly deflated. "I knew you would think that. No one around here knows my name is Calista, except for my family."

Addison laughed and reached out and squeezed Lissa's forearm. "You are both beautiful princesses."

Lissa chuckled. "Yeah we are." She looked down at the cat with love on her face. "Anyway, I kept her name when I brought her home with me."

"She's adorable." Addison stood up and looked down at Callie. "As cute as you are, the growl in my belly is stronger."

"I was about to toast to friendship and food," Lissa said, opening both their beers.

"We can drink to that. But how about to pretty princesses instead?" Addison said with a twinkle in her eyes.

"I don't know, you may be a queen. I have a feeling you are always in charge," Lissa replied with a smirk.

Addison chuckled and clinked her beer bottle to Lissa's. "You're not wrong."

They dug into their food and little sounds of delight came from both of them as they consumed bite after bite.

"You know all about my family and now my cats. Oh shit, does that make me a cat lady?" Lissa said with horror on her face.

"No," Addison giggled.

"Whew. When I said that out loud it sounded kind of pitiful."

"No it didn't," Addison said around another bite of her torta. "It sounds exactly like who you are."

Lissa raised her eyebrows in question.

"You're a person who cares about animals. There's nothing wrong with that," Addison reassured her.

"Thanks. What I was going to say is that you know about me, but all I know about you is that you came here from Dallas."

Addison nodded. "I grew up in Minnesota, the land of 10,000 lakes. I was near water most of my life."

"You said you're a city girl."

"Yep. I grew up in the Twin Cities, but I wasn't far from the lakes."

"How did you get so interested in banking?"

"I worked at the bank while I was in high school. We had a CEO who was so smart and got me interested in finance. I loved it and went on to major in it in college."

"How long do you see yourself staying here?"

Addison eyed Lissa but didn't answer.

"Come on, I know you have aspirations for bigger and better things."

"I do, but it's hard to say," Addison said, sounding noncommittal. "I'm discovering the charm of small-town living."

"Charm?"

"Yes. For example, there are really good people here, like you," Addison added.

"And?"

"And I'm also finding the hazards that go along with it."

Addison leaned closer to Lissa. "People like to get in your business."

Lissa laughed. "It's good that you're finding that out now."

"It is, I suppose. But that doesn't mean I have to like it."

Lissa took a sip of her beer. "I'm sorry folks are so nosy. Some of them mean well and actually care, but then there are others..." Lissa trailed off.

"Like Karen who wants to stir up shit."

"Damn, you learn fast."

Addison chuckled. "There's always someone out to get you when competition is involved. That's true in just about anything."

Lissa nodded. "You proved that you've got my back and just so you know, I've got yours."

"Thanks, Lissa. I need that." Addison stared into Lissa's eyes and smiled.

Lissa couldn't help but wonder what Addison was thinking. Her eyes were the same warm blue from the first day Lissa looked into them, but there was something else there. *What are you looking for, Addison? What do you see?*

5

W*hat a day*, Addison thought as she pulled into her garage. She had put out fires, corrected errors, and solved problems all day long. There was a problem at headquarters that took her most of the day to resolve and when she wasn't involved with that, she handled several customer issues. She smiled, thinking about how her solution at the main office would help all the banks in the system. "That's why you'll be running everything someday," she said softly then chuckled.

As she gazed out her back door, the last golden rays of dusk were quickly disappearing in her backyard. The soft blanket of evening began to fall and suddenly she had an idea. She hurried to her bedroom and quickly changed into jeans and a sweatshirt.

When she walked back into the kitchen, she selected a bottle of wine from the small wine rack at the end of her cabinet. She and Lissa weren't planning to walk this evening, but Addison needed a little Lissa-time to wash away the chaos from this day. Lissa had a way about her that was comfortable, for lack of a better way to explain it.

Addison liked being with her. They laughed, talked, and sometimes were simply quiet, enjoying the moment. That's what she needed right now.

She walked out the back door, through her yard, and out the gate. It wasn't far to Lissa's house through the alley, but in the receding light Addison wasn't quite sure which house was hers. Then she remembered Lissa commenting that she didn't have a privacy fence and was thinking about having one built. She'd said her fence was chain link and didn't have a lock on the gate.

She spied the house, carefully closing the gate as she went through, and knocked on Lissa's back door. When Lissa opened the door, Addison held up the bottle of wine and gave Lissa her best smile.

"Whew, I hoped this was the right house. I wanted a glass of wine and didn't want to drink alone. Would you join me?"

The delight on Lissa's face was obvious. "Come on in."

"Thanks. I hope you don't mind me coming to the back door. It was quicker and I'm carrying a bottle of wine." Addison shrugged. "I figured it was a small town thing and all right to come to your back door. Do you lock your doors at night? Isn't that a small town thing?" Addison realized she was babbling.

Lissa led them into the kitchen and got out a couple of wine glasses. "I like your style, Addison. I don't mind you coming to the back door at all. I do lock my doors. I'm a big chicken. Are you?"

"Um, I don't think so. I've been having to fight my way up in the financial world. There are more women in upper management, but there's still a long way to go."

Lissa nodded.

"Have you had to fight?"

Lissa gave her a measured look. "Do you mean, have I fought to be myself in a small town?"

Addison nodded.

"I was pretty low-key until after my parents died. I didn't want them to have to defend me or anything like that. My family has always been supportive of me. But this is a small town and people have their opinions and some aren't shy to express them."

"My best friend is gay. You'll get to meet her at Fall Fest. She and her wife are coming to visit. I thought that would be a good time to show her the town."

"I look forward to it. Maybe she'll tell me more about my new friend."

Addison chuckled. "I don't know about that. She loves to tease me and tell me I'm missing out. How does she put it..." Addison tapped her finger on her chin. "'You should come to my side and see the difference.'"

Lissa laughed. "I think I'm going to like your friend. And she's not wrong."

Addison joined her laughter and held up her glass for a toast. "To my gay friends."

They each took a sip of the wine and Addison saw Lissa's approving nod. "This is lovely."

"Thanks. I'm glad you like it."

"Did you have a hard day?" Lissa asked, studying Addison for a moment. "Or was Karen talking trash about your gay friend again?"

Addison gave Lissa a slow smile. *This was a good idea.* After just a few minutes with Lissa, all the stress from the day was gone. "No, Karen was one of the few problems I didn't have to deal with today."

"You don't have to defend me," Lissa offered.

"Yes, I do. It isn't really defending as much as it is

showing acceptance to others. It doesn't matter to me who you love," Addison stated.

"Or who *you* love," Lissa added.

Addison gave her a baffled look. "I never thought of it that way. You and Suzanne don't care who I love."

"Suzanne?"

"Oh sorry, that's my best friend. She and her wife, Rachel, will be here for the 5K."

"I can tell you're excited to see them."

Addison couldn't keep the delight from her face and grinned. "I am. Suzanne and I have been friends since we both moved to Dallas right after we graduated from college. We miss seeing each other."

"I'm sure you do."

"Yeah, she wasn't too excited about this move."

"But it isn't forever," Lissa stressed with a smile.

Addison nodded. "The huge problem that took all day to solve will help all the banks under my holding company's umbrella—"

"So, you may be moving up even faster than you expected," Lissa said, finishing Addison's statement. She held out her glass and added, "To Addison, though our time may be brief, I hope you'll remember your first friend in Brazos Falls when you're running *all* the banks."

Addison chuckled and clinked her glass to Lissa's. "I could never forget the old cat lady," she teased.

Lissa gasped and set her glass down on the table. "We're about to find out just how ticklish you are."

"Wait, wait! I'll take it back." Addison giggled. She hurried into the living room and looked around. "Where's Callie? I think I need protection."

Lissa laughed as she followed Addison into the room, bringing the bottle and her glass with her. She offered to top off Addison's glass before sitting down on the end of the couch.

"She is outside wandering through the neighborhood, re-establishing her domain. She does this most evenings," Lissa explained.

Addison studied Lissa from the other end of the couch. In a short time, Lissa had become a trusted friend she didn't think she'd ever forget no matter how long she ended up staying in Brazos Falls.

"What are you thinking about over there?" Lissa asked, meeting Addison's gaze.

"I couldn't forget you," she said softly.

Lissa smiled then her face fell into a pout. "I'm not a cat lady."

"There's not a cat in sight."

Lissa laughed. "Thank you."

They simply looked at each other as they sipped their wine and Lissa finally said, "If we're going to finish this bottle of wine, we should eat something."

"I don't want to be a bother," Addison replied quickly.

"Never," Lissa scoffed. "Do you like pizza?"

A bright smile grew on Addison's face. "I love pizza!"

"Are you a snob about it? Or do you like any pizza?"

"I am an equal opportunity pizza connoisseur." Addison laughed. "I do like a fancy pizza, but trust me, I've had many a frozen pizza or two in my life and will continue to do so."

Lissa checked her watch. "We have just enough time to order from the specialty pizza place and they deliver."

"This may be a test to our friendship. What toppings do you like?" Addison asked cautiously.

Lissa studied Addison. "I don't like onions," she said slowly.

Addison nodded. "Me either."

"I can eat everything else," Lissa said.

Addison raised her eyebrows and let Lissa's statement hang in the air for a moment then she chuckled. "But what's your favorite?"

"Pepperoni, but I like other toppings too."

"We'll be just fine." Addison beamed Lissa a smile. "How about we order two pizzas? You create one and I'll create the other. Then we can share."

"What if we order the same thing?"

Addison laughed. "I guess that could happen."

Lissa took out her phone and called the pizza place. "Hi Kaylee, how are you tonight?"

Addison watched as Lissa listened then she put the phone on speaker.

"I need two pizzas delivered. Make one pepperoni and black olive and the second..." Lissa looked at Addison.

"Sausage and mushroom, with extra sauce," Addison said with a smile.

Lissa nodded her approval.

"We're shorthanded tonight, Lissa. It may take a while because we're down a delivery person," Kaylee said over the laughter in the background.

"Is that my nephew I hear laughing?" Lissa asked.

Kaylee giggled. "Yep. No one laughs like Max."

"You make the pizzas, Kaylee. My payment info is on file. I'll get Max to be the delivery person. Can I talk to him?"

"Sure."

"Hello?" a young man's voice came through the phone.

"Max!"

"Hi Aunt Lissa. Whatcha up to?"

"I'm hungry for pizza, but Kaylee said they don't have a delivery person. Could I get you to do me a favor?"

Max laughed. "Yeah, I'll bring it to you."

"Thanks!"

"For a small delivery fee," he said, giggling.

"Yeah, I'll take care of that delivery fee when you get here," Lissa threatened.

Max laughed again. "I'll see you soon, Auntie."

Lissa ended the call and shook her head. She smiled at Addison. "You'll get to meet my nephew."

"He sounds like fun," Addison said.

"He's a good kid."

"What were you going to do tonight? I'm not messing up any plans, am I?"

"Not at all. I'm glad my back gate wasn't locked."

Addison chuckled.

"I was going to watch a Hallmark movie," Lissa said, looking into Addison's eyes. "What do you think? Are you in?"

"Don't tell me you're a romantic!" Addison exclaimed. She studied Lissa for a few moments then smiled. "I'm not surprised."

Lissa shrugged. "I am what I am."

Addison chuckled. "I like who you are."

Lissa reached for the remote and found the movie. "More wine?"

"Yes, please."

Lissa topped off both their glasses and they settled in to watch the movie.

"Do you watch a lot of Hallmark movies?" Addison asked.

"No. I watch a few around Christmas time. This is a new one."

"They all follow the same formula," Addison commented.

"How would you know if you don't watch a lot of them?"

"It's common knowledge," Addison said. "The two main characters get friendlier and friendlier throughout the movie and then kiss once at the end."

Lissa chuckled. "They kiss once?"

"Yeah. We're supposed to believe that one kiss makes all the difference. And then they live happily ever after from that one kiss."

"You don't think you'd know from one kiss?" Lissa asked.

"It would have to be some kiss," Addison replied.

"It could be all that's leading up to it, you know. It's like they have to kiss—that's where everything has led and they couldn't stop it if they wanted to."

Addison looked at Lissa. "You are a romantic."

Lissa shrugged. "I believe in happily-ever-after, even if I haven't found mine yet. If that makes me a romantic then I guess I am. What about you?"

Before Addison could answer there was a knock at the door. "That must be our pizzas," Addison said.

Lissa held Addison's gaze before getting up to answer the door. "I won't forget my question."

"Delivery," Max said when Lissa opened the door.

"Let me check those pizzas and make sure you didn't eat a slice," Lissa teased, letting Max inside the living room.

"Oh, hi," he said with a friendly smile when he saw Addison sitting on the couch.

"Max, this is Addison Henry," Lissa said. "Addison, this is my nephew, Max."

"Her favorite nephew," Max corrected Lissa.

"You are my favorite right now since you brought us dinner." Lissa grinned.

"It's nice to meet you, Max," Addison said, standing up.

"You're the banker lady that walks with my aunt. It's nice to meet you."

Addison chuckled. "I am the banker lady."

"Sorry," Max said sheepishly.

"It's okay. That's what I do."

Lissa took the pizzas from her nephew and put them on the kitchen table. She reached in her purse for money to give Max and walked back over to them.

"Wait," Addison said. "Let me pay the delivery fee."

"No way. He's my nephew and you brought the wine," Lissa said, handing Max a twenty dollar bill.

"Thanks, but you didn't have to pay me. I was on my way home anyway," Max said, handing the money back to Lissa.

"I like giving you money. Keep it."

Max smiled and gave Lissa a hug.

"Do you want to stay and have pizza and watch a Hallmark movie with us?" Lissa asked.

"Uh, I'm going to pass," Max said politely. "It was nice to meet you, Addison. I'm sure I'll see you at Fall Fest for the 5K."

"Oh, are you running it?" Addison asked.

"I'm not sure."

"Does that mean you haven't figured out a way to get out of it?" Lissa asked.

"You know me so well, Aunt Lissa."

They all laughed and Lissa opened the door. "Love you," Lissa said to Max.

"Love you more," he said and walked out.

"What a great kid," Addison said, walking into the kitchen.

Lissa followed her and took down two plates along with napkins. "He is. You'll get to meet the rest of them at the 5K."

"This is going to be fun. I'll be meeting your family and you'll be meeting mine."

"Yeah, I guess we will." Lissa handed Addison a plate and opened both pizza boxes.

"Ooh, that smells so good," Addison said, taking a whiff. "Hey, are you busy Saturday night after Fall Fest? I hoped you could join Suzanne, Rachel, and me for dinner."

"I'd be happy to."

"I think you'll all get along. It should be fun."

They filled their plates and went back to the couch.

"Do you need anything else?"

"Nope. You can start the movie back. Let's see what happens leading up to that kiss."

Lissa laughed and started the movie again.

6

Fall Fest was only two days away and Addison was getting more and more excited to see Suzanne and Rachel. She wasn't sure where they should go out to dinner Saturday night and decided to call Lissa for advice. Addison smiled just thinking about Lissa. They had talked or texted every day and she had gone to the mill in the evenings to play with the cats and walk with Lissa several times.

"Whatcha doing?" Addison asked when the call connected.

"Hanging out with my friends," Lissa said nonchalantly.

"Oh!"

Lissa chuckled at Addison's startled reply. "I'm reading a sapphic romance."

"Sapphic romance? That's a thing?"

"Yep. They have gay characters and they don't die at the end like they do in most movies."

"I'll have to tell Suzanne. She loves to read."

"I'm pretty sure she already knows." Lissa chuckled.

"Oh yeah?"

"If she's anything like me then she has probably searched for books with gay leads. I read them all the time now. It's like having gay friends."

"Huh, I had no idea."

"I wish our library had a bigger LGBTQ section. I've been trying to get the librarian to add more."

"Maybe that's our next project."

"Our next project?" Lissa parroted.

"What are we going to do after the 5K? Oh I know, I know!" Addison exclaimed.

"Please elaborate." Lissa chuckled.

"We should watch a Hallmark movie each week."

"Are you going to critique it as we watch or can you hold your review until the end?"

Addison threw her head back and laughed. Lissa always made her laugh. "I think we should rate the kiss at the end and see if it's happily-ever-after worthy."

"Oh, now that could be fun!"

"Hey, I can't decide where we should go to dinner Saturday night. Any suggestions?"

"Hmm, you're showing them the town all day Saturday, right?"

"That's the plan," Addison replied.

"There are a couple of great restaurants out at the lake," Lissa suggested.

"You haven't taken me to the lake yet," Addison said.

Lissa chuckled. "Please forgive me. I have failed as the Addison Henry ambassador to Brazos Falls."

"Well, I guess I can forgive you this time, but don't let it happen again," Addison said in mock consternation. "I'm so excited for you to meet them." She wasn't sure why it mattered to her so much, but she imagined the four of them becoming best friends. "I hope you don't have any weekend plans because I'm going to need you the entire time they're here."

Lissa laughed. "Why? They're your friends; why are you so nervous?"

"I'm not nervous. I just don't want them to be bored and I know Rachel will have a ton of questions I can't answer, but you can."

"My plans are to be with you all weekend. I don't want to get in the way, though. I mean, I'm sure you want time with them; they are *your* friends," Lissa said cautiously.

"They'll be your friends, too, after tomorrow night," Addison assured her.

"Addison, would you like to come over for a beer?"

"Can I?"

"Come over and we'll plan the weekend. I have leftovers calling your name."

"Lissa, can I ask you something?"

Lissa chuckled. "Sure you can."

"Do you like me?"

"What? Of course I like you."

"I'm not a pain in your ass? I mean, I'm not a project and you're not my ambassador or whatever you said."

"Addison, you're my friend. Though you may be a pain at times," Lissa replied with a chuckle.

"I'm not a bother or something that's in your way or someone you feel like you have to help—"

"Addy!" Lissa stopped her. "You are a leader and you command that fucking bank. You are never a bother." Lissa paused. "I've never heard you sound so unsure of yourself."

"You called me Addy," Addison said softly. Her family

and Suzanne were the only people she let call her Addy, but it sounded nice the way Lissa said it.

"I did. And I've never heard you like this. Look, I'm excited to spend the weekend with you and your friends. I'm doing this because I *want to*! You are my friend and I like you very much. Now, come over and drink my beer and eat my leftovers so we can plan a weekend that Suzanne and Rachel will never forget."

"I'm on my way," Addison said quickly.

"The back gate is unlocked."

* * *

Lissa looked in the refrigerator and took out a couple of beers. She was still smiling as she recalled her conversation with Addison. She was so confident and in control when it came to her job, but for some reason she had been nervous and at the same time excited that her friends were coming to visit.

Lissa was sure a lot of it had to do with Addison becoming the president of the bank and in some ways this was her town. She probably wanted to prove to Suzanne she'd made the right decision moving here as well. Lissa was determined to help Addison show them a good time. She wouldn't let her friend down.

There was a knock at the back door and before Lissa could open it Callie came scurrying in from the living room, meowing at the top of her feline lungs.

"Okay, okay." Lissa chuckled, opening the door.

Callie greeted Addison with several meows and growls then immediately started rubbing against her legs.

"Well hello there," Addison said, bending down to pet the cat. "Someone is glad to see me."

"I'm glad to see you, too," Lissa said with a smile. "Let Addy come in, Callie-girl."

Addison chuckled and carefully walked into the kitchen.

"A beer for my friend," Lissa said, handing Addison a bottle. She noticed Addison had her dark brown locks pulled into a messy bun on top of her head. A few stray strands framed her face and it occurred to Lissa just how adorable Addison Henry was. This was different from the strikingly professional persona Addison displayed at the bank and Lissa couldn't decide which was more attractive, but then again she shouldn't be having thoughts like this about her straight friend.

Addison tilted her head, catching Lissa's stare. "Thank you," she said softly.

Lissa smiled and led them into the living room. Once Addison sat down on the couch, Callie immediately jumped into her lap.

"She really likes you," Lissa commented.

Addison smiled and ran her hand along the cat's head and down her body. "I really like her, too."

Lissa studied Addison for a moment. "Do you realize how much I like spending time with you? Believe me, Addison, I wouldn't be walking, watching movies and hanging out with you if I didn't. I thought you knew that."

Addison continued to pet the cat's back as she purred loudly. "I do know that, Lissa. I've made such a big deal of Suzanne and Rachel's visit, I was afraid I may have forced you into spending the weekend with us instead of asking you."

"You invited me to hang out with y'all when you first knew they were coming and I gladly accepted. I really am excited to meet them."

"So you'll have real gay friends instead of the ones in books? At least for the weekend," Addison said.

Lissa chuckled. "Are you making fun of my books?"

"Not at all. I'm glad you have them."

"I have other friends in town, Addy, but it's different with you."

"What do you mean?"

"Most of them are married or have things to do with their kids or other reasons that they're busy. You and I..." Lissa paused.

"You and I..."

"We always have something to talk about and we're finding that we like a lot of the same things."

Addison gave Lissa such a sweet smile. "Like Hallmark movies?"

Lissa raised her eyebrows. "I didn't think you were a fan."

"I'm enjoying watching them with you," Addison said. "You make it fun."

"I'm learning all kinds of things on how you have to deal with people and it's fascinating how you seem to make everyone happy."

"That's the secret. You have to make them think you're making them happy." Addison chuckled.

Lissa laughed. "See there? You've got skills, my friend."

"I'm learning about small-town living from you, Lissa. It's so different from anywhere else I've lived. There really is a difference and I don't know what would have happened if I hadn't met you. They may have kicked me out of town already."

"I doubt that. You're doing just fine."

"By the way," Addison said. "Have you wanted to smoke?"

"What?"

"The first day I met you, you told me you had a craving to smoke because your brother did."

"Oh, right. You remember that?"

"I remember everything about you."

Lissa tilted her head and met Addison's gaze. Suddenly she felt a gentle flutter in her stomach. "I figured out that smoking, or wanting to smoke, was a reaction to stress or sadness. I haven't felt much of either of those since I told you that."

"Good. Let's try to keep it that way, but I'm here if you ever want to talk about your brother."

Lissa took a drink of her beer and sighed. "Thank you. Let's see what we can find for dinner and start planning this magical small-town weekend."

"I'm not sure Callie-girl is going to let me up."

"I can help you with that." Lissa got up and went to the kitchen. She shook a box and Callie jumped off Addison's lap, hurrying to the kitchen.

"Cat treats," Lissa said, taking several of the treats out of the box and feeding them to Callie. "Do you like tortilla soup?"

"Oooh, that sounds good. It's a little chilly this evening," Addison replied.

Lissa went about warming the soup and got out chips and salsa to complete their meal.

"I thought we could either order in or go to the pizza place Friday night when they get here. Suzanne loves pizza like I do."

"Okay."

"Then we can go back to my place. Saturday morning they can hang out at the finish line while we do our walk."

"There will be plenty for them to see and do while we're

walking. Some of my family will be at the finish line and they can hang out with them, too."

"Perfect. After that we can check out all the booths and activities around the square. I want to take them to the mill to meet the cats, if that's all right."

Lissa wiped her mouth and said, "Oh, I don't know about that, Addy. Once they see that place they'll think I'm a hick for sure."

"A hick? You are the farthest thing from a hick, Lissa."

"Country bumpkin?"

Addison giggled. "Not even close."

Lissa smiled and for a moment they stared into each other's eyes.

"This is really good." Addison said after another bite. "I want to drive them around town so they can get the full picture of what it's like here."

"Do you want to take them to the lake for dinner that night?"

Addison nodded as she dipped a chip in the salsa and crunched.

"This sounds like a fun weekend to me," Lissa commented.

"It does?"

"Yep. It's a solid plan. Do you feel better now?"

"I do." Addison said. She gazed at Lissa and smiled. "Thank you."

"For what? You planned it all."

"Thank you for being my friend. I like spending time with you, too."

Lissa held up her bottle. "To Suzanne and Rachel. Here's hoping they approve of your small-town life."

"They will, once they see how happy I am. They were

afraid I would move out here and work all the time. I think they thought I'd be lonely."

"Are you?"

"Nope. I have this friend..." Addison trailed off.

Lissa chuckled. "Are you up for another movie tonight?"

"Is there one on?"

"Honey, there's always a Hallmark movie on. That reminds me, you never did answer my question."

"What question is that?"

"Do you believe in happily-ever-afters?"

"Oh, hmm." Addison considered the question. "Do you mean in general or for me?"

"Both."

"I believe in happily-ever-after for some people. Like Suzanne and Rachel; I think they're living theirs."

"And for you?"

"I'm not sure."

"Oh?"

"What I mean is, I'm not sure what my happily-ever-after looks like. I've been so focused on work and moving up the ladder. I haven't really seen myself with a partner."

"Why not?"

"You don't have a partner, so why should I?"

"I'm not saying you have to. I haven't given up on spending my life with someone special."

Addison stared at Lissa as a sincere look settled on her face. "You should have someone special and she would be one lucky person."

A small smile played at the corners of Lissa's mouth. "Thanks, Addy," she said softly.

When the moment passed Lissa got up and began to clear the table. "Maybe you should think about someone special for you, too."

"Maybe," Addison said, getting up to help. "What's the movie about tonight? Are we doing a Christmas setting?" she asked, changing the subject.

Lissa stopped listening as she wondered what a partner for Addison would look like.

"Hey Lis, did you hear me?"

"Oh, the movie. I'm not sure. Let's see."

7

"**A**re you and Addison ready for the 5K tomorrow?" Ben asked.

"We're ready." Lissa chuckled. "We're just walking, remember?"

"Still, not everyone can go out and walk three miles." Ben looked at his sister and smiled. "I'm glad you and Addison have become friends. You're happier."

"What do you mean?" Lissa looked up at her brother and furrowed her brow.

"Just what I said. You've been happier since you and Addison started walking. I know how losing Peter has affected you, sis. Just because you're the oldest now doesn't mean you have to take care of us."

"Peter will always be the oldest and he didn't take care of us anyway. It was more like we took care of him."

"I know, but you shouldered most of the load. You may not have realized it, but the sorrow was all over your face. It's not there anymore; you're happier."

Lissa nodded and changed the subject. "Who is doing the 5K with Addison and me tomorrow?"

Ben narrowed his gaze and shrugged. "Okay. Good talk. Kara and the boys are running it. Last I heard, Marielle and Max are the finish line crew."

Lissa chuckled. "Max was very non-committal the last time we talked about it, so I'm not surprised he opted to be our cheerleader. What about you?"

"I will be joining our sister and nephew at the finish line. You'll hear me cheering you on from a mile away."

"Uh huh. Let me guess, you were too busy here to devote the time to training."

"That excuse works for me." He laughed.

Lissa laughed with him and shook her head as her cell phone rang on her desk. She smiled when she saw Addison's face on the caller id. Addison had taken the picture one day while they were out walking. Lissa remembered her taking several selfies of them because she claimed it was a beautiful day and they had beautiful smiles to go with it.

"Hey, Addy," Lissa said, connecting the call.

"Hey yourself. How's your day?"

"It's been good and it's almost over."

"The work day is almost over, but the fun's about to begin."

Lissa couldn't keep from laughing. "Is someone excited to see her friends?"

"I'm always excited to see you, Lissa," Addison teased.

"Haha. You know what I meant."

Addison laughed and Lissa thought it was such a nice sound.

"I'm already home and they'll be here soon. When are you coming over?"

"Can I go home and change first?"

"Yes, but hurry up. Let's get this weekend started."

Lissa laughed. "Yes ma'am. You can take off your bank president hat now."

"Oh Lissa, just because I'm not at the bank doesn't mean I'm not in charge."

Lissa scoffed. "Oh my God, Addy." She couldn't hold the laughter back. "See you soon."

"Hurry up," Addison said. "Bye."

Lissa looked at the phone, still laughing.

"I'm guessing that was Addison," Ben said from the doorway.

"She is so excited about her friends coming for the weekend."

"You'd better get going then. Aren't you her weekend guide?"

"Not really. She has everything planned. Believe me!"

"Have fun, sis. I'll see you in the morning."

Lissa closed the programs on her computer and grabbed her purse. "Here we go," she muttered. Honestly, she was a little nervous. She wanted Addison's friends to like her, but more than that she wanted Addison to have a fabulous weekend with her friends in her new town.

* * *

Addison was animatedly telling Suzanne and Rachel about their plans for the weekend in between hugs and squeals. She barely heard the knock at the front door in all the excitement, but then realized it was Lissa. Her stomach did a flip and her heart began to pound in her chest. *What was happening?* She couldn't think about that now; she needed to answer the door.

"Do you want me to get that?" Rachel asked with an amused look.

"It's Lissa!" Addison exclaimed. "Hey!" she said, opening the door.

"Hi," Lissa said tentatively then chuckled.

"Suzanne and Rachel," Addison said with a huge grin, "this is Lissa."

Suzanne gave her a measured look. "So, you're the new friend."

"And you're the best friend," Lissa replied with a twinkle in her eye.

Suzanne chuckled. "I like you. We're going to get along just fine."

Lissa laughed. "It's nice to meet you."

"Hi, I'm Rachel, the other friend. I'm married to that one," she said, holding out her hand.

Lissa shook her hand and grinned. "I imagine we'll get to know one another well this weekend while these two catch up."

"So true."

Addison put her arm around Lissa and the delight on her face lit the room. "All of my people are finally together."

They all laughed and followed Addison into the kitchen for drinks. She handed each of them a glass of wine while they stood around the island.

"So tell me about this 5K thing we're doing in the morning," Suzanne said.

"It's a fundraiser for the child advocacy department of the county. It's a 3.1 mile walk or run," Addison explained.

"We will be walking," Lissa added.

"I can't believe you convinced my friend to do it. She's only interested in numbers, mostly the ones that add to dollars and cents."

"Very funny. You act like I don't do anything physical. I'm still doing yoga," Addison said, defending herself. She looked over at Lissa and widened her eyes. "That reminds me, you haven't done yoga with me yet."

"You said we would do yoga after the 5K," Lissa replied.

"Be ready on Monday evening," Addison said with a wink.

Suzanne began to giggle. "Do you remember that time you talked me into doing a yoga class with you."

"How can I forget?" Addison snorted.

"Come on, you have to tell us," Lissa urged them.

"Everything was fine until I bent into downward dog and a little toot squeaked out."

"Oh my God." Lissa couldn't keep from laughing.

"We laughed and giggled through the rest of the class. I'm surprised they didn't ask us to leave."

"Don't worry," Addison said, looking at Lissa. "We'll be doing yoga in the comfort of my spare bedroom."

"That doesn't mean I want to fart in front of you!" Lissa said, horrified. "I'll be thinking about it the whole time."

"It's okay," Addison said softly, touched by Lissa's embarrassment.

"Your cheeks are red, Addy," Suzanne said.

"Lissa had been so good to let me walk with her and this was my way for her to do something with me. I don't want her to be self-conscious or nervous," Addison explained.

"It will be fine. But it's been a long time since I've done yoga. You'll have to be gentle with me," Lissa said.

Addison gave her the sweetest smile. "I will, just as you have with me."

"What will we be doing while you two are walking?" Rachel asked.

"Part of Lissa's family will be at the finish line. You can hang out with them," Addison said.

"My brother, sister, and her son aren't doing the 5K.

They are our cheerleaders. There will be things to do around the finish line while we're walking," Lissa explained.

"I've met them and they'll take good care of you."

"My sister-in-law and her sons are running it," Lissa commented. "They'll be at the starting line with us, but we'll see their backsides get smaller and smaller as they run away from us." Lissa chuckled.

"Did you want to run it?" Addison asked with a hint of distress in her tone.

"No! I told you all along that I was walking. I'm glad I won't be doing it alone."

Addison nodded as Lissa gave her a reassuring smile. "Oh, tell Suzanne and Rachel what you're doing with the library," Addison urged Lissa. "She's a reader, like you, Suz."

"I'm trying to get the library to expand their LGBTQ section. There are very few offerings," Lissa explained.

"Did you know about sapphic books?" Addison asked Suzanne.

"Well, duh. Yes! A lot of gay readers are looking to see themselves represented in books. You do remember that I'm in a book club, don't you?"

"Yes, I do. I thought you read bestsellers. I never thought about sapphic fiction and when Lissa told me about it, I wondered why I never heard you talk about it."

Suzanne shrugged. "The only books you're interested in are about finance—boring, non-fiction money books. When it's my turn to choose the book for book club, I always select a sapphic fiction or romance. You should hear my straight married friends talk about the sex scenes."

"No way!" Addison exclaimed.

"Yep," Rachel commented. "She comes home telling me how these women are missing out."

Suzanne looked at Lissa. "I've been telling Addy for

years that she needs to give a woman a chance. It would change her world," she teased. "At this point, if she'd go out on a date I'd be happy, even if it is with a guy."

Addison gave Suzanne a menacing look. "There's nothing wrong with having goals and working to achieve them. I have said to you over and over that I don't have the time right now. Besides, you seem to love my focus when you need to borrow money!"

"I don't borrow money from you. And I'm just teasing you!" Suzanne exclaimed.

"But it's still nice to know I have it if you need it," Addison said with a smirk.

"I'm surprised you haven't been set up with any of the single men in town," Rachel said. "Isn't that a small-town thing?"

"Have you?" Lissa asked, sounding a bit unsettled.

"No." Addison shook her head. "A couple of hints have been dropped here and there." She glanced over at Lissa and noticed her cheeks were pink. *What's that about?* "Do you know Hunter Wray?"

"Yes, he's a good guy," Lissa said with a smile that looked forced. "His mom is one of the best people I know."

"Sidney?" Addison asked. "I've met her. She told me she was going to suggest that Hunter take me to dinner."

"Have you met him?" Lissa asked, sounding anxious.

"He comes in the bank occasionally and stops by to say hello."

"Is he your type?" Suzanne asked.

"My type?"

"Yeah, is he cute? Where does he work? Maybe he's in finance, like you," Suzanne said excitedly.

"He sells insurance to ranchers for their pasture land and crops," Lissa stated flatly.

"What's that?" Rachel asked.

"Ranchers depend on the weather to feed their herds by growing grass. They can buy crop insurance to help out when there isn't much rain. He also has investment opportunities as well," Lissa explained.

"It sounds like he knows finance," Suzanne remarked.

"The last thing I want to do after working all day is talk about finance on a date. No thanks," Addison said. She glanced over at Lissa and smiled, then chewed on her bottom lip, trying to figure out why this conversation seemed to bother Lissa.

"Are we going out or eating in?" Suzanne asked. "Because I'm drinking more wine if we're staying."

"No," Addison said, tearing her eyes away from Lissa. "There's a pizza place I can't wait for you to try."

"Let's go," Rachel said, taking the last sip from her glass.

As they walked outside Addison turned to Lissa. "Do you mind driving?"

"Not at all." Lissa looked over and gave her a smile.

Addison was glad to see that whatever had troubled Lissa a few minutes earlier seemed to have passed.

They got into Lissa's SUV and from the back seat Suzanne exclaimed, "I can't believe she's letting you drive, Lissa. This one likes to drive and make the plans."

"You should see her at the bank," Lissa said, backing out of the driveway. "She is such a leader and her employees love her even when she's telling them what to do."

"Is there such a thing as a warm ice queen?" Rachel said.

"That doesn't make sense." Addison glanced into the back seat.

"Sure it does. You're a focused professional, but you deliver your expectations in a way that makes people like you," Suzanne explained.

"Exactly," Lissa agreed. "It's pretty damn amazing to watch."

Addison looked over at Lissa and furrowed her brow. "When have you seen me with my employees?"

"Every time I go into the bank." Lissa glanced over at Addison with a smile. "You're usually solving some kind of issue and doing it well."

"Thanks." Addison met Lissa's gaze. When Lissa turned her eyes back to the street Addison studied her friend for a moment. She knew Lissa thought she was good at her job, but somehow it felt different hearing her tell Suzanne and Rachel. Lissa sounded proud of her and maybe a little in awe. Her stomach fluttered as she let Lissa's words wash over her.

After dinner they went back to Addison's and Lissa loved watching Suzanne try to tease Addison. But Addison was always ready with a clever comeback that made Lissa and Rachel laugh.

"Are they always like this?" Lissa asked Rachel.

"Oh yeah. It's a competition on who can out-zing the other."

Lissa chuckled. "They're both very good at it."

"That they are."

"So what did you think of the pizza?" Addison asked.

"It was delicious," Suzanne replied. "I can't believe I'm saying this, but it was as good or better than Carlo's."

"I know!" Addison exclaimed. "I couldn't believe it the first time I had it at Lissa's. And for your information, Lissa doesn't like onions either."

"And we were getting along so well," Suzanne said, giving Lissa a disappointed look.

Lissa chuckled and shrugged. "It's all about the kisses, Suzanne."

"Right!" Rachel exclaimed. "Who wants to kiss you after you've been eating onions?"

"It doesn't seem to bother you, *babe*," Suzanne said, giving Rachel a pointed look.

"I can't help it if I like kissing you," Rachel grumbled.

"I'd better get going," Lissa said, rising from her seat on the couch.

"Oh no you don't," Suzanne said, raising her voice. "Who are you worried about kissing with onion breath?"

Lissa laughed. "I don't kiss and tell."

"I'll walk you out," Addison said, saving Lissa from Suzanne's questions.

"See y'all in the morning."

"Bye, Lissa. This was fun," Rachel said.

"Yeah, and I'm not through with the questions for you, new friend," Suzanne said with a grin.

"Okay." Lissa hurried out the door with Addison right behind her.

"I hope she didn't upset or offend you tonight," Addison said as Lissa got into her car.

"Not at all."

"So... What did you think?"

"They are tall and blonde," Lissa replied.

Addison chuckled. "They are, but you weren't intimidated in the least."

"As long as I had you to defend me." Lissa chuckled.

"I've got you, friend."

"I'll pick you up in the morning."

Addison nodded. "Bye, Lis. This was such a good night."

"Yeah, it was. Thanks, Addy."

On the short drive to her house Lissa thought back to the evening. Suzanne and Rachel were indeed very attractive, but Addison was beautiful. "Why would that even cross my mind?" she muttered. She had to admit it was fun hanging out with them and Addison was right: maybe they were her gay friends now, too. The idea of that made Lissa smile, and the four of them together had almost felt like two couples out for an evening.

"Don't even go there," Lissa mumbled to herself, shutting the thought down.

8

Lissa pulled into Addison's driveway and before she could get out of her car, Addison came bounding out of the house, jumping up and down. She stopped at the driver's side door and Lissa rolled down her window.

"Are you ready?" Addison exclaimed.

Lissa raised her eyebrows and grinned as Suzanne and Rachel followed Addison out of the house.

"You didn't answer me, Lissa. Are you excited?" Addison asked, taking her voice up a notch.

"I am now!" Lissa replied as Suzanne and Rachel got into the back seat and Addison ran around to the passenger side.

"Hi, Lissa. She's been like this all morning," Rachel said.

Lissa chuckled and waited for Addison to get into the car. "I had no idea you were this excited about the race."

"I didn't either." Addison shrugged. "I got up this morning and bam! I'm ready to go!"

Lissa looked into the rearview mirror as she backed out and eyed Suzanne. "How are you this morning?"

"I'm ready for my next cup of coffee and happy to cheer y'all on once the caffeine has had its way with me."

"Okay then." Lissa looked over at Addison and smiled. "I know a place where we can park. A friend has a store near the start/finish line and said we could sneak in the back."

"And that's why you're driving. I knew you'd find us a good place." Addison gave her a big smile.

Lissa drove them the short distance to the downtown square.

"Oh my God! This is right out of one of those Hallmark movies. It's so quaint," Rachel gushed.

"Is that your bank?" Suzanne exclaimed.

Addison chuckled. "That's it."

"It's kind of modern looking compared to all the old buildings on the square. But it's right on the corner anchoring everything."

"That it is. You know I didn't have anything to do with how it looks, right?" Addison said, but she sounded pleased.

"I know that, but it's still a nice building. I like those windows on the upper floors. They look like mirrors," Suzanne said.

"Are you going to show us your office?" Rachel asked.

"It's just an office; there's nothing special about it," Addison replied.

"Maybe so, but it's your office and we love you," Suzanne said.

"We'll see. Let's get this race over first."

"Here we go," Lissa said, putting the car in park. "We're here. Are you still excited?"

Addison chuckled and looked over at her. "Yes, I am. Are you making fun of me?"

"No!" As Suzanne and Rachel got out of the car, Lissa quickly grabbed Addison's arm. "Hey, I've done this race several times, but I'm happy that I'm doing it with you this year."

Addison gave her a slow smile. "I bet you say that to all the girls."

Lissa's eyes widened. "Suzanne is rubbing off on you."

"Probably." Addison chuckled. "Thanks, Lissa. I'm glad you invited me to do this, but you have to promise me that even though we won't be walking every week anymore, we'll do something together."

"I thought we were doing yoga and watching Hallmark movies."

Addison nodded. "Okay. Just checking."

"Are you chickening out?" Suzanne asked from where she was waiting for them at the back of the car.

"No way!"

They walked out from behind the building and headed for the starting line. When Lissa sneaked a look behind her to make sure Suzanne and Rachel were with them, she saw them holding hands. A warm feeling spread through her chest and she smiled. Man, she loved holding hands and didn't realize how much she missed it.

"Hey, are you okay?" Addison asked softly, putting her hand on Lissa's forearm.

"Yeah, sure."

"You had a sad look on your face," Addison explained.

"How could anyone be sad today?" Lissa held out her arms. "The sun is shining, we get to do the walk we've been training for all these weeks, and your best friends are here with us."

Before Addison could reply, two teenage boys came running up to them.

"Aunt Lissa, Joe and I got your packets. You've got to put

your numbers on," Leo said, his cheeks bright red in the crisp morning air.

"Hi guys!" Lissa said, grinning.

"Are you nervous, Addison?" Joe asked with a shy smile.

She grinned back at him. "No. I'm just walking with your Aunt Lissa. I think we can handle that. But are you nervous? You're running. Are you going to beat your older brother?" she asked in a hushed tone.

"No, he is not!" Leo said loudly.

"Hey guys, I want you to meet Addison's friends," Lissa said, chuckling at her nephews.

"We're your friends now," Suzanne said, winking at Lissa.

"This is Suzanne and this is Rachel," Lissa said. "And these helpful fellows are my nephews, Leo and Joe."

"It's nice to meet you," Suzanne said.

"You're going to run it!" Rachel said, clearly impressed.

"Yes ma'am." Leo beamed a smile. "We play a few sports in school so we run a lot as it is."

"But he barely beat me in our last training run, so watch out, big brother," Joe warned.

Lissa looked in her packet and found her race bib with safety pins, along with a T-shirt and other goodies.

"I forgot we were getting a shirt," Addison said, pulling her number out of the envelope. "Hey, our numbers are right together."

"Yep. I hadn't signed up yet when I asked you to walk with me, so I signed us both up the next day," Lissa explained.

"Will you pin this on me?" Addison asked. "Where does it go?"

"Pin it on the front," Leo said, proudly sticking out his chest.

"Here," Lissa said, taking the number from her. "I'll pin it on your stomach, just below—"

"Don't stick me," Addison warned her with a giggle.

Lissa looked into Addison's eyes and could see her amusement. She took one of the pins Addison offered her and attached one corner of the bib just below Addison's breast.

"Be careful, Lissa. You don't want to get her more excited," Suzanne teased.

"Suzanne!" Addison said, sounding horrified.

Lissa didn't look up, but was sure her cheeks were bright red. Thank goodness it was chilly this morning and maybe no one would notice. She fastened the last pin and chanced meeting Addison's eyes. "There you go. I didn't poke you once."

"Your turn," Addison said, taking Lissa's number and one of the pins.

"Be careful," Lissa teased.

Addison stared into her eyes and for a moment Lissa couldn't breathe. A small smile crossed Addison's face. "I'll be careful."

"But what if you weren't careful for once in your life?" Suzanne commented.

"Suzanne!" Addison and Lissa both yelled.

"Okay, okay. Come on, I was just having a little fun. You're playing with each other's boobs!"

Lissa could see that Addison's cheeks matched hers now and wondered if she was embarrassed...or could it be something else.

"There you go," Addison said, staring at Lissa's number. "Not one drop of blood from either of us."

"Where are your parents?" Lissa asked the boys.

"They have a place staked out at the finish line. They told us to come get you," Joe said.

They walked over and found Lissa's sister, brother, sister-in-law and nephew encouraging the runners and walkers as they warmed up.

Lissa and Addison introduced Suzanne and Rachel to the rest of Lissa's family. As they all started talking at once, Kara walked over to Lissa and Addison. "I want to walk with you for a while."

"I thought you wanted to run it," Lissa said.

"I do, but I want the boys to get way ahead of me so I won't be tempted to try and keep up with them."

Addison chuckled. "Lissa told me last night that they would start with us but become smaller and smaller as they sped away."

"I'm not sure what we'll do if Joe finishes before Leo. It could happen. I'll need Aunt Lissa to come to the rescue," Kara said.

"Hmm, my suggestion is to trip one of them so we don't have to deal with this until next year." Lissa grinned.

Addison laughed. "We'll come up with something if we have to," she assured Kara.

They called the participants to line up at the starting line and the cheerleaders waved their pom poms at the runners and walkers.

"As soon as they take off, we'll get coffee at that booth over there," Marielle told Suzanne and Rachel. "I happen to be Lissa's smart sister and have a little something we can add to it to warm us up," she said with a wink.

"I love your family, Lissa," Suzanne called to Lissa as she and Addison walked away.

"What was that about?" Addison asked, craning her neck around to see Suzanne waving wildly at them.

"If I'm guessing, my sister probably has a little something to take the chill off," Lissa replied.

"What? Like liquor?" Addison said, her eyes widening.

Lissa nodded. "Bourbon or Kahlua or maybe brandy. She adds it to coffee."

"Suzanne will love that. No wonder she loves your family. They are her people." Addison chuckled.

"Does that mean they're your kind of people, too?" Lissa asked quietly.

Addison tilted her head. "Yeah, why wouldn't they be? You're my people, Lis."

A man began to yell through the PA system to get ready to race.

"Since we're walking, let's start over to the side so we won't be in the runners' way," Lissa suggested, taking Addison's hand and pulling her through the crowd. Lissa felt Addison lace her fingers through hers and for just a moment the most magical feeling passed through her. It was odd and also familiar at the same time. She and Addison were holding hands and she knew it didn't mean the same thing to Addison as it did to her, but she reveled in it anyway.

Leo and Joe lined up in front of them and Kara stood beside Lissa. As the gun went off to start the race, the wave of participants moved forward and cheers were heard from the people gathered on either side of the starting line.

Lissa grinned at Addison as they began walking. Some people passed them easily then there were others that they had to sidestep to keep from walking into them.

"This is wild!" Addison said, walking quickly. Her breaths were coming faster and her cheeks were flushed from the excitement all around her.

"People will spread out and It will calm down soon," Lissa assured her.

"There go the boys. You're right, Lissa, they're getting smaller and smaller." Addison laughed.

"You don't have to walk so fast," Lissa said, glancing over at Addison. "It's the excitement from starting the race. Let's slow down."

Addison followed Lissa's lead and they slowed their pace.

"It's crazy at the start," Kara said. "Hey! Watch out, Jacob!"

"Sorry, Mrs. Morgan," a young man said as he ran by. "Hi, Lissa."

"That little shit almost knocked me down," Kara lamented.

Lissa chuckled. "You're okay, Mrs. Morgan."

"He calls you Lissa?" Addison asked.

"Yeah, he's one of Joe's friends. He's probably trying to catch up to him."

"Lissa has played with all the kids and their friends since they were little; that's why they call her Lissa," Kara explained.

"Oh." Addison considered Kara's explanation. "But they call you Mrs. Morgan because you're Joe's mom?"

"Yes, because I'm the mom and Lissa gets to be the fun aunt."

"Gets to be?" Lissa chuckled. "I *am* the fun aunt."

Kara laughed. "That you are. Okay, you two, I think it's time for me to run."

"Have fun!" Addison said.

"Next year you'll be running with me, Addison," Kara said as she started to run.

"Oh, I doubt that!"

Kara opened her arms and turned as she ran backwards. "Be open to the possibilities! See y'all at the finish line."

Lissa chuckled and watched her take off. She looked over at Addison and saw a serious look on her face.

"What's wrong?"

Addison met Lissa's eyes and smiled. "Nothing. I was just thinking about what Kara said."

"Do you want to run the race next year?"

"Oh, no. I'd much rather walk with you. What she said about being open to possibilities is a little out of my comfort zone, but I'm trying."

"Moving to a small town to further your career and get the experience of running a bank is being open, isn't it? I mean, you're from the city. I'm sure Brazos Falls is way out of your comfort zone," Lissa said.

"I guess you could look at it that way. I was thinking more about something Suzanne said last night."

Lissa said hello to two people as they passed them then looked at Addison. "Suzanne said a lot of things last night."

Addison chuckled. "That she did. I was referring to when she went on and on about you driving."

"Oh, that." Lissa shrugged. "I figured it was just easier because I'm from here."

"I've been here long enough that I know where everything is. Suzanne was talking about my tendency to be in control. She's right. But I don't feel like I have to be in control with you. I trust you."

Lissa looked over at her and smiled. "I'm glad you do."

"You seem like you're the one that's usually in control though," Addison commented.

"Yeah, I guess I usually am. With my family, someone has to lead us or at least suggest things. But you know, I've seen you at the bank and believe me, you are the boss!

You've got this," Lissa said. "You know, I don't have to be the one to decide everything. I guess what I'm trying to say is that sometimes it's nice to let someone else take the lead, you know."

Addison gave Lissa a sideways glance. "No! I don't know!"

Lissa laughed. "Yes, you do. It's something as simple as letting me drive."

"I guess, if you say so. Maybe I'm being open to possibilities," Addison said in a dreamy voice.

9

"Oh Addy, you've been open to more than you realize by simply moving to Brazos Falls," Lissa said, continuing their conversation.

"If you weren't concerned about finding a job, would you leave Brazos Falls?" Addison posed the question and raised one eyebrow at Lissa.

"Hmm, interesting question." Lissa stole a glance at Addison and smiled. "Are you going to take me with you when you're promoted to run all the banks?"

"Run all the banks?"

"Yeah, isn't that the goal? Don't you want to be the CEO of the company that owns all the banks, hence, run all the banks?"

"It's the way you said it." Addison chuckled. "Run *all* the banks!"

Lissa laughed with her. "But?"

"Yes, that is the ultimate goal. It will be several years with stops along the way, but I may as well aim for the top, shouldn't I?"

"Of course you should! You didn't answer my question," Lissa reminded her.

"You didn't answer my question and I asked first," Addison replied.

"Okay, okay. Yes, I would leave Brazos Falls."

"Hey, is that the finish line?" Addison said as the cheers began to reach them.

"It is. Does that mean you won't take me with you?"

"What? Oh! Yes, I'll take you with me and I'll get you a job, too. Be open to possibilities, Lissa," Addison said, her eyes gleaming.

Lissa laughed.

"Hey, that would be awesome. It would be my turn to show the small town girl the city," Addison marveled.

"Uh, you forget that I lived in the city."

"Oh, that's right. Well, I could show you *my* Dallas."

"Maybe we can do that sometime."

Addison imagined showing Lissa the city she'd called home for so many years and would eventually return to as her responsibilities grew in the company. That brought on all kinds of thoughts of things they could do together, like travel or go to concerts. She could probably talk Lissa into going to those dreaded parties the company had that she needed to attend, but didn't have a date for. Lissa could be her date!

"What is going through that head of yours?" Lissa asked. "You are smiling from ear to ear."

"I'm just thinking about all the fun we could have in Dallas," Addison explained. "Doesn't it feel good!" she exclaimed as they got closer and closer to the finish line.

"Doesn't what feel good?" Lissa said, her face brightening at Addison's contagious excitement.

"We made a goal and prepared in order to attain it. Here

we are, my friend, about to achieve our goal! It feels so good."

Now Lissa was laughing and sharing Addison's exuberance. "It does feel good. I'm so glad you walked this 5K with me, Addy!"

They could hear and see Lissa's family along with Suzanne and Rachel, all cheering for them. Everyone was smiling and Addison couldn't remember when she'd felt so happy and loved. Yeah, that's what the feeling was that she couldn't quite describe as they approached the end of the race. It was happiness and love.

She grabbed Lissa's hand and raised their arms as they crossed the finish line together.

Leo and Joe hurried over with their finisher's medals and a bottle of water for each of them.

"Way to go, Aunt Lissa," Joe said, placing the medal around Lissa's neck.

"Congrats, Addison," Leo said, mirroring his brother's move. "I'm so glad my aunt has you for a friend."

Addison gave him a bewildered look.

"Aunt Lissa is one of my favorite people," he said quietly. "I haven't seen her this happy in a long time. It must be you."

"Aw, thanks, Leo. She's made my life a lot happier, too," Addison said.

"Who has?" Kara asked, coming to congratulate her.

"Lissa has. It seems we have come into each other's lives at just the right time." Addison beamed a smile at Lissa.

She gave her a confused look, but shrugged and smiled back at Addison.

"Come on, let's get some food. Aunt Marielle and Max are holding a table for us by the food trucks," Joe said to the group.

As Addison followed everyone, Suzanne sidled up next to her and slung her arm over her shoulders. "I'm so proud of you."

Addison chuckled. "For what? Walking three miles?"

"That, and for letting these people embrace you."

Addison smiled over at her. "And here I thought you'd be jealous that Lissa has become my friend."

Suzanne guffawed. "I deserve that, but she knows her place. I'm the *best* friend."

"Yes you are. But this is going to be my home for a while."

"But... I think Lissa could be another kind of friend to you," Suzanne said cautiously.

"Cut it out, Suz," Addison said. "You wouldn't say that if Lissa was straight. Don't make her uncomfortable. She's my friend and she matters to me, just as you do."

"Okay, okay. I just wish that you'd open your eyes, Addy."

"Why? Why would I risk my friendship with Lissa for something that I don't have time for and isn't in the cards for me at this time? Drop it. Okay?"

Addison could feel Suzanne staring at her. "I'll drop it for now. But you and I both know you didn't dismiss the idea of Lissa because she's a woman. That's progress. Maybe your eyes are beginning to see."

Addison shook her head and rolled her eyes. "Hey, Lis! Wait up!" She hurried ahead, leaving Suzanne and her musings behind.

* * *

They spent the rest of the morning eating, playing games, and visiting the different booths at Fall Fest. The director of the race asked Addison to come up on stage and present the age group winners of the 5K. It was great publicity for the bank and Addison was a natural in front of the crowd.

"Hey sis," Marielle said, standing next to Lissa. "Would y'all like to come over and play games tonight? Ben and his crew are coming and we can order pizza."

"Thanks, Mari, but Addison wanted to take Suzanne and Rachel to the lake for dinner," Lissa replied.

Addison walked up, hearing the end of the conversation. "Did I hear games?"

"You did. We'd love for you to come play with us sometime."

"Lissa told me y'all have some pretty heated game nights," Addison said.

Marielle chuckled. "She does, that's for sure. Ms. Competitive loves to win."

"Then we'll make a fabulous team." Addison gave Lissa a grin.

"Okay, we'll do it another time. Y'all enjoy the lake."

"Thanks, sis."

"Thanks for supporting us today, Marielle. I could hear y'all cheering and it was so nice!" Addison said.

"Of course! We have to cheer on our friends." Marielle gave Lissa a wink and walked off.

"What was that wink?" Addison asked.

"Oh, you saw that, huh," Lissa said. "She was just teasing me a little. I promise they do not think we're together, Addy. I've told them!"

"It's okay. She was just teasing."

"I imagine several people saw us walking together and wondered," Lissa absently mumbled.

"Who cares. Let's go play with the cats," Addison said, giving Lissa a smile.

"I care," Lissa said, turning to face Addison. "I'm sorry. I don't want to harm your reputation."

"Hey, it's okay." Addison reached out and grabbed Lissa's hand. "But now?"

"I know, you want to show Suzanne and Rachel the mill and the cats."

"And I'd like you to smile."

Lissa stared into Addison's eyes and when Addison widened hers comically, Lissa grinned.

"That's better." Addison looked around and found Suzanne and Rachel talking to Kara and Ben. She walked over to get them and thought about how upset Lissa seemed at the thought of other people thinking they were together. It didn't bother her so much, but she wondered why it upset Lissa.

Lissa gave Suzanne and Rachel a brief tour of the mill. When the four of them walked into the large room where the cats lived, felines began to come out from behind pallets and machinery. The women were greeted with a chorus of meows and Suzanne and Rachel gasped.

"Wow!" Suzanne exclaimed. "This is wild!"

Lissa laughed. "No, the cats are wild!" She stood next to Addison and watched Dart hurry over and stop in front of her. He looked up, meowed, then head-butted Lissa's shin. "Hey, buddy," Lissa said softly.

The cat raised his head and seemed to notice Addison standing still next to her. He took a step over to where he was standing in front of her and lowered his head.

Addison looked up at Lissa with wide eyes.

"Slowly bend down and touch his head," Lissa said softly. "He remembers you."

Addison reached down as Lissa instructed and ran a finger between the cat's ears. Dart raised his head and nuzzled into Addison's hand. She began to run her hand from his head down his back and he turned in circles, following her pats.

"I can't believe this," Addison said, awed. "He does know me."

Finished with this brief moment of tameness, the cat looked up at her and then scurried on top of a pallet of feed.

Lissa chuckled. "And that's how he got his name."

Addison turned to Suzanne and Rachel. "His name is Dart because he never walks or slinks along like the other cats; he darts everywhere."

Lissa stepped back and sat down on a pallet of sacked feed as Addison told Suzanne the cats' names.

"Can we feed them?"

Lissa nodded. "You know where the cat food is."

Rachel sat down next to Lissa and asked. "Are they always like this?"

"They are always happy to see me. It may be because I feed them, but still, it's a nice welcome."

"I'll say."

They watched as Addison and Suzanne tried to coax the cats closer. "Addison has been coming by and playing with them while I close up for the day then we go walk around the neighborhood," Lissa explained.

"They'll let you pet them when they have their heads down eating," Lissa heard Addison instruct Suzanne, just as Lissa had told Addison a few weeks ago. This made Lissa smile.

"Look, babe. This one likes me," Suzanne said from across the room.

"I noticed several looks earlier today when Suzanne and I were holding hands," Rachel commented.

Lissa whipped her head around. "Oh no! Did anyone bother you?

"No, no. The looks weren't bad. A few people stared, but they also smiled," Rachel said. "It made me wonder..."

Lissa looked over at her and waited.

"Do you wonder what others think when you're with Addison?" she asked softly.

Lissa sighed. "I warned her at the beginning that some people might be looking at us and imagining things. I worry about it. I don't want to cause any problems for Addison at the bank."

"She wouldn't stand for it. She would shut down any kind of discrimination or gossip that had to do with you. I assure you," Rachel stated.

"Why do you say that?"

"Because I see how she looks at you. I know Addison, and she wouldn't work for a company that isn't inclusive. Let me ask you." Rachel paused. "If there was something going on between the two of you, would you still care what people are saying?"

10

L issa stared at Rachel. "There's nothing going on between us but friendship. Addison is straight."

Rachel smiled. "Humor me, please. What if there was? Would you care what people are saying?"

Lissa pursed her lips and thought about Rachel's question. "I would care, but I would also show them that we are just people, like everyone else. There's no reason to be threatened or afraid. We're just two people, trying to be happy like any other couple."

"It's that simple. I don't know why people have to make it so hard," Rachel said.

"Addison will be good for our town. She cares and people have already seen that with the changes she's made at the bank." Lissa continued to watch Addison and smile.

"She also cares for you."

Lissa looked over at Rachel and grimaced. "Rachel, I hope you're not trying to see something that isn't there. Addison is my friend. We have a good time together and that's it."

"Addison is my friend, too, Lissa. I've known her for,

gosh..." Rachel paused. "I guess it's been ten years now. I've never seen her befriend someone as quickly as she has you. She's had acquaintances at work and gone out with a couple of different guys, but Suzanne and I are her closest friends. You are who she talks about when she calls us and I haven't seen her this excited to see us in forever."

"Did you ever think that she misses you?" Lissa said flatly. "She talks about me because I'm the one who's been showing her around town. She knows she can ask me anything and I'll help her navigate this small town, which is a new environment for her."

A slow smile crossed Rachel's face. "Okay, Lissa." She leaned in. "Even though I don't know you very well, yet, I can tell you feel it and I see how you look at Addison, too."

Lissa took a deep breath and slowly let it out. She was about to reply when Addison grabbed her arm.

"Lissa," Addison said sweetly, looping her arm through Lissa's and taking her hand.

A smile quickly grew on Lissa's face. "Yes?" she replied in a cautious voice.

"Do you think Dart would be happy if he left the mill?"

Lissa studied Addison for a moment. "Do you mean...do I think Dart would be happy living down the alley from his sister?"

Addison looked at Suzanne and Rachel. "Dart's sister lives at Lissa's house," she explained. She looked back into Lissa's eyes and chuckled. "Yes, that's exactly what I mean. I want to adopt Dart if you think he'd be happy at my house."

"What? I've never known you to have a pet," Suzanne said.

"I haven't had one because I work so much, but I'm home a lot more here and, I don't know, I really like playing with them when I come to see Lissa."

"They like you and are getting accustomed to you coming around," Lissa observed.

"But...will you let Dart come live with me?"

Uh oh, how could she say no to those blue eyes when they sparkled at her like that? Lissa had felt a familiar tug in her heart as she watched Addison. It had been years since she'd felt it, but there was no mistaking what was happening. She knew she needed to shut it down before it complicated her friendship with Addison.

"You know, you are kind of the opposite of Dart," Suzanne said. "You are one to process things and think them through before you act. I'm not saying you can't make a quick decision, but you always think before you leap."

"That's not Dart." Lissa chuckled. "He jumps right in."

"Maybe that's what you need in parts of your life, Addison," Rachel suggested.

"What?" Addison looked at her, confused.

"Sometimes you need to jump right in," she explained. "Like you've done with Lissa."

Addison gave Rachel a stern look. "What are you trying to say, Rachel? There's nothing wrong with me hanging out with Lissa and if you're trying to imply that I need to consider the optics because Lissa is gay then you're wrong. Lissa is my friend and has been from the beginning. What we do is our business and no one else's."

Surprise overtook Lissa's face. She knew Addison had set Karen straight, so to speak, at work, but she'd never heard Addison speak in her defense before. A smile threatened to curve her mouth, but she bit her bottom lip instead. Addison was clearly upset.

"Whoa, Addy. I didn't mean it like that," Rachel said, walking over and resting her hands on Addison's shoulders. "I meant you're slow to make friends."

"It shouldn't matter who I do what with. But because my friend happens to be gay, it seems to change everything," Addison said, stepping towards Lissa. "I know it bothers Lissa and I'm sorry all of you have to think about things like that. It shouldn't matter, but I'm not naive and I know it does."

"Hey, hey, hey," Lissa said, smiling at Addison. She reached for both of her hands and took them in hers. They gazed into one another's eyes for a moment. "Thank you for defending me. I don't want the gays to dampen your day."

Addison scoffed. "The gays are my friends—oh, I see what you're doing." Addison giggled and began to laugh. "Sorry, I got a little defensive and serious there. I know you all have to think about things like this to keep yourselves safe. Just know that you're always safe with me."

"We know that, honey," Suzanne said, putting her arms around Addison and pulling her into a hug.

"I think Dart would love to come live with you. We can begin his transition next week. What do you say?" Lissa said.

"I say yes!" Addison jumped from Suzanne's arms into Lissa's.

Rachel met Lissa's eyes as she felt Addison's arms tighten around her shoulders. Rachel gave her a slight nod and Lissa wrapped her arms around Addison. Just for a moment she relaxed into the hug and closed her eyes.

Addison pulled away with a smile that lit the rather dark expanse of the warehouse. "Let's show them our town, Lis."

"Let's go," Lissa replied.

* * *

Lissa drove them around town while Addison narrated their tour.

"Where are the falls?" Suzanne asked. "I mean, the name of the town suggests there is water somewhere nearby."

"They're just outside town. We'll pass them on our way to dinner," Addison said.

"This is a nice town," Rachel said. "I can see why you like it, but Addison…"

"What?" Addison asked, turning to look at Rachel in the back seat.

"It's just that it's so small. What do you do? Where do you go? I know how you love to shop!"

Addison chuckled. "I do love to shop. And that's why I'll be doing plenty of it when I come in for Friendsgiving at your house."

"We're not going to see you until Thanksgiving?" Suzanne exclaimed.

"It's only a few weeks," Addison said, turning back to look out the front windshield.

"You can come visit anytime you want," Lissa said, looking at Suzanne and Rachel in the rearview mirror.

"Thanks, Lissa. We may take you up on that."

"I thought it was understood that my door is always open to you, anytime," Addison said.

"It is, but it's nice to know Lissa isn't sick of us yet." Suzanne laughed.

"What? No way. This has been the best weekend I've had in a long time," Lissa said.

"But you have a big family. I figured y'all are doing something all the time," Rachel said.

"Sometimes, but they're family. It's been nice to hang out with friends," Lissa explained.

"We hang out together most weekends. Are you saying you're tired of me?" Addison asked, seriously. She and Lissa walked on the weekends and she knew Lissa enjoyed it as much as she did, but it was also fun to tease Lissa.

"No!" Lissa cut her eyes toward Addison.

Addison couldn't keep the grin from curling the corners of her mouth.

"You're teasing me!" Lissa exclaimed then laughed. "You little shit."

"What was that?' Addison asked, her brows shooting up her forehead.

"You heard me." Lissa chuckled.

Suzanne and Rachel laughed from the back seat. "You do know the real Addison," Suzanne said. "She loves to tease and pester."

"But usually it's aimed at you, isn't it?" Lissa asked.

"Yep, but you're here and I'm so far away," Suzanne crooned.

"It's not that far." Rachel chuckled.

"Let's go change for dinner. I know walking three miles wasn't that big of a deal, but I could use a shower," Addison said.

"Me too," Lissa agreed. She dropped them off at Addison's then went home to shower and change.

While Lissa was in the shower she thought back to everything that had happened that day. She was trying to figure out what had changed because she was sure something had shifted in her relationship with Addison. *Is it just me?* The way Addison had sidled up next to her and asked if the cat could come live with her... it felt so natural for her to grab Lissa's arm and intertwine their fingers.

Lissa stuck her face under the stream of water and

closed her eyes. *Don't do this!* There was something about Addison that had drawn Lissa in since the first time they met. They had hit it off and formed a fast friendship. Lissa could remember a time or two when Addison had looked at her and her heart had fluttered in her chest, but today there was a sense of togetherness. They were showing Addison's friends *their* town.

Stop this silliness! Lissa finished rinsing her hair and chuckled. "It's good to know you're not too old to imagine," she said out loud. After quickly toweling off and drying her hair, Lissa changed clothes and applied a little make-up. Satisfied with the results, she looked into the mirror and smiled.

"You're Addison's friend, that's all and that's enough," she said to her reflection. "Addison is hyper focused on her career and don't forget, she's straight."

She picked up Addison and her new friends and headed for the lake. Lissa pulled over so Suzanne and Rachel could see the waterfall that had given the town its name.

"I hope you weren't expecting something larger and more dynamic," Addison remarked. "Our little falls are subtle and mystical."

"Mystical?" Suzanne asked.

"Well, maybe not mystical, but I think they're peaceful and soothing," Addison said earnestly.

"Hmm, I can see that," Rachel said. "This would be a good place to contemplate what worries you."

"My worries include hunger and a craving for seafood," Suzanne said. "Your falls are beautiful, Lissa and Addison, but will you please feed me?"

Lissa chuckled and pulled the car back onto the highway. When she glanced over at Addison, clear blue eyes were staring at her.

"Your hair looks nice." Addison reached over and brushed a few dark blonde strands behind Lissa's ear. "I don't get to see you wear it down like this very often. We're usually wearing ponytails."

"Would you still like it if I cut it short?"

Addison ran her fingers through a few more strands and tilted her head. "Are you going to cut it?"

"I'm thinking about it."

Addison nodded. "I think it would look cute."

Lissa smiled at her and turned her attention back to the road, but not before she glanced into the rearview mirror and saw Suzanne and Rachel share a look.

11

A few minutes later, Lissa pulled into the restaurant's parking lot. The moon sparkled off the surface of the dark water, welcoming the four friends into the brisk evening air.

"Oh, this is cozy," Suzanne commented. "I can imagine how lovely it is in summer."

Once inside they were seated at a table next to the large windows that offered a view of the lake. They ordered drinks and discussed the menu options.

"Don't look now, but Chris Albritton is headed our way," Lissa said quietly.

Addison leaned toward her. "Isn't he on the city council?"

Lissa nodded discreetly.

"Good evening, ladies," Chris said, smiling down at Lissa and Addison. "Congrats on your race today."

"Thanks, Chris." Lissa chuckled. "It was a nice walk."

"Nice walk? It was three miles! We didn't walk three miles!" Suzanne exclaimed.

"She's right. You should be proud," Chris replied.

"Thank you." Addison smiled.

"I don't want to interrupt your dinner, but I wanted to ask a quick question."

"Okay," Addison said cautiously.

"I know the bank and the feed mill sponsored the race today. We have the Christmas parade and stroll coming up in December. I was wondering if you'd both be interested in sponsoring two of the middle school hot chocolate teams?"

Addison looked at Lissa, then back at Chris. "I know about the parade and stroll, but what are hot chocolate teams?"

"The clubs at the middle school have hot chocolate teams that compete during the stroll," Lissa explained. "Organizations sponsor them to help with the costs and decorations of their booths on the square."

Addison smiled at Lissa. "So we'd be competing against one another?"

"Sort of," Chris replied. "The people vote that night on which hot chocolate they like the best."

"That sounds like fun," Addison said, giving Lissa a look.

Lissa could see the mischief in Addison's eyes and chuckled. "We'd be happy to sponsor a team," Lissa said to Chris, but challenged Addison with a look.

Addison laughed. "Chris, the bank will be happy to also sponsor a team, and I know we've already promised to sponsor the parade and will have a booth for the stroll."

"Thank you both! This will be fun. I'll leave you to enjoy your dinner."

"Are you challenging me, Lissa Morgan?" Addison asked after Chris walked away.

"I thought you were challenging me!" Lissa laughed.

"I understand the parade, but what is the stroll?" Rachel asked.

"On the evening of the parade, all the stores are open around the square, serving goodies," Lissa explained. "The mill isn't on the square so we sponsor the parade."

"We're on the square so we'll have some kind of refreshments and we'll give away stuff," Addison added.

"Like money?" Suzanne asked. "I'll be back for that!"

Addison laughed. "You're welcome to come back. It's a couple of weeks after Thanksgiving."

"Count me in," Rachel said as their server came to the table.

They placed their orders and Lissa explained more about the parade and stroll. It didn't take long to get their food and the conversation was lively with this new competition brewing between Lissa and Addison.

"We'll have to come back that weekend for sure now. Lissa will need her gay friends to support her," Rachel said, taking another sip of wine.

"Hey, wait a minute," Addison grumbled. "You were my friends first."

"I do have gay friends, y'all," Lissa said in self-defense. "They just don't live here and I don't see them very often."

"And you have your friends in your books," Addison added, quirking her brow.

"Are you making fun of me?" Lissa asked.

"No. But what is it with gay friends? Do you want someone you can sit around with and talk about women?"

"No, it's not like that!" Lissa exclaimed.

"Oh yeah, Addy. That's what we do, we sit around and talk about women." Suzanne laughed.

"No you don't," Addison scoffed. "You only have eyes for each other."

"That's the way it should be," Lissa said softly.

"Oh, is it?" Addison asked, resting her chin on her hand and leaning towards Lissa.

Lissa met Addison's gaze and paused. "That's the way it is for me. You see, when I'm in, I'm all in. If I'm interested, it's just her."

Addison studied Lissa and couldn't help but wonder what that would be like—what would it feel like to be Lissa's focus, Lissa's only one.

"But what if they're not gay?" Rachel asked. "Surely that's happened to you."

"Oh yeah." Lissa sighed.

"Then there are those who haven't been with a woman before..." Rachel began.

"And break your heart when they decide it isn't for them," Suzanne added.

"Is that different from breaking up with someone or deciding they aren't for you?" Addison murmured.

"It is for me," Suzanne said. "In a way, you feel like you've been deceived. They're trying it out and it makes you feel like you're not good enough."

"That's terrible. You're one of the best people I know!" Addison exclaimed.

Suzanne smiled at her. "That's why you're my best friend."

"And that's why I married you," Rachel said, kissing Suzanne on the cheek.

"We need to think about our friends and set Lissa up," Suzanne said.

Lissa's eyes widened. "Oh no, I'm okay. Really."

Addison watched this exchange and felt a stab of fire ignite in her stomach. The idea of Lissa going out with one of Suzanne and Rachel's friends didn't sit well with her. But why would it bother her? Didn't she want Lissa to be happy?

"Hey," Suzanne said, snapping her fingers in front of Addison's face. "Where did you go?"

"Sorry." Addison shook her head, trying to get the idea of Lissa on a date out of her mind.

"I was telling Lissa I think it's so cute that you walk down the back alley to her house. How small-town is that?"

"Is this like a mini vacation for y'all?" Lissa chuckled.

Suzanne looked over at Rachel and grinned. "Kind of. We haven't been anywhere in ages."

"You know, that tells me what you're doing in my spare bedroom," Addison said, with a smirk.

"And what would that be? Sleeping?" Suzanne said, amused.

Addison chuckled. "You're having vacay sex in my extra bedroom."

"I wouldn't expect anything less from you when you come to visit us," Suzanne said matter-of-factly.

"Oh my God!" Lissa chortled. "You two are too much!"

"Of course, that would mean Addison would have to meet someone, which isn't likely," Suzanne commented.

"Why do you say that?" Lissa asked.

"Because she's so focused on that bank and what comes next," Suzanne explained.

"People do come into the bank. You know that, right, Suzanne?" Lissa said, defending Addison.

"That's how I met Lissa and look how that turned out," Addison said, smiling over at Lissa.

"I'd say it's been a wonderful surprise for both of you," Rachel commented.

Neither of them said anything or broke their gaze.

"Can we walk down to the water before we go back?" Rachel asked.

"Sure," Addison replied, getting up. "I'll go settle the bill and meet y'all by the water."

"Wait, let me help." Lissa stood up.

"I've got this. You've done so much for me... Please?" Addison said softly.

Lissa nodded and led Suzanne and Rachel out of the restaurant and down to the lake.

"This is nice," Suzanne said.

"We've got to come back and see it in the summer," Rachel added.

"You're always welcome."

Addison walked up next to Lissa and put her arm in hers. They watched Suzanne and Rachel step closer to the water, holding hands. "No wonder they wanted to walk down here; it's very romantic," Addison said.

"Especially in the moonlight," Lissa remarked.

Addison's heart began to beat a little faster. She realized she was holding Lissa's arm as if they were a couple and almost pulled away. But when she saw Lissa quietly taking in this beautiful scene she didn't even think; she simply put her arm through hers. She'd do the same thing if it were Suzanne or Rachel standing there. *Wouldn't she?*

Suzanne and Rachel turned around and they started to walk back to Lissa and Addison. "It's really beautiful here. Now I'm in the mood for a little vacay sex."

"Oooohhh!" Addison exclaimed and dropped Lissa's arm. "You had to ruin it!"

Suzanne laughed and kissed Rachel. "You started it!"

* * *

Lissa had been home all afternoon and couldn't get Addison out of her mind. They'd laughed and talked after dinner last night and Lissa went back to Addison's this morning to help with brunch. At times she'd catch Addison looking at her, but couldn't read her expression. Lissa wondered if Suzanne's teasing and comments about being gay were bothering Addison.

She liked Suzanne and Rachel and they'd be back for the Christmas parade. Maybe she should talk to Addison and make sure they were okay. The last thing she wanted was to make Addison uncomfortable.

Callie jumped up on the couch and walked around and around in Lissa's lap. She meowed right in her face then jumped down and lazily walked to the back door. "Okay, okay." Lissa grabbed her phone and went out the back door.

Callie took off on her neighborhood rounds and Lissa walked down the alley to Addison's. She texted her and within a minute the back gate opened.

"Hey," Addison said with a smile.

"Are you tired of me yet?" Lissa asked, crinkling her nose.

"Never. Come on in." Addison stepped back to let Lissa into the backyard and closed the gate. "Let's sit in the sun; it's nice this afternoon."

Lissa joined her on the back porch where the sun bathed Addison's chairs in warmth.

"Suzanne texted me and said they made it home," Addison commented.

"Oh, good. Did the weekend turn out like you hoped?"

"Yes! Thanks for helping me show them around, and thanks for spending time with us," Addison said with a smile. "You know, we made a good team this morning. Brunch was wonderful, didn't you think?"

"It was. I had a really good time all weekend. Suzanne and Rachel are great."

"Yep. You've made new friends."

Lissa nervously chuckled. "Yeah, uh, I wanted to ask you..."

"Hey, is something wrong?"

Lissa looked up at Addison and took a deep breath. "Does it bother you the way Suzanne teases you about dating a woman? And then the whole gay friends thing," Lissa blurted. "I was afraid she made you uncomfortable and I never want to do that to you, Addy."

"You didn't," Addison assured her. "I know how Suzanne is. Believe it or not I used to just let her tease me, but then I learned to give it right back to her."

Lissa smiled. "You definitely hold your own with her."

"The thing about gay friends bothers me. I don't quite understand it and it makes me feel like I can't be a complete friend, you know?"

"Oh? I never thought of it that way. It's hard to explain, Addison. Although every gay person's journey is different, there's something about knowing they've been through it, too. It doesn't make them a better friend or a closer friend. It's just different somehow," Lissa said, trying to explain.

Addison nodded and Lissa could tell she was thinking about what she said.

"I will tell you this," Lissa said, waiting for Addison to look at her. "I wouldn't trade you for all the gay friends in the world."

"Yeah?" Addison chuckled.

Lissa loved the sparkle in Addison's blue eyes and it made her even happier to know she put it there. "I know we haven't known each other long, but you've become my best friend. I can talk to you about anything. It doesn't matter if you're gay or straight or neither. All that matters is that we—"

"Like spending time together," Addison affirmed.

"Exactly." Lissa beamed. She exhaled a relieved breath.

"I will admit, when Suzanne was talking about setting you up with someone, it made me hesitate," Addison said.

"Hesitate?"

"Well." Addison wrinkled her forehead. "I may have been a little jealous."

Lissa raised her eyebrows and her heart began to pound in her chest.

12

"Jealous and selfish," Addison added.

"You could never be selfish," Lissa said.

"Oh yeah, I can. If you find someone then where does that leave me? You won't have time for me anymore. You'll be with her." Addison shrugged.

"That's not true. I don't have to spend time with you, I *want* to. I'll always want to spend time with you, Addy. So, it's not about having time, it's who I choose to spend time with and I'd choose you."

Addison smiled and narrowed her brows. "But would you choose to spend time with me if you met your dream woman? You'd want to be with her. Tell me, Lis, what is she like?"

Lissa chuckled. "She'd be kind."

"Well duh, like you'd be with someone who's mean. It'd never happen."

"I don't mind if she has a little snark about her if she can back it up."

Addison laughed. "That would keep things interesting."

"What about you? What is your person like?"

"My person," Addison began thoughtfully, drumming her fingers on the arm of her chair. "Would have to be someone who isn't hyper-focused on their career. Because there's only room for one of us in this relationship."

Lissa laughed. "And that's you!"

"I'd want them to be settled and okay with themselves," she said wistfully. "Does that make sense?"

"I think so. You want them to be supportive of your goals, as well as know what they want."

"Yeah. And I'd support their goals, too."

"I do know my person is a woman," Lissa stated.

"I understand that."

"You know, being gay isn't the same for everyone. I worked with a woman who had only dated men and then she fell in love with a woman. They got married and have been for over twenty-five years. I'm not sure she considers herself gay, bi, or what."

"Wow, that's something."

"It is, but I know for me, my person is a woman and I believe we'll be together someday." Lissa shrugged.

Addison smiled. "I love your confidence."

"Don't you believe that for yourself someday?"

"Um, not really."

"I hope you don't find yourself as the CEO in fifteen years and end up lonely," Lissa said.

"Don't worry. I've thought about that, but now I'll have you, right, Lis? You'll always have time for me."

Lissa chuckled. "Yeah, Addy. You'll have me."

Addison visibly released a relieved breath. "Will you be ready for yoga tomorrow after work?"

"As long as you'll come watch a movie with me this week."

"There's nothing I'd rather do." Addison grinned at Lissa.

* * *

Addison walked Lissa out of the backyard and was about to close the gate when she saw Callie slinking towards them in the alley.

"What about Dart?"

Lissa turned back to Addison and smiled. "I can bring him to you when we do yoga tomorrow."

"Really?" Addison was excited, but she was also nervous.

"He can roam around the house while we exercise. Maybe I can get Callie to come with me. It will be interesting to see how they react to one another."

"Do you think they'll remember each other?"

"We'll find out."

Addison couldn't contain the excitement bubbling up inside her. "Thank you, Lissa!" she exclaimed and suddenly wrapped her arms around Lissa's shoulders, pulling her into a hug.

She could feel Lissa's surprise as her back muscles tensed under Addison's hands, but then she felt Lissa's arms encircle her waist and for a moment they both relaxed into the embrace.

"I know you'll give Dart a good home," Lissa said softly.

Addison could feel Lissa's breath next to her ear and a shiver ran through her body. She started to pull away, but something kept her there and instead she held Lissa a little closer.

They pulled apart when they heard Callie loudly meowing at their feet.

Addison looked down as the cat was rubbing against her legs and purring loud enough for the neighborhood to hear.

"What the..." Lissa said.

Addison chuckled. "I think someone else might be jealous."

Lissa chuckled then gave Addison a serious look. "Are you going to steal my cat away from me, too?"

"You can come visit," Addison teased.

Lissa stood there with her mouth open.

Addison threw her head back and laughed. "Where have you been all my life, Calista Morgan? This just gets better and better."

"I'm glad you're having a good time as my life implodes," Lissa whined.

It was Addison's turn to be surprised. "Oh, right. Your life has been so horrible since I came into it. Let's see, you have someone to laugh with, walk with, share meals with, watch silly movies with, and generally hang out with. Do you want me to keep going?"

Lissa narrowed her gaze. "What makes you think I didn't have that before?"

"Do you have another friend that I don't know about?"

"I have lots of friends," Lissa scoffed.

Addison chuckled. "You do, but as you once told me they have kids and husbands and not much time for friends. But I, on the other hand," Addison grinned, "have time for you and love being with you. So?"

"So?"

"So I'd say your life is much, much better since my timely arrival," Addison said boldly, crossing her arms over her chest.

"Okay, okay, you win. My life is better, but please don't steal my cat," Lissa pleaded.

Addison grinned. "I'm not stealing your cat. She clearly loves to mess with you, just as I do."

As if on cue, Callie began to circle Lissa's feet and rub her legs. She even stretched her front legs up and rested her paws on Lissa's thigh then began to rub them over and over, gently patting Lissa's leg.

"Aww, that's so cute," Addison said.

"Yeah, it's cute until the claws come out," Lissa said, reaching down and picking up her cat. "Come on, sweetness, let's go home before you change your mind. See you tomorrow."

Lissa took a few steps then let the cat down. Addison watched as Lissa and Callie walked down the alley side by side until they reached her gate. Lissa turned and waved.

Addison returned her wave and smiled. She went back into her own yard and shut the gate. There were times last night when she couldn't keep her eyes off Lissa. She wasn't sure why, but she didn't look away when Lissa's eyes met hers.

She thought back to what Lissa said earlier about being gay, that it wasn't the same for everyone. Suzanne had been teasing her off and on for years about dating a woman, but Addison had never seriously considered it. Her reason was always the same: she was focused on her career.

Maybe she'd never entertained the thought because there had never been a woman who interested her. But now, this move to Brazos Falls had not only helped her career, it had also given her more free time that she was spending with the most interesting woman she'd met in, hmm, she couldn't remember when.

Addison sighed as she walked back into the house and started to unload the dishwasher. Her thoughts drifted back over the weekend. Suzanne and Rachel had immediately hit it off with Lissa and that made Addison happy. She wondered if people who didn't know them saw them at different points during the weekend, say at Fall Fest or out at dinner, and thought they were four friends out having fun... or maybe they thought they were two couples spending the weekend together.

One thing Addison knew for sure, whoever was lucky enough to be Lissa Morgan's girlfriend would have to be exceptional herself. Again, Addison found herself wondering what it would be like to have all of Lissa's attention.

A smile crossed her face then she nearly dropped the plate she was holding. "Holy shit! I have the majority of Lissa's attention!"

She put the plate away, but not the thoughts of Lissa. Had something changed over the weekend? "I did just jump in her arms in the alley." Addison chuckled, but that was because she was excited about the cat. Would she have done that with any other friend?

Then she gasped. *Am I interested in Lisa?* "Surely not," she said aloud. "She knows I'm straight." Addison walked into the hallway and looked into a mirror that hung on the wall.

"Am I straight?"

* * *

"Are you checking me out?" Lissa asked. "You'll give a gay girl hope."

"What? No!" Addison exclaimed as she turned her attention back to the yoga instructor on the TV screen.

They had been doing yoga for three weeks now and Dart had settled into his new home. He loved to peek into the room, crawl through their outstretched arms and legs, then dart away, true to his name. He'd just dashed from the room when Addison's gaze landed on Lissa's firm butt. *Yoga definitely looked good on her.*

Lissa chuckled. "It's okay, Addy. I was teasing. I know your mistress is spreadsheets and deposits and bank services to help your customers."

"You make that sound tiresome and very unflattering." Addison said, horrified.

"Not at all! I think it's incredible and amazing."

"You do?"

"Yes! I think for me, I knew I would always have to come back here, so I made the most of my time in the city while I was there."

They twisted into another pose. When Addison looked over at Lissa, Lissa winked at her. Addison chuckled. "Stop that, you'll make me fall." She knitted her brows together and stared at Lissa before standing and reaching for the sky as the leader instructed. "I really like your new haircut. The shorter style suits you."

"Thanks. I'm still getting used to it."

"We were in Dallas at the same time, but we never met," Addison said, steadying herself.

Lissa scoffed. "Don't forget I'm a lot older than you. We probably didn't hang out in the same places."

"You're not that much older than I am," Addison said. "I moved there after grad school; I was twenty-four."

"Let's see, I'd have been thirty-eight? What was I doing then?" Lissa mused.

"I was working at headquarters and starting my career. Oh, and Suzanne and I were neighbors."

"I lived in North Dallas then and worked near downtown. I hated that commute," Lissa said, bending down to touch her toes.

"Why didn't you live closer? I had to commute to a bank in east Dallas and almost moved there, but Suzanne talked me out of it."

"That wasn't an option at the time. I was living with my girlfriend and she owned the house."

"Oh! Did you live together long?"

"We were together for five years."

They both followed the instructor into downward dog.

"That's a long time. Why'd you break up?" Addison looked under her right arm and found Lissa staring back at her. "Oh shit, too much?"

Lissa chuckled and stepped her feet back into plank pose. Then she lowered down and raised her chest off the floor into up dog. "No, it's okay. The short answer is that she thought I was the one and I didn't feel the same way about her."

"The one? As in being together forever?" Addison glanced over at her.

"That's the one. I loved her, but I don't know, I just couldn't see spending forever with her."

"Why not?"

"Wow, aren't you the inquisitive one?" Lissa said, cutting her eyes toward Addison.

"I'm sorry. Do you not want to talk about it? Did she break your heart or did you break hers?" Addison pressed her. Why she wanted to know was beyond her right now. What she did know was that she loved being with Lissa and they were both learning more and more about each other every time they were together.

"We had a good life, but something was missing. I don't know if it was the idea that this was as good as it gets or what? I understand that there will be times in a relationship when things aren't exciting, but..." Lissa paused.

"Even when things aren't exciting you're still in love with that person and like being with them."

Lissa swung around and sat crossed-legged, facing Addison. "That's it exactly."

Addison mirrored Lissa's posture and the way Lissa was looking at her made her heart speed up. "Do you think you'll find that someday?" Addison said, her voice just above a whisper.

"God, I hope so," Lissa said, her eyes never leaving Addison's.

Dart came running into the room and crawled into Addison's lap then meowed in her face.

"Are you sure you weren't checking me out?" Lissa said with an amused look on her face.

Addison quirked an eyebrow. "Oh, you'll know when I'm checking you out," she stated confidently, petting Dart between the ears.

Lissa laughed. "Addison Henry bringing the charm."

"Is it charm or snark?"

"Ah, with you it's a fine line, but mostly, it's adorable," Lissa said, beaming Addison a smile.

Addison felt caught in the warmth of Lissa's gaze. It was mesmerizing and she couldn't look away. *How can a woman resist you when you're looking at them like this?*

"I think someone wants to play with his sister," Lissa said, nodding toward the cat and breaking their stare.

"**D**o you think it's unusual that Callie and Dart remember each other?" Addison asked as Dart purred in her lap.

"Not really. What I find amazing is how they come to our houses and want to play with each other. It's like they're visiting and then they go back to their homes."

"Callie is probably on the back porch right now waiting for me to let her in or let Dart out." Addison chuckled.

"Let's go see," Lissa said, getting up and offering Addison her hand.

Addison smiled up at Lissa and took her hand. They had settled into a nice routine since Fall Fest: they watched at least one movie together each week and did yoga three times a week. Most weekends they went out to dinner or cooked at one of their respective houses.

For a while Addison had compared the things she did and how she felt about Lissa with feelings she'd had for other friends. She'd decided to stop thinking about it and trying to define what was happening between her and Lissa.

They were friends and liked being together. Why put a label on it?

When she opened the back door, Callie was waiting for Dart on the back porch. They shared a couple of head butts and meows before tackling one another and falling off the porch.

Lissa chuckled. "They are so funny."

"You know, I *was* checking you out earlier," Addison said, bumping her shoulder into Lissa's.

Lissa's eyes were comically wide when they met Addison's. "I knew it!"

"Do you remember when Suzanne was here and she mentioned that she could tell I'd been walking because I looked fit?" Addison began. "I'm not sure that's the right word, but we've been doing yoga for a few weeks and I can see a difference in you, Calista Morgan."

"Please, go on," Lissa said, giving Addison her full attention.

Addison could feel her cheeks warming under Lissa's stare, but she didn't look away. "Let's just say—uh oh, I can already tell this isn't going to come out right."

Lissa chuckled. "Keep going, you can do it," she urged her on.

Addison giggled. "Parts of your body appear firmer. There, I said it!"

"Parts?" Lissa asked, obviously amused.

"Yes, parts. You'll have to figure out which ones," Addison stated with a twinkle in her eyes.

"Uh huh. Well, I have also noticed a change in our bodies. Our backsides may be firmer, but my belly is still jelly because of all the pizza we eat on movie night," Lissa said, wiggling her butt and patting her belly.

"Who said anything about backsides?" Addison asked innocently.

Lissa gave her a pointed look. "I know where you were looking."

Addison burst out laughing. "Caught in the act."

"Are we still on for a movie and pizza tomorrow night?" Lissa asked.

"I wouldn't miss it, but if you'd rather have salad..." Addison shrugged. "You'll have it alone because I'm eating pizza!"

Lissa laughed as they watched the cats continue to prance around the yard.

"We're getting good at figuring out what's going to happen in the movie," Addison said.

"And you're beginning to believe in that kiss at the end of the movie," Lissa added.

Addison narrowed her eyes. "One kiss...that's still hard to imagine."

"It depends on the kiss," Lissa said with a lilt in her voice.

Addison studied her for a moment and decided maybe some of Lissa's romantic ways were rubbing off on her after all.

"Hey, I've been meaning to ask you about Thanksgiving. You're going to Suzanne's for the weekend, right?"

"Yeah, the bank can't be closed that many days in a row and since it's my first holiday here I wanted to be an example," Addison said in a lofty voice.

"Of course you are," Lissa said in mock seriousness. "But that means you will be here Thanksgiving Day."

"Yep, I will."

"Would you please spend it with me and my family?" Lissa asked earnestly.

Addison tilted her head. "All kidding aside, really? You want me at your family Thanksgiving?"

"Yes!" Lissa smiled. "We'd love for you to join us."

"I'd like that, Lis. Thank you."

Lissa grinned. "We're having it at Marielle's this year. I'm sure there will be some kind of video game competition. Which reminds me, I need to practice."

"What can I bring?" Addison asked.

"All you have to bring is you." Lissa smiled sweetly.

"No way. I have to bring something," Addison insisted.

"I'll check with Marielle and see what's on the menu. We can make something together."

"We are a good team." Addison said, nodding.

"That we are." Lissa bumped their shoulders together again.

* * *

Addison's phone rang on her desk and she tore her eyes away from the report she was analyzing on her computer. "Addison Henry," she answered in a pleasant voice.

"How's my bff?" Suzanne asked on the other end of the call.

"Hey, Suz. Why are you calling me on the bank phone?" Addison asked.

"I realized I didn't have your work number in my phone. So I took to the internet, looked it up and what do you know? It works!" Suzanne explained.

"You could've simply texted me," Addison replied.

"Ah, where's the fun in that." Suzanne laughed.

Addison chuckled. "I'm looking forward to seeing you next weekend. Thanksgiving is almost here!"

"I know! I've already warned Rachel that we will be in super shopping mode."

"I'm ready!"

"What are you taking to Lissa's family Thanksgiving?"

"I'm not sure yet. We're supposed to figure it out this weekend."

"Hey, you should ask Lissa to come with you next weekend," Suzanne suggested.

"That would be fun," Addison replied. A smile played across her face at the idea of Lissa joining them for shopping and she could meet her other friends. "I'll ask her."

"Ugh, I should get back to work," Suzanne lamented. " Let me know if Lissa can come. Love ya, bye," she added hurriedly.

"Bye," Addison's voice trailed off as Suzanne had already ended the call. "Okay then." She chuckled.

"Hey, boss," Maise said, sticking her head into Addison's office.

"Hi, Maise."

"A few of us get together for happy hour occasionally and we wondered if you'd like to join us. We're meeting at Mi Familia after work."

Addison raised her eyebrows. "It's hard to say no to a margarita."

Maise laughed. "They have the best ones in town."

"Okay. Count me in."

"We'll save you a seat."

Addison knew they did this from time to time, but they hadn't asked her to come along until now. She understood that they didn't want the boss tagging along, so she was pleased to accept the invitation. It would give her a chance to get to know her employees in a more relaxed setting.

Before turning back to her computer, she revisited her

conversation with Suzanne. She hoped Lissa would go with her next weekend. *Why hadn't they thought of that sooner?*

Addison finished the report and emailed it to her superiors at the home office in Dallas. When she looked out her office windows she noticed the lobby was empty and the tellers were putting on their coats to leave.

She saw Maise look towards her office door as she walked to the exit. Addison got up and called to her. "I'll be right there."

"Okay." Maise waved and left the bank.

Addison closed the programs on her computer and grabbed her coat and purse. The restaurant wasn't far from the bank, but then again nothing was very far away in this small town.

She walked into the restaurant and a blast of heat along with the aroma of Mexican food hit her. Maise waved to her from a table not far from the entrance.

"Hey," Addison said, taking her coat off and putting it on the back of her chair.

"It's just Karen and me tonight. Everyone else had plans. I hope that's okay," Maise said apologetically.

"I'm just happy you invited me," Addison said. She turned to Karen and smiled. "What are you having?"

"I'm having the strawberry margarita. We're glad you could join us," Karen replied.

"That sounds good, but I think I'll have the traditional margarita," Addison said.

"Me too," Maise added.

They placed their orders and talked about their day until the drinks came.

"I know you don't want to talk about bank business all evening," Addison said, taking a sip of her drink. "Oohh, that's good."

That was all the invitation Maise and Karen needed. They talked about their families and their plans for Thanksgiving until their drinks were empty.

"Look who's here," Karen exclaimed, waving at a man as he came into the restaurant.

Addison looked up and saw Hunter Wray walking towards them.

"Is this a bank meeting?" he asked good-naturedly.

"Hi Hunter," Karen said, a little too loudly. "Join us."

He nodded at Addison and Maise then sat in the empty chair next to Addison.

"Can I get you ladies another round?" he asked politely.

"Not for me," Maise said. "One is my limit. I've got to get home."

"Me too. Why don't you two stay and have dinner?" Karen suggested.

Hunter looked at Addison and smiled.

This felt a bit orchestrated to Addison, but she couldn't think of a reason quick enough not to stay and she didn't want to be rude. She smiled at Hunter and nodded.

"Have fun," Maise said, patting Addison on the shoulder. "Thanks for joining us tonight."

"Thanks for inviting me. I'll see you in the morning," Addison replied.

"You two enjoy your dinner," Karen said, a little too aggressively.

Addison rolled her eyes. "See you tomorrow, Karen."

Once they'd left, Addison looked over at Hunter and smiled. "How are you?"

Hunter chuckled. "Sorry about Karen. She's a little..."

"Oh, I know." Addison laughed.

"You know, you're helping me out by staying for dinner."

"How am I doing that?"

"My mother will be thrilled and hopefully stop asking me if I've taken you to dinner yet."

Addison chuckled. "Mothers just want their kids to be happy. Isn't that right?"

"I suppose."

"How is your mom? My friend, Lissa Morgan, once remarked that she's one of the best people she knows."

"Lissa is one of my favorite people," Hunter exclaimed. "And there's her brother."

Addison looked towards the entrance and saw Ben Morgan. He gave her a smile and nodded. Suddenly Addison had a bad feeling in her stomach and felt her cheeks start to burn.

"I'm sure they feel a little lost without Peter."

"What was that?" Addison said, looking back at Hunter and realizing he was talking to her.

"The Morgans. They lost their brother, Peter, not long ago."

"I know," Addison said. "That's how I met Lissa. She came into the bank to close his account."

"She took really good care of him."

Addison smiled, put her chin on her hand and smiled at Hunter. "You've known Lissa for a long time."

"I have." Hunter grinned. "Oh, that's right. Y'all walked together in the 5K and I heard you are sponsoring hot chocolate teams at the Christmas stroll."

"We are. To say we are both competitive would be an understatement," Addison chuckled. Once they started talking about Lissa she felt better.

* * *

Lissa heard a knock at her door and smiled when she opened it. "I'm not tipping the driver," she said to her brother.

Ben laughed. "What if I have a secret, will you tip them then?"

"Who did you see at Mi Familia?" Lissa said, taking the bag from Ben and setting it on the coffee table.

"Addison was having dinner with Hunter Wray," he stated.

Lissa tried to hide the surprise on her face. "Really?"

"Yeah. She gave me an odd look when I spotted them. Are they dating?"

"Not that I know of," Lissa said. She had a sinking feeling in her stomach and she knew why. Even though she knew Addison was straight, at times they felt like more than friends. Lissa knew it was all in her mind and Addison had never given her any reason to think she was interested in anything but friendship with her.

"Well, they were definitely having dinner. Speaking of, I'd better get this food home before my family wonders where I am."

"Thanks for bringing this by," Lissa said, walking him to the door.

Once Ben had left, Lissa sat down and took her nachos out of the bag. She was no longer hungry since Ben had delivered not only her food, but also the news about seeing Addison with Hunter. Who was she kidding? She slumped down on the couch and frowned. Addison saw her as a friend. How could she not go out with someone eventually? Even if she didn't, Lissa knew she wouldn't be in Brazos Falls long. Her aspirations were much loftier than a small town bank.

Lissa was puzzled that Addison hadn't told her she had a

date though. She thought they told each other everything. Maybe they weren't as close as she thought.

She didn't know how long she'd been sitting there when a knock at the door brought Lissa out of her dark thoughts. Ben must have forgotten something.

When she opened the door she was shocked to see Addison.

"Hey," Addison said shyly. "Could I come in?"

14

Lissa stepped out of the way so Addison could come inside. As surprised as she was to see Addison, Lissa was just as bewildered by her timidness. Addison Henry commanded any room she entered and she'd been to Lissa's house many times before.

Addison sat down on the couch and looked up at Lissa. "I've had the strangest night."

"Yeah?"

"Yes, but first I need to ask you something," Addison said.

"Okay?"

"Why don't you go with me next weekend to Suzanne and Rachel's," Addison stated.

"What?"

"Come to Dallas with me. You can go shopping with us and meet our other friends," Addison said with a smile.

Lissa could see that Addison was acting more like herself now and in a strange way it calmed Lissa too. But why would she ask Lissa to go with her for the weekend if she was dating Hunter Wray? LIssa shook her head in an effort to rid those thoughts and focused on Addison's question.

"Uh," Lissa said. "I'd like that, but my niece will be in from college and I promised her we'd spend some time together. Can we do it another time?"

"Nope, it's now or never."

Lissa's face fell. But before she could say anything Addison added, "Yes, we can go another time." Addison chuckled. "You should've seen your face."

"Ha ha," Lissa deadpanned. The sick feeling in her stomach was still there.

Addison had just noticed the food on Lissa's coffee table. "Is that from Mi Familia?"

Lissa nodded.

"You're right. They do have the best nachos."

Lissa couldn't keep from smiling. "I told you. Did you finally try them?"

Addison studied Lissa's face and stared into her eyes. She took a deep breath and slowly let it out. "You already know I did, don't you?"

"I may have heard that you were at Mi Familia tonight having dinner, but I don't know what you had to eat," Lissa confessed.

Addison shook her head. "Small town?"

Lissa nodded.

"I'd like to tell you about my evening. I don't know why I feel the need to share all of this, but there's something inside me that needs you to know. Okay?" Addison asked, never letting her eyes leave Lissa's.

"Okay." Lissa sat down next to Addison on the couch and tried to make herself relax.

"You know how there's a group of people at the bank that meet for happy hour sometimes?"

"Did they finally invite you?" Lissa asked excitedly.

Addison nodded with a grin. "They did, but only Maise and Karen showed up."

Lissa shrugged. "Well, it's a start."

"Yeah, that's what I thought. We had a margarita and I was about to say goodbye when Karen made a big deal about Hunter Wray walking in," Addison explained.

"Oh," Lissa said, suddenly understanding Addison wasn't on a date after all.

"Yeah, well, Karen suggested Hunter join us and she and Maise immediately left."

"Hmm," Lissa murmured.

"Yeah, I thought the same thing. Anyway, Hunter said it would be a favor to him if I'd stay because then he could tell his mother we had dinner and she'd hopefully leave him alone about asking me out."

Lissa chuckled. "That sounds like Sidney. However, Addison, I can't blame her."

"Thank you, Lis." Addison gave Lissa a crooked smile. "I was kind of uncomfortable, then Ben walked in." Realization dawned on Addison's face. "Oh, that's how you knew I was there."

Lissa shrugged. "His family ordered take-out, so he brought me dinner."

Addison looked down at the food then back at Lissa. "Why haven't you eaten this?"

Again Lissa shrugged. "You said you were uncomfortable when Ben walked in," Lissa prompted Addison.

"I was, then the funniest thing happened."

Lissa raised her eyebrows in question.

"We started talking about you."

"About me!"

"Yeah, Hunter Wray is one of your biggest fans. And you know what else?"

Lissa shook her head and raised her shoulders.

"I'm a big fan, too."

Lissa could feel her shoulders soften and her heart smile. *Do hearts smile?* That's what her heart felt like.

"I need something from you, Lis," Addison said earnestly.

"Name it," Lissa stated.

"I don't know why, but I didn't want to be there with Hunter and when Ben walked in, all I could think was: I have to tell Lissa. You know I'd tell you if I ever went on a date, right?" Addison inched closer to Lissa.

"Well, I was surprised when Ben told me you were with Hunter because I thought you would've told me, so yes, I know you'd tell me."

"What I need from you is an excuse," Addison said.

Puzzled, Lissa looked at her. "An excuse?"

"I couldn't think of anything quick enough to get out of dinner with Hunter. I don't want to go out with anyone, but I can't be rude either. It would be a bad look for the bank."

"Oh," Lissa murmured.

"I need to have plans with you."

"You do have plans with me pretty often," Lissa remarked.

Addison chuckled. "I know, but if anyone asks me out, from now on I'm going to say I have plans with you. So if someone comes up to you and asks, you have plans with me."

"Oh!" Lissa smiled and began to laugh. "Now I get it."

Addison reached over and took Lissa's hand. "Is that okay?"

"Yeah, Addy. I'll be your plan." Lissa knew Addison

didn't realize how upset she was at the thought of Addison going out on a date. *Maybe she didn't need to know.*

A look of relief washed over Addison's face. "Are you going to eat your nachos?"

"Yeah, I'm kind of hungry now." Lissa got up and took the plate of nachos to the microwave and warmed them. "They won't be as good this way." She set the plate back down on the coffee table. "You have to help me," she said, looking at Addison.

Addison reached over and took one of the nachos. "I wasn't very hungry earlier, but now I am." She bit down and grinned at Lissa.

They shared the plate of nachos and Lissa couldn't stop sneaking looks at Addison. She shouldn't feel relieved that Addison had no plans to date while she was in Brazos Falls, but she did. In all the scenarios that occasionally played in her mind there was no way she and Addison would end up together, but that didn't mean she couldn't dream.

* * *

Addison wiped her fingers on her napkin and looked down at the empty plate. "What now?"

Lissa gave her a confused look.

"I'm so glad tomorrow is Friday. What do you want to do tomorrow night?"

"Oh! Yoga?" Lissa replied.

Addison considered Lissa's answer then shook her head. "Let's binge watch something and make our own margaritas. Wanna be lazy?"

Lissa's eyes brightened and she grinned. "That sounds perfect."

"It's a date," Addison said, getting up and walking to the

door. She chuckled, thinking how earlier the idea of a date had her in a near panic. "Where's Callie?" She opened the front door and the cat came scurrying inside.

"I'm sure she's been wandering the neighborhood with Dart," Lissa said as the cat came in sniffing the air.

"You missed out," Addison said, bending down and petting the cat. "Dart's in the house and we ate all the nachos." She stood up and smiled at Lissa. "What a night."

"Everything's okay, right?" Lissa said.

Addison met Lissa's eyes and noticed what a beautiful shade of light brown they were tonight.

"What?" Lissa asked as Addison stared.

"Your eyes are beautiful, Lis. I don't think I've ever seen that shade of brown." She squeezed Lissa's arm and walked to her car. When she got behind the wheel she saw Lissa's silhouette standing in the doorway.

Lissa was such a beautiful woman. It wasn't that Addison hadn't noticed, but tonight when she and Hunter were talking about Lissa she felt a sense of pride. Being Lissa's best friend and knowing Lissa trusted her gave Addison such a warmth in her heart.

She pulled into her garage and Dart met her at the door. "Hey buddy, sorry I'm getting in late," she said, smoothing the fur down his back. He began to purr and Addison took a moment to pet him.

Thoughts of Lissa still played through her head. She was trying to understand all the feelings that had surged through her tonight. When she was with Hunter she had such a feeling of not wanting to be there. She couldn't get to Lissa's fast enough to tell her what happened. There had been an underlying feeling that she couldn't quite put her finger on.

She set her things down and was about to go to her

bedroom when she stopped and looked at her reflection in the hallway mirror. "Why were you afraid Lissa would be upset?" She continued to stare into her own eyes. "Just say it," she whispered. *You didn't want Lissa to think you were out with someone else because you want to be with her.* Addison couldn't say the words out loud and sighed. "You can't say it, but you could come up with this stupid idea to always say you have plans with Lissa going forward."

Addison continued down the hall and started to take her clothes off. The cat followed her into the room, jumped onto the bed, and plopped down in the middle of it.

"What am I doing, Dart?" she said to the cat. "Why do I care if Lissa is upset with me for going on a date?" She hung up her clothes and dropped down on the bed next to the cat.

Dart looked at her and meowed.

Addison signed. "You're right. I care because the only person I want to be with is Lissa. How in the fuck did this happen?" She splayed across the bed and closed her eyes. "Just wait until Suzanne finds out."

Dart replied by nuzzling against her with a little growl before he closed his eyes and went to sleep.

"It'll be okay," she said, gently stroking the cat's head. "There are only a few days until Thanksgiving. If I can't figure this out, I know Suzanne will know what to do."

Dart purred a little louder.

Addison smiled. "You love Lissa, don't you. Suzanne and I have been best friends for years, but there's something about Lissa. There's a difference and I have to figure out what it is before I screw up this amazing friendship."

She sat up on the bed and looked down at the cat. "That's one thing I will not do, Dart. I will not mess this up."

Dart rolled over on his back with his feet in the air and stretched. Then he hopped down and left the room.

Addison followed him into the kitchen to make sure he had food and water.

She took her phone out of her purse and noticed a text from Lissa.

"I'm glad you came over tonight."

Addison smiled and sent her a reply. "Me too."

A moment later Lissa texted again. "You know, Karen will have questions about your 'date.'"

Addison chuckled and typed her response. "I'll handle Karen. You get the margaritas ready."

Lissa quickly texted back, "Yes ma'am!"

Addison laughed and put her phone away. *What am I going to do with you, Lissa Morgan?*

15

"Have you been holding out on me?" Lissa asked Addison as she slid the sweet potato casserole into the oven.

Addison giggled. "You know I don't cook much, but I can make a few things."

"Maybe we should start cooking more instead of ordering out," Lissa suggested.

Addison watched Lissa as she wiped off the kitchen counter. She knew what she was thankful for this year: Lissa Morgan. The past few days had been hectic at work with the Thanksgiving holiday, some employees traveling to visit family, and others taking personal time off, but Lissa seemed to be around at just the right time to make Addison smile or laugh.

Lissa turned around and noticed Addison smiling at her. "Well?" Lissa asked.

"Well what?"

"Should we start cooking more instead of ordering out?"

Addison shrugged. "It probably depends on the day."

Lissa chuckled. "That's true. Will you be glad when this week is over?"

"We've made it through the hard parts. Friday won't be too bad at the bank and we're closing early."

"And then you'll be off to Suzanne and Rachel's. I know you're looking forward to that."

Addison smiled and nodded. A part of her was very excited about getting away for the weekend, but she wished Lissa was going with her. Since the night she'd shown up at Lissa's to tell her about the dinner with Hunter and admitted to herself there was more going on between them than just friendship, Addison had indulged her imagination from time to time and had even pictured this very scene of them cooking together.

They had spent even more time together the past weekend under the guise of getting ready for Thanksgiving. Addison was more aware of their body language and it felt like their eyes met more often with a sweet smile or soft look exchanged. And now here they were in her kitchen, cooking together on Thanksgiving morning, and there wasn't any place she'd rather be.

"Do we need to go early and help Marielle set the table or do anything else?" Addison asked.

"I asked and she said Blythe and Max would help her. We can go a little early to have a drink before we eat."

"When the sweet potatoes are ready, the pies are next?"

"Yep. They have to bake for forty-five minutes and we'll be done."

Addison nodded. She walked over and took Lissa's hand. "Let's sit while that's cooking."

Lissa followed Addison into the living room and they sat down on the couch.

"I know today might be hard for you at times," Addison

said compassionately. "I'm sure all of you will be missing your brother. Just know that I'm here for you if you want to talk." Addison squeezed Lissa's hand and gave her a soft smile.

"Addison," Lissa said softly. She shook her head and Addison could see tears in her eyes.

"You don't talk about him very often, but I'm here," Addison offered again.

"You are something else. Thank you," Lissa said. "I have thought of him several times this morning."

"Have you wanted to smoke?" Addison asked carefully.

A big smile grew on Lissa's face. "No, I have not. You're probably going to always remember that about me, aren't you?"

Addison chuckled. "I don't know. Maybe. Did you have nice memories of him this morning?"

Lissa nodded. "I did. My mom always asked him to carve the turkey. I don't know why, because he didn't cook."

"What else?"

"Oh, nothing specific. It just feels a little weird that he's not here."

"I'm sure it does. Did you always come home for holidays when you lived away?" Addison asked.

"Yeah, I did."

"Did you bring your girlfriends?" Addison asked, wiggling her eyebrows.

Lissa laughed. "Only one."

"The one who thought you were the one?"

"That would be the one." Lissa paused. "Or not."

They both started laughing.

"Thank you, Addy. You seem to turn sadness into laughter for me or at least make it better."

"Anytime. I can't count how many times you saved me this week with a text or a phone call or a visit."

Lissa tilted her head. "Really?"

"Yes! Well, you may have saved my employees, not just me."

Lissa sat back on the couch and looked over at Addison.

Addison smiled. There had been moments like this all week where they simply took a moment to look, or rather, see one another. "What?" Addison finally asked.

"I'm thankful for you, Addison. You have..." Lissa smiled. "It's hard to put into words, but you've made my life happy."

"Happy?" A line appeared between Addison's brows. "You weren't happy before?"

"Not really. I mean, I wasn't unhappy, but I was just kind of taking up space."

"Oh, Lis. No way! Do you know how many people I've met and once they find out we're friends they share a story or a nice comment about you."

Lissa shrugged. "I told you it was hard to put into words. I just...look forward to the day now."

"Oh yeah? Because you wonder what kind of shit I'm going to get us into or what I need your help with?" Addison rambled.

"Let's just say, you brighten my days." Lissa grinned.

"Brighten doesn't even begin to describe what you've done for me, Lis. I don't even want to think about what my life in Brazos Falls would be like had you not come into the bank that day."

"You saw a woman with a sad look on her face and wanted to help."

Addison smiled and studied Lissa for a moment. "I saw more than that. Anyway, we both know what we're thankful for this year. Don't we."

The oven timer sounded from the kitchen, they looked at one another and paused.

"It's your turn," Addison said, hopping up and going to the kitchen.

She took the sweet potatoes out and checked to be sure they were done. Then she turned the oven over to Lissa. Addison watched her carefully place the pies inside. A smile played across Addison's face. She had a surprise for Lissa a little later and Max was going to help her deliver it. That was another thing that amazed Addison, how Lissa's family had welcomed her like they'd known her forever.

"I'm going to run home and change clothes while the pies are baking. I'll be back before they're done," Lissa said.

"Okay. I'll be ready when you get back."

Addison watched her leave and went into her bedroom to change. She had decided not to worry about what was going on in her heart where Lissa was concerned. There was something to be said for just letting things happen. If she could find the courage, she wanted to say something to Lissa, but she could do that after the holiday weekend. She wanted to enjoy Thanksgiving with the Morgans and then go to Suzanne and Rachel's.

* * *

Lissa changed into jeans and a sweater to wear to her sister's. Addison had seemed different since the night she came by after her dinner with Hunter. Neither had really talked about why Addison felt like she needed to explain things to Lissa, but Lissa had her own ideas.

She'd felt jealous at the idea that Addison was on a date without telling her, which she had no right to be. But then

Addison had shown up at her house, explaining the situation as if she was afraid she'd hurt Lissa.

All Lissa knew was her feelings for Addison were growing deeper and deeper and she needed to stop because she was going to get her heart broken. Addison had her sights set on moving up in the bank. She didn't plan to stay in Brazos Falls for long and a relationship was the last thing on her mind.

Lissa sighed. "It would be so easy to fall in love with Addison Henry," she whispered.

Callie meowed at her as if agreeing with her statement.

Lissa chuckled. "It can't happen, sweet girl. But that doesn't mean I can't be thankful for our friendship and enjoy what we have while she's here."

With that Lissa went to get Addison and drove them to her sister's for Thanksgiving.

"Wow, it smells heavenly in here," Addison said, carrying the food into the kitchen.

"Thanks," Marielle said. "You can set those right here. We're going to have a buffet style dinner."

"There's another pie in the car. Max, will you get it for me?" Lissa said.

"Sure thing," he replied.

"Addison, I'd like you to meet my niece, Blythe," Lissa said, introducing her.

"It's so nice to meet you." Addison smiled at the young woman who reminded her of Lissa.

"I've heard so much about you," Blythe said, returning her smile. "I hear you and Aunt Lissa are on rival hot chocolate teams. My team won when I was in middle school."

"Oh, we'll have to talk later so you can give me all the secrets on how to beat your aunt," Addison said with a wink.

"Hold on," Lissa objected. "I'm your aunt. You should be helping me."

Blythe laughed and hugged her aunt. "You know I will."

Ben, Kara, and the boys came in next and the volume rose along with the laughter.

"Hi Addison, we're happy you could join us," Kara said, setting down a large bowl of salad.

"Where do you want this, Mom?" Joe asked, walking into the kitchen. "Hi Addison, how's it going?"

"Hey, Joe. Why don't you set that right here," Addison said, clearing a space on the counter.

"How's the cat settling in at your place?" Ben asked, opening a bottle of wine.

"He loves it, especially since his sister lives a few houses down. They play together nearly every day."

Lissa scrutinized her brother. "Why in the world would you ask about one of the cats? You don't like them."

"It's one less that you're feeding at the mill." Ben grinned.

"Come on, be honest. You like them, just a little," Lissa said, holding her thumb and index finger close together but not quite touching.

Ben chuckled. "I'll never admit it." He poured each of the adults a glass of wine.

They helped Marielle get the food ready to serve and sipped their wine while the boys played video games in the living room.

"Okay, Addison," Kara said. "You've lived here long enough, tell me who you've been set up with. Some of these nosy old ladies just can't help themselves."

"Who said that single women need to be set up in the first place?" Marielle commented. "If someone comes along that I want to go out with, I'm capable of asking them myself."

"Listen to you, Mom!" Blythe whooped.

"Who have you asked out?" Kara said. When Marielle didn't answer, Kara added, "That's what I thought."

"There's no one to ask out. Lissa knows what I mean."

"Hold on. Don't drag me into this," Lissa replied. She looked at Addison and grinned.

"I have had a few comments dropped here and there, and Sidney Wray did tell me she was going to have Hunter take me to dinner, but I've got an excuse ready if someone asks," Addison explained.

"Why? There are a few nice guys who also happen to be single here in town," Kara said.

"Because some single women like being single," Marielle said.

"Is that right?" Kara said. "Do you like being single, Marielle?"

"Sometimes." Marielle shrugged.

"Since I represent the single gay women in this crowd I will admit that I don't necessarily like being single, but there is nothing wrong if our dear sister does like it. Own it, Mari!" Lissa said, defending her sister.

Marielle grinned at Lissa. "You have to understand that there aren't many good guys like our brother in this town. So give us a break, Kara."

"You're right. Ben is a good guy," Kara agreed. She turned to Addison. "Hey, what's this excuse you have ready if someone asks you out?"

Addison smiled at Lissa. "I have plans with Lissa."

Lissa chuckled and shook her head.

"Really? You don't think that makes people wonder?" Kara said, skeptically.

16

"Make them wonder what? That Lissa and I are friends so we do things together? I don't think so. I have a question for y'all," Addison said, changing the subject. "Lis and I watch Hallmark movies and you know how they follow a set plot?"

"Yeah, like they meet, and are either old friends or were once enemies. Then they find themselves falling in love and kiss at the end," Marielle said.

"Yeah, something like that. It's the kiss at the end. We're supposed to believe that this one kiss makes them want to be with this person from now on," Addison said with a grin aimed at Lissa.

"I've tried to explain to Addison that it's everything they've gone through leading up to the kiss that makes it even more special. Once their lips finally meet, it's all over, like magic," Lissa said, clapping her hands and returning Addison's grin.

"I want one of those kisses," Marielle said.

"I believe it can happen," Kara said. "It was like that with Ben and me. Wasn't it, honey?"

"What?" Ben said, coming in from the living room.

"Our first kiss," Kara said, putting her arm around his shoulder. "It was Hallmark worthy."

He looked at her, confused.

"Did you know from our first kiss that we'd be together forever?" Kara prompted.

"I knew that I wanted to keep kissing you," Ben said.

Everyone chuckled.

"Come on," Addison said. "You couldn't tell from that first kiss that you wanted to spend your life together."

"From that first kiss, I could see the possibility that this could be forever," Kara said with a smile at Ben.

"I had asked her out several times and finally convinced her to go out with me, so I hoped that was the best kiss I had in me." Ben chuckled.

Lissa laughed. "See there, Addy. I'm telling you, it can happen."

"I'll have to take your word for it." Addison shrugged.

"You never know, you could be living in a Hallmark movie right here in Brazos Falls," Kara said. "We're a small town, a lot like the ones in the movies."

Addison chuckled. "I don't think I've seen that one yet. Because I'm the one who is focused on her career and not looking for any kind of relationship."

"Oh, they make it," Lissa said quietly, standing next to Addison.

Addison looked over and raised an eyebrow. "Really?"

Lissa nodded. She didn't notice Marielle and Kara smile at each other while they looked on.

"Is it time to eat yet? We're getting hungry," Leo called from the living room.

"We're ready," Marielle said. "Let's eat."

Everyone gathered around the island and filled their

plates. Addison followed Lissa to the dining table. "Does it matter where we sit?" she asked.

"Peter usually sat at one end of the table," Lissa replied. "You should sit there, Ben."

"You're the oldest," he said.

"No I'm not. Peter is still the oldest in our little sibling circle. You sit at one end and Marielle at the other. It's her house," Lissa suggested.

"Good idea," Kara said.

"Let's sit here," Lissa said to Addison with a smile.

When everyone took their seats, Lissa leaned back and chuckled. "I like this. My niece and nephews lined up across from me. Catch me up."

"Uh, we're having our Thanksgiving video game tournament after we eat," Max said, giving Addison a quick glance.

"Prepare to lose, my children."

"We'll see about that," Joe said, elbowing his cousin.

Lissa stared across the table. "Y'all are up to something. I can feel it."

"I hope you've been practicing, Aunt Lis," Leo asked.

"Oh this is going to be fun," Lissa said, her eyes sparkling.

Blythe shared how her semester was going at college.

"You're majoring in music therapy?" Addison asked.

"Yes. I hope to work at one of the children's hospitals in either Dallas or Ft. Worth," she replied.

"That is so interesting. Do you play instruments and sing or what?"

"It depends on the patient. Sometimes we teach them to play a simple instrument or join in singing a song. Sometimes I sing to them or play music on my phone. Do you listen to music?" Blythe asked Addison.

"I do. I have playlists for different moods or whatever I'm doing."

"Sometimes music can reach people when other methods can't," Blythe said.

"That's so cool," Max said. "You know, video games speak to me."

"Uh huh," Marielle said. "They speak to you when you should be doing homework, that's why you have a timer."

The rest of the meal was spent in spirited conversation and laughter. Lissa loved how comfortable Addison was and everyone welcomed her like she was part of the family.

"I want your recipe for sweet potatoes, Addison," Kara said as they cleared the table.

"I'd be happy to share it with you."

"What did you think of Lissa's pie? Her pecan pie is the best I've tasted," Marielle said.

"Including your mother's?" Kara asked.

"Yep. It's that good."

"Seriously though, is there anything Lissa can't do?" Addison said with a grin.

"We'll see if she's been practicing, because it's her turn to play," Max said, handing Lissa the game controller.

Ben and the kids gathered around to watch.

"Let me help with the dishes," Addison said to Marielle.

"No way. I'll have plenty of help with that later. Let's watch this match."

Max and Joe had finished their game and it was Lissa and Leo's turn.

"Well, that didn't take long," Lissa said after easily winning. "Are you sure that controller is working?" she teased.

"I'm next," Max said. "Let's see what you've got." He glanced at Addison and grinned.

In a close race Lissa passed Max at the finish line to win.

"I am on fire!" Lissa whooped. "Who's next?"

"Hmm, how about I give it a try?" Addison said, taking the controller from Max and sitting next to Lissa.

"Have you played?"

"I've been paying attention. I think I know what to do." She gave Lissa a sweet smile.

The game started and Lissa took the lead. "That was a good start, Addy," she said, steering her car around the slower ones ahead.

"Thanks. I'm coming for you, Lis."

Lissa chuckled and kept pushing the buttons and sliding the joy stick.

"Do you see me?"

"Huh?" Lissa grunted.

"Yeah, that's me that just whizzed by you. Come and get me."

Lissa grimaced and concentrated on the screen. She could hear Addison tapping the keys and her car got smaller and smaller as it pulled away from her.

Addison's car crossed the finish line and everyone cheered.

"What the?" Lissa said, staring at the screen. She looked over at Addison and saw her grinning proudly. Lissa tilted her head then realization dawned on her face. She couldn't keep from smiling. "I've been set up."

Everyone began to laugh and Max and Leo highfived in front of the TV.

Addison chuckled and bumped Lissa's shoulder with her own. "Aww, it looks like I put out your fire."

"You never told me you played video games." Lissa grinned.

"I haven't much, but I had a little help," Addison said, holding her hand up for Max to slap.

"What did you do?"

"I asked Max to give me a few lessons so I could challenge you."

"Turns out she's a natural, Aunt Lis. You should've seen your face."

Lissa looked around. "Were you all in on it?"

"I might have heard something about it," Ben said, laughing.

"Do you want to go again?" Addison asked, wiggling her eyebrows.

Lissa gave her a menacing stare then chuckled. "You bet I do."

For the next hour they took turns playing and then played partners. Lissa and Addison were undefeated when they teamed up.

"Would you look at us!" Addison exclaimed. "I knew we were a good team."

"Yeah, you say that now, but what about the hot chocolate contest in a couple of weeks?" Kara said. "You'll be rivals."

"Hmm, that might be fun to watch," Marielle commented.

"We should make some kind of wager on it," Addison said.

"Oh, I know," Lissa began. "Whoever loses has to cook dinner for the winner for..."

"A week? A month?"

"A month! That's a lot of dinners!" Lissa exclaimed.

"Okay, a week?" Addison acquiesced.

"A week," Lissa agreed, holding out her hand.

Addison took it and held it for a moment. "You're our

witnesses. I can't wait to sit back and let you cook for me," she teased.

Lissa chuckled. "I'll be over after work, waiting to eat your good cooking."

"The Christmas stroll and parade just got a lot more interesting," Ben commented.

"Yeah it did," Marielle agreed and glanced at Kara.

* * *

"What a fun day," Addison said as Lissa pulled into her driveway.

"It was for you!" Lissa exclaimed, looking over at her.

"You can't believe that I beat you," Addison teased with a smirk.

"Oh, you are so gonna—" Lissa unbuckled her seat belt and reached over with both hands and tickled Addison.

"No! No!" Addison screamed, but it was too late. She was trapped and Lissa's fingers found the most ticklish spots around her waist.

Addison somehow managed to push the latch on her seatbelt and open the door. She fell out of the car and ran, still laughing. "Oh," she said breathlessly. "You got me good."

Lissa chuckled and went to the back of the SUV. She reached for the dishes they'd taken to Thanksgiving dinner when Addison jumped on her back and wrapped her arms around Lissa's neck. Lissa squealed and grabbed Addison's legs that were wrapped around her middle.

"What now!" Lissa exclaimed.

"I may not have thought this through." Addison giggled.

Lissa began to spin around and Addison said, "You're going to make me dizzy."

"And?"

Addison laughed. "I'll throw up on you!"

Lissa immediately stopped and let go of Addison's legs. She slid off her back and Lissa quickly turned around.

"Gotcha!" Addison laughed, backing away.

"Addison Henry," Lissa said warily. She leaped forward and grabbed Addison just as she turned to run. Lissa held Addison so that her back was pressed against Lissa's chest and her arms were wrapped around Addison's middle.

Addison leaned her head back on Lissa's shoulder and held her hands over Lissa's hands and laughed. "Okay, okay," she said, turning her head. Her eyes met Lissa's and they both stopped. Addison's heart was already pounding from their wrestling, but she felt a flutter in her stomach and for a moment she lost her breath. She could see wonder in Lissa's eyes and then something she couldn't read.

"Are you going to let me go?" Addison asked softly. She watched as Lissa realized how tightly she was holding them together and felt her grip loosen.

"I will this time. But now I know you don't play fair," Lissa said, glowering at her.

Addison chuckled. "Where's the fun in that?"

They both walked to the back of the SUV, grabbed their dishes, and went inside.

"Your sweet potatoes were a hit," Lissa said, putting the dish on the counter.

"Thanks for letting me have the last piece of pie. I'll wash your plate—" Addison started.

"You will not," Lissa said, taking the pie plate from her hand. She reached in the cabinet for a plate and put the piece of pie on it. "I'll clean this at home."

"Are you working tomorrow?" Addison asked.

"I'll probably go in for part of the day," Lissa replied.

"You'll be working, the kids will be sleeping in, so I may as well work."

"Or you could lie around and hang out with your friends." When Lissa gave her a confused look Addison chuckled. "You know, your gay friends in your books."

"Oh! Very funny." Lissa grinned. "But that's not a bad idea. What time are you leaving for Suzanne and Rachel's?"

"The bank closes at 3:00. I'll run by here to change and tell Dart goodbye. By the way, thanks for keeping him for me."

"He and Callie will have a great time."

"And thanks again for inviting me to spend the day with you and your family."

"You made what could have been a sad Thanksgiving much happier. I heard Ben say he missed Peter when we were in the kitchen talking about 'girl stuff,' as he put it." Lissa chuckled.

"Yeah, I noticed him quickly leaving the room."

"You may have underhandedly tricked me playing video games, but you made my Thanksgiving happy. Thanks, Addy."

"There was absolutely nothing underhanded about it. I learned and practiced fair and square. You just didn't know it. You made my Thanksgiving happy, too, Lis." Addison held out her arms and raised her brows.

Lissa grinned and walked into the hug.

They held each other for a moment and Addison took just an instant to enjoy how her head fit perfectly on Lissa's shoulder. *This is nice, really nice.*

Addison stepped back and walked Lissa to the door. "I'm going to start packing, but I was wondering if you'd be interested in sharing that piece of pie with me later."

"I could do that. I could also bring you lunch tomorrow," Lissa said.

"Leftovers?" Addison said, her face hopeful.

"Do you like leftover turkey sandwiches?"

"With Marielle's cranberry relish on top?"

Lissa smiled. "Of course. It wouldn't be a leftover sandwich without cranberries."

"Oh, Lissa. I'd love that."

Lissa nodded. "I'll see you later."

Addison watched Lissa walk to the car and waved as she left. She sighed and smiled as she closed the front door. She stood against it and images of the day popped into her head. The look on Lissa's face when Addison's car passed hers in the video game. The high fives when they won every challenge as partners. She remembered how they had worked side by side in her kitchen that morning cooking together.

She put her hands on her waist and could feel where Lissa's fingers had tickled her and then where her hands had held her tight. What was that look in Lissa's eyes? There was happiness and joy, but what else?

Addison sighed again. "I like you, Lissa Morgan. I really do," she said softly.

17

"Thanks for sharing the leftovers with me," Lissa said as she prepared sandwiches for lunch.

"I'm glad Addison was here yesterday. I hope it won't be the only holiday she spends with us."

Lissa looked over at her sister. "What do you mean?"

"I thought yesterday was going to be weird without Peter. Don't get me wrong, I missed him. But with Addison here it was different. In a good way."

Lissa smiled. Addison always seemed to make her days better.

"She fit right in with our family. It was like we were missing a piece, but added another. In our sadness we were still able to be thankful."

"Wow, that's kind of deep, Mari," Lissa said, glancing at her sister.

"We've never really seen you with a girlfriend," Marielle commented.

"What are you talking about?" Lissa asked, confused. "I've brought girlfriends home with me before."

"Not really. You didn't have a girlfriend until you went off to college. And you've never brought your friends home much, especially during holidays," Marielle explained. "Seeing you with Addison yesterday kind of gave me a peek at what you're like with a partner."

Lissa looked over at her and tilted her head. "Oh wait— no, no, no. Addison and I are just friends!" she exclaimed.

"Are you sure about that?"

"Yes, I'm sure. She has never been with a woman," Lissa said, going back to making their sandwiches.

"Hmm," Marielle murmured. "Just because she hasn't been with a woman doesn't mean..." she trailed off.

"Doesn't mean what?" Lissa gave her sister a look.

"I'm telling you, sis. You may not want to admit it, but there's something going on between the two of you. Who learns a video game to surprise their friend?"

"We happen to be competitive," Lissa said.

"Competitive? You work out together several times a week, watch movies every week, go out to dinner. Do I need to keep going?" Marielle raised her hands. "Before you say anything, this is a good thing, Lissa."

Lissa continued to make the sandwiches. What Marielle said was true. It was a good thing that she and Addison were friends.

There had been times lately that she and Addison would share a look or a smile and it felt different. But yesterday, when she grabbed Addison and held her tight, there was a moment when their eyes met and it felt like everything stopped. There was such joy and mischief in Addison's eyes, along with wonder. They sparkled and for a second Lissa almost leaned over and kissed her. It felt like exactly the thing to do, but Lissa had quickly realized what she was doing.

"Hey, what's that look?" Marielle asked.

Lissa took a deep breath and slowly let it out. "Addison has her career, Mari. She is focused and has a plan. There is no way she has feelings for me, except as friends."

"Not from what I saw yesterday," Marielle stated.

Lissa packed the sandwiches in a container and snapped the lid shut. She met Marielle's gaze and smiled. "Addison is a wonderful person and I like her so, so much. Since we have become friends my life is much happier, but Marielle, if we crossed that friendship line I'd lose her and I don't want that to happen."

"You don't know that! What if you crossed that line and it was wonderful?"

Lissa shook her head. "I won't take that chance. She's here for a couple of years, then she'll be promoted and oversee several banks."

"Or she could fall in love with the best person I know and live happily ever after, wherever that happens to be."

Lissa smiled at her sister. "Thanks, Marielle."

"Enjoy your lunch with your friend," Marielle said with a smirk.

* * *

"Mmm, oh my gosh, this is so good," Addison said between bites. "I think Thanksgiving leftovers may be better than the actual meal."

Lissa chuckled. "But we don't have your sweet potatoes or pie."

"We don't need them. This turkey sandwich," Addison said, pointing to her plate, "is a masterpiece."

"I'm glad you like it."

"Maybe that's what I'll request when you have to make my dinners for a week." Addison smirked.

"Oh, I don't think so. It'll be *you* making *me* dinners."

Addison leaned back and wiped her mouth. "What if our teams aren't as into this as we are?"

Lissa shrugged. "I guess we'll have to motivate them."

"Oh." Addison nodded. "I guess I could pay them. You know, promise them a bonus if they sell so many cups."

Lissa gave Addison a horrified look.

Addison laughed. "I'm kidding. Relax, Lis."

Lissa chuckled. "Are you packed and ready to go as soon as you lock the bank?"

"I am. What are you going to do all weekend without me?" she teased.

"Hmm, that's a good question. I'm going shopping with Blythe tomorrow. While she's here, we like to check out all the shops around the square and start Christmas shopping."

"You're not going to find someone else to watch movies with are you?" Addison asked, eyeing Lissa.

"Now, why would I do that? I am not that kind of friend," Lissa stated firmly.

Addison smiled. "I was just thinking about what you said yesterday about being single."

Lissa wrinkled her forehead. "What'd I say?"

"You said you didn't particularly like being single."

"Mmm," Lissa mumbled as she took a drink of water and nodded. "I don't." She shrugged.

"Because?" Addison prompted. She'd been curious about this and had meant to ask Lissa last night when they finished off the pie, but they'd gotten to talking about something else.

Lissa sighed. "Well..." she stammered and stared at Addison.

Addison could tell Lissa was holding back and this

surprised her. "Hey, you can tell me. I mean, it's me... Addy," she said with a soft smile.

Lissa smiled. "I watch those Hallmark movies and read sapphic romance for a reason. I'm a romantic, Addy."

"I know that!"

"It would be nice to have someone to share stuff with. You know." Lissa shrugged again.

"We share stuff, don't we?"

"Yeah, but..." Lissa sighed. "For example, it would be nice to, let's say, go shopping or out to dinner with someone and simply hold hands. Or, when I wake up in the night, it'd be nice to roll over and see someone you love sleeping beside you."

Addison listened and could hear the dreaminess in Lissa's voice. She couldn't help but smile. "That sounds nice," she said softly.

"Why, Addison Henry, is there a bit of a romantic hiding inside you?" Lissa smiled.

"The way you described it makes it rather appealing, or maybe your movies are rubbing off on me," Addison said.

Lissa chuckled. "Whatever it is, it looks nice on you."

Addison drew her brows together. "How so?"

"I don't know. You're more lighthearted than when we first met. Don't worry, I know you are still focused on your goals: making this the best bank it can be, then running all the banks," Lissa said, ticking off each goal on her fingers.

Addison laughed. "You and your 'running all the banks.' I'm not focused on banks all the time."

Lissa dropped her chin. "Are you sure about that?"

"Yes, I'm sure. I think about other things. Like video games," she teased.

Lissa laughed and shook her head.

Addison met Lissa's eyes and smiled. For a moment

neither of them looked away. Finally, Addison sighed. "I'd better get back. Thanks again for bringing me lunch."

"You are very welcome." Lissa got up and quickly put their trash into a bag while Addison cleaned off the table.

"Hey, would you do something for me?" Lissa asked tentatively.

"Name it," Addison said, turning to face her.

"Would you mind texting me when you get to Suzanne's?"

Addison felt her heart fill with warmth. "Of course I will. I'll need to check on Dart."

Lissa nodded and grinned. "Have fun!"

Addison walked out with Lissa then drove back to the bank.

The afternoon passed quickly, but Addison found herself thinking about Lissa several times. She'd admitted to herself that she was going to miss Lissa this weekend. Although she was happy to get to spend time with Suzanne, there was a strange little ache inside of her when she thought about leaving. *What the hell!*

After the bank closed, Addison hurried home and changed clothes. She grabbed her bag and made sure the back door was locked. Lissa had taken Dart with her after lunch, so she knew he would be taken care of. But...maybe she should swing by Lissa's and leave her an extra key, just in case she needed anything for the cat.

She pulled out of her driveway and drove around the corner to Lissa's. "Yeah right," she mumbled, getting out of her car. "Like Lissa needs anything for Dart."

"Hey!" Lissa said, pleasantly surprised when she opened the door.

"I meant to give you the key to the house," Addison said, handing it to Lissa. "In case you need it."

"Oh, okay."

"Is Dart okay?"

"He and Callie were asleep on my bed the last time I checked. Do you want to come see him?"

"No, no," Addison said, nervously shuffling from one foot to the other. She smiled at Lissa. "I'll text you when I get there. Maybe I'll call and check on him tomorrow or something."

"We'll miss you, Addison. But I hope you have a great time," Lissa said.

Addison nodded. "Well, I'd better get going." She turned to walk back to the car then stopped. When she turned back around Lissa had the softest smile on her face. Addison took a step and wrapped her arms around Lissa's neck. She felt Lissa's hands press firmly against her back. They stayed this way for a few moments and Addison felt Lissa nuzzle her hair ever so slightly.

"Be safe, Addy."

Addison slowly pulled away. "I will. Have fun with Blythe."

Lissa nodded.

Addison hurried off the porch to her car. *Why was it so hard to leave?*

She waved at Lissa as she backed out of her driveway then sped away. "Oh, Suzanne. Do I need to talk to you," she muttered.

* * *

Lissa watched Addison drive away. "What the hell?" she mumbled. She walked back inside and fell onto the couch. "What are you doing, Addy?" she sighed.

Lissa hadn't been expecting to see Addison since they'd

said their goodbyes at lunch. When she opened the door and saw Addy standing on her porch, her heart had jumped in her chest. Lissa knew where Addison hid her extra key outside her house, so she didn't have to bring one by.

Had Addison wanted to see her again before she left? *That hug.*

Lissa's heart started pounding again just thinking about the hug. Addison had laid her head on Lissa's shoulder and she couldn't keep from turning her head slightly and nuzzling her hair. The scent of Addison's shampoo still lingered in her nose. Lissa knew all of this had to be in her head.

Marielle's words echoed around her. "You may not want to admit it, but something is happening between you two."

"Is there?" Lissa said out loud. A flutter erupted in her stomach and she groaned.

Lissa had the weekend to figure out what to do because she meant what she'd said to her sister. She did not want to lose Addison.

18

"I'm so glad you're here," Suzanne said, handing Addison a glass of wine.

"Me, too." Addison took a sip of the wine and her eyes widened. "Mmm, this is good."

"Rach discovered this while listening to a podcast, of all things," Suzanne replied.

"That's random."

Rachel shrugged as she walked in from the kitchen. "How's Lissa?"

Addison smiled and took another sip of wine. "I invited her to come with me."

Suzanne's face lit up. "Where is she?"

"Her niece is in from college and they planned a day to shop around the square tomorrow."

"Aw, that's nice. Those shops around the square are so cute," Rachel said.

"You'll get a chance to enjoy them when you come for the parade," Addison said.

Suzanne stared at Addison. "What's different about you?"

"Yeah, you've got a healthy glow about you," Rachel added.

Addison wondered if they could tell what was going on inside her confused brain. "Uh, we've been doing yoga three times a week."

"Let me ask you, Addy," Suzanne said in a thoughtful tone. "Do you do yoga just to spend time with Lissa?"

"That's part of why we do it. I actually wanted to talk to you about Lissa if you can keep from losing your mind," Addison said, giving Suzanne a pointed stare.

Suzanne's hand flew to her chest and she gasped, but Rachel took Suzanne's hand and held it in her lap. "I've got her. We are your friends and we're here to listen," Rachel said with a kind smile.

Addison looked at their clasped hands and could hear Lissa's voice. *It would be nice to hold hands.* She sighed and looked back up at her friends' eager faces.

"You may not believe this, but Suzanne, when you used to suggest that I give women a chance, I took it seriously. I thought about it when I'd meet your other friends and their friends, but I wasn't attracted to anyone." Addison sat up and set her wine on the table. "Let me ask you this. I know you're married and have been together a long time, but are you still attracted to other women?"

"I appreciate a woman's beauty. It may be their looks or their actions or the things they say. I am attracted to some characters on TV or in movies, but..." Rachel trailed off.

"But she doesn't want to jump anyone's bones but mine." Suzanne grinned.

Rachel chuckled and gave her the most loving look. "That's right. I'm only attracted, like that, to you."

"For me, I find all women beautiful! All shapes, all sizes, all backgrounds; I adore women!" Suzanne kissed the back of Rachel's hand. "But Rachel has my heart. She's the only one I want to kiss, hold hands with, make a life with."

Addison nodded. "I'm finding myself attracted to Lissa and it's been happening for a while." Addison took a deep breath, let it out, and continued. "So, I've been looking at women who come into the bank or women I see at the grocery store or when I'm out shopping, and there's nothing. It's just Lissa; it's just her."

Suzanne smiled. "I can see why you'd be attracted to Lissa. You go together."

"Yeah, you complement one another," Rachel added.

"What?"

"Look, Addy. You're extremely driven whereas Lissa is more laid back. You don't have to compete with her."

"Wait," Rachel said. "There was the video game incident."

Suzanne looked at Rachel. "That was all in fun. Yes, you wanted to beat her, but it was for amusement and joy."

Addison listened to them and thought about how she liked to tease Lissa because sometimes it led to Lissa grabbing her and holding her close. And yeah, she liked that very much.

"You can be the relaxed yet inquisitive Addison, not the I'm better than you Addison," Suzanne continued.

When Addison started to protest Rachel interrupted. "She means that in a nice way."

"Yeah," Suzanne said. "You are cutthroat when you need to be in business, but with Lissa you're learning about the town and how people live there. You're getting to know her and you like who she is."

Addison reached for her glass and sat back. "Yeah I do like her, but I don't know if she likes me that way."

Suzanne and Rachel exchanged a look. "How could she not?" Suzanne said. "You are amazing."

"Thanks. But to her, I'm her best friend, Addy." Addison took a drink of her wine and then continued. "There was that date fiasco thing."

"What? You had a date?"

"No. Did I not tell you about this?"

"No! Spill it," Suzanne demanded.

Addison explained about dinner with Hunter and then going to Lissa's. "It was the strangest feeling. I felt like I was hurting Lissa by being there. All I wanted to do was leave and tell her how it happened, but then Hunter started talking about her."

"About Lissa?" Suzanne asked.

"Yeah, Lissa once told me that Hunter's mother was one of her favorite people. As it turns out Hunter thinks a lot of Lissa. Once we started talking about her I felt less anxious and was able to calm down somewhat."

"Then what happened?"

"Dinner was over and—"

"You went straight to Lissa's," Rachel interrupted with a smile.

"I did. But...she already knew!"

"What?"

"Small towns." Addison held up her hands. "Anyway, we talked and I could tell she was relieved when I told her what happened. But I also know it upset her because her cold, untouched dinner was on the table when I got there."

Suzanne stared at Addison. "What aren't you telling us?"

Addison sighed. "I came up with this dumb idea that whenever someone asks me out, I'm going to tell them I have plans with Lissa. She agreed to go along with the idea."

Rachel smiled. "That's not a dumb idea."

Suzanne chuckled. "It sounds like you agreed to be exclusive although neither of you want to admit you're dating."

Speechless, Addison stared at Suzanne with her mouth agape.

"How was Thanksgiving with the family?" Rachel asked.

"It was great. I had such a good time. They welcomed me like I was part of the family. Check that—I felt like one of the family. On the drive here, I got to thinking that maybe it's a good thing we're apart this weekend. It'll give me a chance to step back." Addison sighed and rolled her eyes toward the ceiling.

"What's that look for?"

"I had to go by and see her before I left," Addison said, then groaned.

"Had to?"

"Yes. I made up an excuse in my head to go by and see her before I left town. Of course she did ask me to text her when I got here."

"That's sweet. She wants to make sure you're safe," Suzanne said. "Don't forget that I texted you to let you know we were home when we visited that weekend."

Addison smiled and nodded. She could see Rachel studying her.

"Has anything happened..." Rachel trailed off.

"We've hugged a couple of times, and I hugged her when I went by earlier today. But yesterday..." Addison smiled at the memory. "I was trash talking about beating her and she started tickling me." Addison chuckled. "We were in the car and I managed to get away. But she was at the back of the car getting our dishes out and I jumped on her back."

"Oh." Suzanne covered her mouth and giggled.

"She grabbed my legs and started spinning around and I

told her I'd throw up on her, so she stopped and let me go." Addison laughed.

"You weren't going to throw up on her!" Suzanne exclaimed. "I've seen you at the carnival."

"Yeah, she realized I was kidding and when I started to run away she grabbed me. We were both laughing and I leaned my head back on her shoulder and looked into her eyes and..."

"And what!" Suzanne shouted.

"There was wonder and joy in her eyes and for a second I thought she was going to kiss me." Addison shook the memory out of her head and looked across at her friends. "I wanted her to kiss me."

"So she feels it too," Rachel said.

"I don't know," Addison said. "What I do know is that I spend a lot of time with her and I like it."

"She'll never make the first move," Rachel stated.

"What? Are there things I should know about being gay? Are there rules?"

"Since the beginning of time, straight women have been coming on to gay women then changed their minds, thus hurting the gay woman," Rachel explained.

"I will not let you hurt that wonderful woman by not being sure of what you want," Suzanne said.

"I'd never want to hurt Lissa."

"I know that, but I'm sure this has happened to Lissa before."

"She hasn't mentioned it," Addison murmured. "But she did tell me about her longtime girlfriend and how they broke up."

"And?"

"The girlfriend thought Lissa was the one." Addison

made air quotes with her fingers. "But Lissa couldn't see them together forever."

"I'm telling you, Lissa will never make the first move. You will have to start the conversation or whatever..." Suzanne trailed off.

Addison gave her a puzzled look. "Why? If she feels the same way—and I don't know if she does—but if she does, why wouldn't she make the first move?"

"She will wait because she doesn't want to push herself on you."

"Lissa would never do that to me or anybody," Addison said sharply.

"I know that," Suzanne said, closing her eyes. "Just trust me, Addy. She'll want you to be sure and will not in any way pressure you."

"But I'm not gay. At least I don't think I am," Addison said softly.

"Do you have to be gay or straight? Can't you just be Addison? If you're attracted to Lissa or have feelings for her, you don't have to put a name on it." Suzanne smiled at Addison and added, "You know what you're feeling and you know how Lissa makes you feel inside, so why hold back on that? Can you take a chance for once in your life and embrace something besides your job?"

"But I may not be in Brazos Falls that long," Addison said quietly. "It would be wrong to fall for her and then leave."

"Whoa!" Rachel said. "Slow down. You are both smart people and can figure that out when and if it happens. For now, why don't you see what it would be like to admit you have feelings for Lissa and go on a real date?"

"A real date?" Addison murmured. "I never thought of

that." She gasped. "There's a lot to consider. It's a small town and I am the president of the bank."

"Stop!" Suzanne yelled. "You are talking yourself out of something that hasn't happened."

"That's why I needed to talk to you!" Addison raised her voice. "I'm so fucking confused!"

Suzanne gave her a compassionate smile. "That's how it goes when you're falling—"

"Don't say it!" Addison exclaimed. "For God's sake, I haven't even kissed the woman."

"Okay, okay," Rachel said, trying to calm everyone down. "Let's take a breath."

Addison finished off her wine and set her glass on the table. She leaned over and rested her chin in her hands. "I like her so much," she said softly.

"Like?"

Addison sighed. "It's more than like, so much more."

19

"Aunt Lissa, look at this one," Blythe said as Lissa walked towards her. "Smell." She held the candle under Lissa's nose.

"Hmm, that reminds me of your mom," Lissa said with a smile.

"I thought so too. Should I get it for her?"

"You know how much she likes candles," Lissa commented.

"Oh, smell this one." Blythe once again held the candle under Lissa's nose.

"Mmm, I like that," Lissa said.

"It's for Addison. See?" Blythe turned the candle so Lissa could read the scent.

Lissa laughed. "Winner Celebration! That would just add fuel to her trash talking. I'm never going to hear the end of how she beat me on Thanksgiving."

"But it smells so good. You have to get it for her," Blythe said, sniffing another candle. "I like her."

"I like her, too." Lissa chuckled.

Blythe tilted her head and looked at her aunt. "Y'all go together."

"What?"

"You go together. Just like me and Caris," Blythe explained. "She's my best friend at school. We do everything together."

"You do? Have you talked to her since you've been home?" Lissa asked.

"Yeah, several times. We text all the time."

Lissa thought about what Blythe said. She and Addison texted often. She'd actually texted with her last night and this morning. Maybe that wasn't unusual.

"I'm glad Addison moved here," Blythe said.

Before Lissa could comment her phone rang. "Oh, there's Addison now. She must've known we were talking about her," Lissa said in a loud whisper.

Blythe chuckled. "Yeah right, Aunt Lis."

"Hey," Lissa said, connecting the call.

"Hey, yourself. I wanted to tell you and Blythe not to buy everything. You have to leave a few things for me. You know how I love to shop," Addison said cheerily.

Lissa chuckled. "Oh, there'll be plenty left for you. Aren't you shopping with Suzanne and Rachel?"

"Yes, we're out shopping right now, but I was thinking of you and thought I'd call. Besides, I need to check on Dart," Addison rambled.

Lissa smiled. "Dart is fine, but he misses you."

"How can you tell?"

"He and Callie have played a little, but he's been lying around the house and when I let them go roaming this morning he went straight to your house."

"Aww, that makes me happy. Maybe I am a good cat parent."

"He's not the only one that misses you," Lissa said softly.

"Calista! You don't mean it. I haven't even been gone a day," Addison said.

"Calista? You're using my whole name?" Lissa chuckled.

"Yeah, I'm trying it on for size. I kind of like it." Addison laughed.

"Okay," Lissa said slowly, not sure what was going on.

"I'd better let you go; I don't want you to miss any bargains. But Lis, just so you know, I miss you, too," Addison said.

"Addison Henry, don't say that so loud, someone will hear you," Lissa teased.

Addison giggled and Lissa thought that was the nicest sound she'd heard in a long time.

"Bye, Lis. I'll see you tomorrow."

Lissa chuckled and put her phone back in her pocket.

"That's a really nice smile on your face, Aunt Lissa," Blythe said with a smirk.

Right now Lissa didn't care if Blythe teased her. *Addison missed her.*

"Lissa Morgan, give me a hug."

At the sound of the familiar voice behind her, Lissa turned to find Sidney Wray standing across from her with both hands on her hips and a wide smile on her lips. "Sidney!" Lissa exclaimed and gave her a hug. "You remember my niece, Blythe?"

"Of course I do," Sidney said, smiling at Blythe. "You've gone and grown up, young lady."

"Hi," Blythe said with a grin. "I'm going to try this on, Aunt Lissa."

"Okay." Lissa watched Blythe walk to the dressing room in the back of the store. When she turned back to Sidney she was looking around the store.

"Who are you looking for?" Lissa asked her.

"Why, Addison, of course."

Lissa rolled her eyes.

"I hear you two are spending a lot of time together."

Lissa shook her head and didn't say anything.

"You know how people talk," Sidney commented.

"You don't listen to gossip, do you?" Lissa challenged her.

"Oh honey, you know I listen to gossip. But that doesn't mean I believe it,"—Sidney leaned in—"or redirect it."

Lissa chuckled as Sidney continued, "Hunter had dinner with our new bank president the other day."

"I heard," Lissa replied.

"All they talked about was you."

Lissa shrugged.

"I like her," Sidney stated.

Lissa gave her a careful look. "Yeah, she'd make a great daughter-in-law."

Sidney scoffed. "Oh lord, no. That girl is too ambitious. She won't be here long. Hunter needs a woman who will be happy right here in our small town."

"Then why did you insist he ask her out?" Lissa asked.

"Because it's the neighborly thing to do. Isn't that what you're doing, being neighborly?" Sidney asked, tapping her foot with one hand on her hip. "I'm sure that's what everyone thinks."

Blythe came out of the dressing room and stopped in front of them. "Well?"

"Oh honey, that looks lovely. Your Aunt Lissa will buy it for you," Sidney gushed.

"It's not Christmas yet!" Lissa exclaimed.

"You don't need a reason to buy your niece a cute outfit," Sidney said with a grin.

"She's right. You should have it," Lissa said with a laugh.

Blythe clapped her hands together. "Thanks, Aunt Lissa!" she exclaimed and hurried back to the dressing room.

Lissa sighed and shook her head. "You know, Sidney, if people didn't know I was gay, I wonder if they'd be talking about Addison and me at all. Would they think we were just two women out having a good time?"

"Isn't that what you're doing?"

"It is. How do you know Addison isn't gay?" Lissa said quietly to Sidney.

Sidney's face lit up. "Oh, I never considered that."

Lissa tilted her head. "She's not, but—"

"No, you're right! People never consider things like that. They would simply look at you."

Lissa smiled and leaned in. "But you would redirect any of that gossip, wouldn't you."

Sidney chuckled and looked Lissa up and down. "You know, I sometimes wondered..."

"Stop that! Now, you're just messing with me." Lissa laughed.

"It was so good to see you," Sidney said, hugging her tight. "Come visit me."

"I will." Lissa stepped back and smiled.

Sidney started to walk away then turned back to Lissa. "Maybe this town is ready to see what a happy gay relationship looks like." She gave Lissa a wink and left the store.

Lissa stood there a moment and considered all that Sidney had said. She wasn't surprised that people were talking about Addison and her, but it was nice to know Sidney would set them straight, so to speak. Lissa chuckled at the thought as Blythe came back out of the dressing room with a wide smile.

"Where'd Sidney go?" Blythe asked.

"Oh, she's off spreading joy to others." Lissa chuckled.

Lissa paid for the dress and candles and left the store. As they walked down the sidewalk Blythe said, "I know you and Addison aren't together, but why not?"

"Well, it's not that easy. You said Caris was your best friend. Are you two together?"

"No. We don't like each other that way," Blythe said. "But you and Addison do. It's obvious."

Lissa stopped. "What?"

Blythe turned around to face her aunt. "It's obvious. I mean, I know you're not together, but you could be."

"Addison isn't gay," Lissa said quietly as she began to walk again.

"So? Maybe she hasn't met the right woman yet." Blythe reached for her aunt's arm and stopped her. "You're the right woman, Aunt Lis."

Lissa scoffed. "I don't know about that."

"I do." Blythe smiled. "Why don't you just ask her?"

"Addison has a set career path with her company. She will only be here a couple of years before they move her up."

"Go with her."

Lissa chuckled. "I wish it was that easy, kiddo. Besides, she's just my friend," Lissa stated firmly.

"But she could be more," Blythe said with a grin.

"We're supposed to be shopping." Lissa opened the door to another store.

"We are, we're finding you a girlfriend." Blythe laughed. "Maybe it's time you come visit me and we'll find you someone. You can at least go on a date."

"Look at this," Lissa said, ignoring her niece.

Blythe chuckled. "Okay, okay. But we're not through with this discussion, auntie."

. . .

Later that evening, Lissa was feeding the cats and thinking back on her conversation with Blythe. Of course Lissa had thought about Addison as more than a friend, but she'd shut those feelings down because it would only lead to her getting hurt.

But Marielle and now Blythe had commented on them being more than friends.

Could Addison have feelings for her? No, Addison had her goals and stuck to them. Or did she?

Still, there was no way Lissa was going to risk losing this friendship. Addison meant too much to her. But to protect the friendship did they need to put a little distance between them to stop the rumor mill?

Lissa had never worried about gossip. She knew people would find something else to talk about. But this was different because someone else was involved. Someone that she liked very much. She'd warned Addison at the beginning, but she hadn't seemed to be bothered by it. What about now?

Lissa grabbed her book and got ready to escape into other people's problems. She chuckled at how Addison called them 'her friends.' But then her phone pinged with a text from Addison.

"I can't wait to tell you all about the weekend. Suzanne and Rachel say hi."

Lissa smiled and replied. "Can't wait. Hi back."

"What am I going to do?" she said aloud.

* * *

The next day Addison was packing her things when Suzanne came into the bedroom.

"Hey, what are you going to do about Lissa? You've been texting her all weekend."

Addison turned around with an amused look. "Are you jealous?"

"Addy, no! I'm concerned," Suzanne said seriously.

Addison sat down on the bed and Suzanne plopped down beside her.

"I don't know how to talk to her about it. I've never done this. I don't want to mess up what we have."

Suzanne took Addison's hand in hers and nodded. "I get that."

"I thought I would ask her to go to the bank's Christmas party as my date," Addison stated. "We go to dinner all the time. This would be around other people, but she knows them all. Would it be a terrible idea for a first date?"

"Hmm, I don't know. It'd be like you're coming out to the whole town, wouldn't it?"

"Well, I was thinking. The town is used to us being together, so it wouldn't be unusual. Maybe it would be a date between the two of us. You know?"

"Kind of like a secret date?"

"I guess. I don't know how else we could go on a real date around there without someone knowing. The date is for the two of us, not the town."

"Oh, I see how you're thinking now. That might work. It would be a special occasion for the two of you. It would be around the bank people, but they wouldn't know it was a real date for you."

"Yeah. Is it a dumb idea?"

"Not at all. It would at least get the conversation started and you can see how Lissa feels."

"You said I'd have to make the first move."

"It's definitely a move." Suzanne chuckled. "Do it. And call me immediately after and let me know what she said."

Addison laughed. "You know I will. Why do I feel like I'm back in high school all of a sudden?"

Suzanne chuckled. "Have you ever asked anyone out?"

"Nope. This is a first in a lot of ways: first date, first woman."

"It'll be great. You'll see. Now, let's go to lunch."

"Thanks, Suzanne. I'm really nervous and will probably talk myself out of it on the way home."

"No you won't. You like Lissa, remember? And you wanted her to kiss you."

"I did." Addison nodded. "I do," she said softly.

20

"Hey," Addison said as Lissa opened the front door.

"Come in," Lissa said with a big smile.

Addison thought Lissa's smile seemed a little brighter and her eyes were sparkling. She felt Dart bump against her legs and heard him meow loudly.

"See! I told you he missed you." Lissa laughed.

"Oh, my boy," Addison cooed as she bent down to pick him up. He continued to meow and began to purr. Just then Addison felt Callie rubbing against her legs and meowing along with Dart.

"He wasn't the only one," Lissa said.

"Wow, I wasn't expecting this." She put Dart back on the floor and he and Callie weaved around her legs then began to play.

Lissa and Addison sat down on the couch and watched them play for a moment.

"The cats weren't the only ones that missed you," Lissa repeated, giving Addison a smile.

"Is that right?" Addison replied with a lopsided grin.

Lissa chuckled and nodded. "As a matter of fact, Sidney Wray asked about you yesterday."

"What? When did you see her?"

"Blythe and I were shopping and we ran into her. She asked where you were since we're together all the time. At least that's how she put it," Lissa explained. "You know, people talk about us sometimes."

Addison scoffed. "I'm sure they do."

"That doesn't bother you?"

"Not at all! Look, Lis, I've lived here long enough to know how small towns operate. It's hard to be welcomed or find your place if you're not like everyone else. New people who move here have good jobs, are married with kids, and usually have family nearby. I have the good job, but I'm not married with kids and don't have family here, so people aren't sure what to make of me, and it's hard to be accepted. I expect to be talked about and who better to be associated with than the sweetheart of Brazos Falls? Everyone loves you and I can't be all bad if you're letting me hang around with you." Addison gave her what she hoped was a dazzling smile.

"Letting you? I love spending time with you."

"I don't care if people are talking about us. I value your friendship more than anything in my life right now. That's how important you are to me and I wouldn't want to do anything to jeopardize that," Addison said earnestly.

Lissa's mouth opened with surprise. "You are important to me, too," she said softly.

"You know, I made up an excuse to come by and see you Friday so I could hug you. That tells me there's more going on between us than just friendship." Addison watched Lissa's face and was relieved to see a smile. "I can tell you know what I'm talking about."

Lissa's smile widened. "Yeah, Addy, but I have to be careful not to—"

"I know what you're thinking," Addison said, holding up her hand. "I'm not gay. I haven't been with a woman. I talked to Suzanne and Rachel and they explained to me that you would never make the first move because you'd want me to be sure."

Lissa nodded and sighed. "That's part of it."

"But if I'm making excuses to come see you before leaving town and texting you the entire time I'm gone, then there's something happening between us. And...I want to see where it will go. I know you can't believe I'm saying this and I have no idea what I'm doing, but I think we should go on a date," Addison babbled nervously.

Lissa sat up a little straighter on the couch and said, "Okay."

"Going on a real date in this town would be kind of hard. I mean, we go out together all the time and we spend time at each other's houses. Suzanne and Rachel will be here next weekend for the parade, but the week after that is my bank's Christmas party." Addison paused as Lissa took all this information in.

"Oh, okay," she murmured.

"So, Calista, would you go to the party with me as my date?" Addison said with a hopeful look. The smile on Lissa's face made Addison's stomach flutter. "It won't be a surprise to anyone that you're there with me, but to us it can be our first date. I think our first date should be special, don't you?"

"I do and you're right, it would be kind of hard to have a special first date here since we've done so much together already."

"No one else at the party has to know, but we'll know," Addison said with a shy grin.

"I like it," Lissa said.

"So... will you go with me?"

"I'd love to," Lissa replied, giving Addison a brilliant smile.

Addison released a deep breath and chuckled nervously. "Are we still on for yoga tomorrow?"

"Yes!" Lissa exclaimed.

Addison grinned. "By the way, I've done a little research on this hot chocolate thing. It's not really a contest. The parents pay for votes for the kids. That's not a real competition."

Lissa scoffed. "I know that and it reminds me, I got you something this weekend." She got up and went to the kitchen. When she came back she handed Addison the candle.

Addison inhaled deeply. "Oh, I love this," she said.

"Read the label," Lissa said, reaching over to turn the candle in Addison's hand.

"Winner celebration!" Addison laughed. "You knew I was going to beat you!"

Lissa laughed along with her.

"Besides, I don't want to compete with you." Addison grinned and reached for Lissa's hand. "I want to date you."

Lissa shook her head in disbelief. "You're sure?"

"I'm sure," Addison said. She intertwined their fingers and smiled at how perfectly they fit together.

"You're home earlier than I thought you'd be," Lissa said.

Addison giggled. "I wonder why."

Lissa chuckled. "It's really pretty outside. Would you like to take a drive with me? There's something I want to show you."

Addison smiled. "How about I take Dart home, unload the car, and you come get me?"

Lissa nodded and for a moment they paused not wanting to let go of each other's hand. She helped Addison put Dart in the pet carrier. On the short drive to her house, Addison smiled into the rearview mirror. "I've got a date!"

* * *

Lissa picked Addison up and began to drive through town.

"Where are we going?"

"Well, I promised to take you to my friend's place at the lake and whenever we had time the weather was always too cold. But today turned out to be beautiful and since you got home early, I thought, why not."

"Oh! This is the place you go paddle boarding?"

"Yeah, and sometimes I drive out here and look at the water. It can be relaxing."

"I know what you mean. I told you how much I like the water."

"You did. Now, tell me about your weekend," Lissa said, glancing over at Addison.

Addison entertained Lissa with stories from her shopping exploits and their friendsgiving dinner Saturday night while Lissa navigated the winding lake road.

Lissa pulled into a driveway and got out to open the gate. "I'll be right back." She drove them down the unpaved road until a house came into view. They could just see the water behind it.

"Oh wow. This is lovely," Addison said in a dreamy voice.

"Isn't it?" Lissa grinned. She pulled down by the water and parked. "I don't have a key to the house, but this is what I come here for." Lissa spread her arms wide and smiled.

"This is beautiful."

They got out of the car and Lissa grabbed a blanket from the back seat. She spread it on the grass at the edge of the sand where the water gently lapped the shore.

Lissa smiled at Addison as she sat down and patted the blanket next to her. Addison plopped down and stretched her legs in front of her.

"You can come here whenever you want?"

"Yeah. They let me know when they're coming into town, but most of the time it's empty." Lissa leaned back on her hands and looked over at Addison. "So, we're going on a date."

Addison looked over at her and smiled. "Yeah, we are."

Lissa grinned, then her face fell. "You're sure about this?"

Addison nodded. "I'm sure."

"You know, crossing that friends-line might be hard to go back to if..."

Addison's forehead creased. "I thought about that. There's no way I want to lose you as a friend, Lis, but how do we..." Addison took Lissa's hand. "How about this? We agree right now that if this first date is a disaster, we recover our friendship and can laugh about it."

"But," Lissa said, "if it's as amazing as we both hope it is, then we agree to go on another date."

"You know, it's been a long time since I've been on a date," Addison said, wincing.

"You think it's been a long time for you?" Lissa laughed, squeezing Addison's hand. "It's been forever for me!"

They laughed and Addison stared at their intertwined fingers.

Lissa could feel her heart begin to pound in her chest at Addison's touch. Their fingers fit together perfectly and Lissa couldn't quite explain the feeling in her heart. It was like going home after being away for a long time. Or like that first taste of Christmas fudge after not having it for a year. It felt exciting and comforting and so simple and satisfying all at the same time.

Neither of them said anything as they looked out over the water, holding hands and being present in the moment.

"I now know why you miss this," Addison said, squeezing Lissa's hand.

"Miss this?" Lissa frowned then remembered what she'd said about being single. "Oh! Yeah, isn't it nice?"

"Would you hold my hand if we're walking around the downtown square?" Addison asked.

"Of course I would," Lissa said, then quickly added, "If you wanted me to."

"Why wouldn't I want you to?"

Lissa looked over at her. "Do you worry about what people will think and how that might affect the bank?"

Addison sighed. "Unfortunately, I do have to worry about how the bank looks, but I don't see how my holding your hand will make a difference."

"You know that I don't ever want to make things difficult for you," Lissa said earnestly.

"I know that and I don't want to make things difficult for you."

Lissa tilted her head. "You know what I mean, Addy. It matters to some people."

"Lis, we haven't even been on our first date yet."

Lissa smiled and nodded. "And I can't wait."

"Me either."

"Are you cold? I think we're in for a beautiful sunset."

Addison sat a little closer to Lissa and pulled their hands into her lap. "Let's stay."

They gazed out over the lake as the sun crept closer to the water.

"Hey, I played a fun game with the kids Saturday night. You pull up your music library on your phone and hit shuffle then see what song begins to play."

"I'm sure that was interesting. Did you even know the songs on the kids' phones?"

"All but Max. His music knowledge and library are extensive."

"What song came up on yours?"

"A song I hadn't listened to in a long time. My dad used to play it for me," Lissa said.

"I want to hear it."

"You do?"

"Yeah. I'm sure it's an old song that means a lot to you," Addison said, squeezing her hand.

"Okay." Lissa got her phone out and pulled up James Taylor's "Secret O' Life."

The soft notes began to play and the words echoed around them.

"Lissa, that's beautiful," Addison said as the song ended.

"It is. Dad used to tell me when things get hard, listen to this song, and it would simplify things. Remember to enjoy the ride."

"Did it work?"

"Most of the time."

"So the secret to love is opening your heart. Isn't that what he said?"

Lissa looked over at Addison and smiled. The cartwheels in her stomach made her know Addison was already in her heart; that was no secret.

"Opening your heart can be scary," Addison said, looking back over the water.

"It can, but I think this time it's worth it," Lissa said softly. She felt Addison squeeze her hand.

"I don't think I've ever heard that song before. I've heard of James Taylor, but not that particular song. I really like it. Will you send it to me?"

"After the sunset. I don't want to let go of your hand," Lissa said with a shy grin.

Addison smiled and gazed into Lissa's eyes. "I love looking into your eyes. I never know what shade of brown they'll be. Right now they're golden."

"You're going to miss the sunset," Lissa said, holding Addison's gaze.

"Maybe what I'm looking at is better." Addison said softly.

Lissa's mouth went dry. "Damn, Addy," she whispered.

Addison smiled and looked away. "I don't know what I'm doing," she murmured.

Good God! Lissa's heart was about to beat out of her chest. If Addison could make her feel like this with a look and a few words, then she was certainly going to enjoy the ride, just as the song said.

"You're watching the sun set and holding my hand. What's there to know? Let's just feel." Lissa sighed. Addison replied by gently placing her head on Lissa's shoulder.

The sun sank into the water and Lissa was pretty sure their hearts were beating in rhythm as they leaned into one another, still holding hands.

21

L issa smiled to herself as she stared at her computer screen. *Addison asked her on a date!* She'd been replaying their conversation over in her head and still couldn't quite believe it. Who was she trying to fool? She'd had feelings for Addison almost from the beginning. She'd been pushing them down, down, down and talking to herself daily. But now, she didn't have to hide those feelings any longer. She could let them spread through her entire being and that's why she was smiling. She couldn't help it.

A bell rang, indicating someone had come through the door into the mill storefront. Lissa glanced up and saw her sister walking towards her office. She hadn't shared her news with anyone yet, instead choosing to keep it to herself and enjoy it without her family's teasing.

"Hey, Lis," Marielle said, stepping into her office and sitting in the chair across from Lissa's desk.

"Hi. Thanks for coming by." Lissa gave her a big smile.

"What are you up to, big sister?" Marielle eyed her warily.

Lissa chuckled. "Addison asked me out," she said, with a huge smile.

Marielle's face lit up. "On a date?"

Lissa nodded and grinned.

"That's fucking awesome!" Marielle squealed. "Tell me all about it!"

"She invited me to go to the bank's Christmas party with her as her date."

"Oh wow! That's kind of big, isn't it?"

"Well, no one will be surprised we're together, but to us it will be our first date."

"Oh, Lissa! I hope it's the beginning of a ton of happiness for you both."

"Me too. Anyway, I asked you to come by because I need something to wear," Lissa said.

"Oh." Marielle sat back in her chair. "You have nice clothes. You just don't get to wear them very often."

"I know, but I'd like to get something new. I can't decide if I want to wear a killer suit or maybe a dress." Lissa shrugged.

"Hmm, you do look good in a suit, but so does Addison. She wears them for work."

"I was thinking about a dress."

"Maybe something appropriate, but also alluring," Marielle said, wiggling her eyebrows.

"I don't think Addison would expect me to wear a dress."

"But you look good in a dress," Marielle said, staring at Lissa. "Yeah, you should wear a dress."

"Would you go shopping with me?"

"Of course! When can you get away?"

"I thought maybe we'd run into the city one morning next week," Lissa suggested.

"I can do that." Marielle clapped her hands together. "This is going to be so much fun!"

Lissa laughed. "I can't wait."

"Addison won't know what hit her."

"Hey, I haven't told anyone else. I don't want to overwhelm her. I was surprised, but not shocked, you know?"

"I'm happy for you. I may have to share this wonderful news with Blythe. She's determined to get you and Addison together while she's home for Christmas."

Lissa chuckled. "Oh, she is?"

"Yes. She'll be so excited when I tell her."

"Thanks, Mari. I really want this to go well."

"What about until the party? You could go out before that?"

"Her friends are coming in this weekend for the parade and Addison wants our first date to be special, so we're waiting until the party. Besides, she's been so busy this week, I've barely seen her."

"Okay," Marielle said, getting up. "Just let me know what day next week."

"I will," Lissa said with a big smile.

* * *

A couple of days later, Lissa counted the cash and totaled the deposit then put all of it in the money bag. She walked out of her office and stopped at the counter. "I'm going to the bank. Do you need anything while I'm out?"

"Tell Addison hello for me," Ben said with a grin.

"I should've never told you we were going on a date," Lissa said, shaking her head.

Ben chuckled. "I'm happy for both of you. By the way,

everything is ready for the parade tomorrow. I had one of the guys paint a sign for the hot chocolate stand."

"Oh, good. You'll be around if I need help at the stand, right?"

"Yes, but I don't think they'll need either one of us. Those kids know what to do. The boys will be there, too. They've done it before."

"Okay. I'll see you later." Lissa left the mill and drove to the bank. Addison had been so busy this week that they'd only done yoga once and had a quick dinner at Lissa's one other night this week.

. When Lissa walked into the bank she made her way back to Addison's office. Lissa could see her through the windows that also doubled as walls. She was sitting at her desk, staring at her computer screen, and for a moment Lissa lost her breath. Addison was so beautiful and Lissa could let herself feel every quickened heartbeat and no longer had to push those feelings away.

Lissa stood in the doorway and smiled. "You ask me on a date and then disappear for days. I see how you are, Addison Henry."

Addison turned her head and the look on her face was pure joy. It made Lissa suddenly weak in the knees. "Hey," Addison said affectionately. "Will you please come sit for a minute?"

Lissa grinned and walked over to the chair across from Addison's desk.

"I need to look into your beautiful eyes. I've missed you," she said softly.

Lissa tilted her head. "It's Friday. You're almost finished for the day."

"Unfortunately not."

"What?"

"I have another report I have to get done before I can leave."

"What can I do to help?" Lissa offered.

"You're doing it." Addison smiled. "You know what I really need?"

"Tell me."

"I need to be at the lake, sitting at your friend's house with you, watching the sunset."

"Let's do it."

"I won't be done in time. But I've thought about it several times this week and imagined the next time we get to go there. The water is calling me."

Lissa had an idea. Maybe she could help after all.

"I know you're tired, but when you get finished can we spend some time together?"

"That's exactly what I want to do." Addison smiled warmly.

"Text me when you're done."

Addison took a deep breath and sighed. "You have no idea how happy I am to see you."

"I've missed you, too, Addy."

"Are we turning into those sappy people in the movies we watch?" Addison grinned.

"Romantic, honey, not sappy."

Addison laughed. "Oh, how I needed this visit."

"Finish that report so you can come home." Lissa got up and paused.

The smile on Addison's face and the sparkle in her eyes made Lissa's heart skip a beat once again. "See you tonight," Lissa said.

"Okay," Addison said softly, staring into Lissa's eyes.

Lissa had a hard time leaving Addison's office, but she had an idea how to make Addison's evening better. She went back to the mill and after they closed she didn't go right home like usual.

* * *

Addison pinched the bridge of her nose and moaned. She was the only one left in the bank since they'd closed over an hour ago. This was the third time this week that she'd stayed late. It wasn't unusual for her to work long hours, but since coming to Brazos Falls she hadn't needed to until this week.

Her phone pinged on her desk and she glanced over at the screen. A smile grew on her face when she realized it was a text from Lissa. She opened the text and gasped.

"Oh my God, Lissa! You are something!" Addison said, staring at her phone. Lissa had gone to the lake and taken several pictures of the sunset and sent them with the text.

Addison read the message out loud. "This will be waiting for us Sunday evening. Until then, I hope this gives you enough calm to get finished tonight."

Addison scrolled through the pictures. She did indeed feel the connection to the water that gave her peace, but she also felt so much emotion at what Lissa had done for her. What she wanted to do right now was to put her arms around Lissa Morgan and kiss her. She wanted that kiss to show Lissa what she was feeling inside because right now she couldn't put it into words.

She quickly thanked Lissa and told her she'd see her soon. With renewed energy she dove into the report, working quickly because she couldn't wait to get home.

Addison pulled into her driveway and saw Lissa sitting in the rocking chair on her front porch. She'd texted Lissa when she left the bank, but hadn't expected her to be waiting at her house.

"Hey," Addison said, giving Lissa a wide smile.

"You have three minutes to run in and change," Lissa stated, looking at her watch.

"What?" Addison chuckled.

"I know you're tired, but if you'll give me...twenty minutes, I'll have you back in your warm house with Dart in your lap."

Lissa's excitement was contagious. "Could I at least stop and thank you for the sunset pictures? They were gorgeous and just what I needed, kind of like you." Addison grinned.

Lissa's smile widened. "You're welcome." She looked at her watch again. "Three minutes. Ready, go! Oh, and grab your warm coat."

Addison laughed and ran inside. Once in her bedroom she quickly changed into leggings and a bulky sweater. She grabbed her big coat out of the hall closet and yelled hello to Dart. Her laughter bubbled out when she slid onto the porch. "Did I make it?"

"Right on time," Lissa said. She grabbed Addison's hand and hurried them to the car.

"I don't guess you'll tell me where we're going?" Addison said as Lissa turned on the car. She reached over and took Lissa's hand in hers, running her thumb along the back of it before intertwining their fingers.

"You have been so busy this week. I remember you telling me that when you're stressed, being near the water calms you."

"It does."

"So, maybe this will be a quick little stress reliever for you." Lissa drove them out of town and then pulled off the highway onto a dirt road. A few moments later they could see a waterfall gleaming in the moonlight.

"Oh, Lissa!" Addison exclaimed, squeezing her hand. "It's beautiful."

"Come on," Lissa said, opening her door.

Addison met her at the front of the SUV.

Lissa put her hands on Addison's shoulders and gently turned her to face the waterfall. "Listen closely and you can just hear the water," she said softly into Addison's ear.

In the still of the night, she could hear the water rushing over the rocks below the falls, then softly rippling into the stream and beyond. The sound soothed her tired soul. She leaned back into Lissa's chest and felt Lissa's arms tighten around her.

It was magical and for a moment she closed her eyes and took it all in. The sounds, the smells, and the feel of Lissa's arms wrapped around her. But just as the water soothed her stress, Lissa being near ignited a fire inside her.

She slowly turned in Lissa's arms and looked up into her beautiful face. Addison's hand cupped Lissa's cheek and she stared into rich brown eyes. She could see the moonlight reflected off the falls glistening in those gorgeous orbs.

Addison reached up with her other hand and ran her finger along Lissa's jaw, over her lips, then trailed it down her chin and neck until her hand rested on Lissa's chest. She stared at Lissa's lips and could see them part slightly. At the same time, she felt the quickened rise and fall of Lissa's chest.

As if drawn by an undeniable force, Addison dropped her hand behind Lissa's neck and leaned up until her lips gently touched Lissa's. Addison had wondered for a while now how Lissa's lips would feel pressed to hers, but she wasn't ready for the electricity that shot through her body. She was aware of everything.

Addison could feel Lissa's hands gripping her shoulders through her coat. She could feel the wisps of Lissa's hair trapped between her fingers where they pressed into Lissa's neck. And she felt the softest most perfect lips kiss hers. That's where all this electricity was coming from! Those pillowy lips touched hers softly at first, a bit tentative, but Addison was sure and pressed a little harder. That's when she heard the softest moan. Did it come from Lissa? Or was it Addison's own heart sighing with relief from waiting so long for this to happen?

She felt Lissa's hands pull her even closer and now she could feel their thighs pressing together. Addison slid her hand from Lissa's chest and wrapped her arm around Lissa's shoulders, trying to get even closer. She could feel Lissa's fingers tangling in her hair as she held the back of Addison's head. Their lips were nipping, pressing, caressing.

There was that little moan again and now Addison could hear the water. Her heart was pounding in her ears, electricity was flowing through her body, and a warmth surrounded her like she'd never felt before. Her hands slid down and around to cup Lissa's face and together they pulled away just enough to separate their lips.

This had to be the best first kiss Addison had ever experienced. She felt a shy smile lifting the corners of her mouth. All she wanted right this moment was to kiss Lissa Morgan again.

22

"Damn," Addison whispered.

"Yeah," Lissa softly breathed, still holding them together.

Addison's hands slid down and rested on Lissa's shoulders. She suddenly thought about those kisses at the end of the movies they'd been watching. She understood now. All she wanted to do was keep kissing Lissa.

"I feel a bit exposed out here," Addison said, rubbing her thumb under Lissa's bottom lip. "Do you think we could go back to my place and..."

"Keep kissing?" Lissa whispered.

A smile grew on Addison's face and she nodded.

Lissa drove them back to Addison's house and as soon as they walked through the front door, Addison pushed Lissa against it. She stared into Lissa's eyes and could see they were a dark silky brown. With a lift of her chin she claimed Lissa's lips with her own.

This kiss was a bit more desperate. Addison now knew how wonderful Lissa's lips felt on hers and she wanted more. Encouraged by Lissa's quiet moan, Addison sucked

Lissa's lower lip into her mouth. She ran her tongue along the pillowy softness and Lissa responded by opening her mouth in invitation.

This made Addison groan and when their tongues collided she was surrounded by pleasure. It felt like a warm blanket pulling her into Lissa. She explored and at the same time let Lissa in. Once again she could feel every part of her body that touched Lissa's. Addison's leg was pushed between Lissa's legs and they were chest to chest. She could feel both of them struggling to breathe, but who needed air when lips tasted this good?

Addison reached up and grabbed Lissa's face then pulled away, panting. "We should've been doing this a long time ago."

Lissa chuckled.

Addison took her hand and led them to the couch. "That was the most romantic thing that's ever happened to me, Lis. It was so…"

Lissa smiled. "I just wanted you to hear the water. And…"

"And that was the best first kiss ever!" Addison exclaimed.

Lissa laughed. "I'm just glad you finally kissed me!"

"You were waiting on me? Don't do that. I don't know what I'm doing, remember?" Addison chuckled.

"Oh, you know what you're doing," Lissa assured her, leaning in and kissing her softly.

"Do I?" Addison whispered.

"Mmm, you do." Lissa brought their lips together in another soft kiss. When they parted, Lissa tentatively asked, "You're okay with this?"

Addison dropped her chin and gave Lissa a look. "Can you not tell?"

"You know what I mean," Lissa said hesitantly.

"I see an amazing woman who is more than my friend, Lis. I see you," Addison said, cupping Lissa's face. "You are who I want to spend my time with." She dropped her hands and chuckled. "I knew it when Hunter and I had dinner. I wanted to have dinner with you, and no one else. That's why I came rushing to your place as soon as we finished eating." Addison shook her head. "I came up with that lame excuse of always having plans with you when what I was trying to say is I wanted to only be with you."

"But you had to wrap your head around us. I understand that, Addy."

Addison looked down at their hands. "I've been thinking about tomorrow. I'm not sure how open I want to be out in public just yet." She looked into Lissa's eyes. "I love holding your hand. If we were hanging out in Dallas I wouldn't think twice about it, but I realize it's different in a small town."

Lissa nodded. "It is because people will start talking."

"I don't really mind people talking. I do worry about the effect it could have on the bank, though."

Lissa sighed. "I get it."

"People will be talking after the Christmas party; that's for sure. And I'm ready for it. Are you?"

"Addy," Lissa said sadly. "I'm sorry it's like this. It shouldn't matter who you're with, but small towns can be tough." Lissa looked up and smiled. "You know, Sidney told me that maybe the town is ready to see what a happy gay relationship looks like."

"She said that!"

Lissa nodded. "I guess she knew something we weren't quite ready to admit to ourselves."

"I'm still working through all the labels, Lis." Addison put her arm around Lissa and scooted closer. "It's you who I want to be with. It's you who I want to know everything about. It's you who I want to kiss." Addison pulled Lissa to her and as their lips met she felt her heart leap in her chest. She wrapped her other arm around Lissa and deepened the kiss.

Their tongues met and Addison felt such a rush of heat and emotion. Sure, it had been a while since she'd kissed anyone, but her heart and body were responding as if this was who she should be kissing from now on.

When they pulled apart she stared into Lissa's eyes. "I can't believe you went to the lake to get sunset pictures for me then took me to hear water because you knew it would ease the stress from this crazy week. Lissa, you beautiful, romantic soul. You're making me swoon."

Lissa smiled. "I may be romantic, but I'm also a little self-ish. I missed our time together this week. I wanted to make you feel better."

"I used to work late hours all the time, but since coming here I haven't had to do that much. This week was long because there are several end of the year reports coming up. One of the things I do is try to find more efficient ways for the bank to operate. Since I'm the president, I can try things at this smaller bank and hopefully share it with the other banks. Then I'll adapt it for the bigger banks, too. This week was a lot of information gathering and trying new things. That's why I was working late."

Lissa smiled. "My smart, accomplished...uh." Lissa stopped and her eyes widened.

"Girlfriend?" Addison said. She chuckled. "You can say it. I am your girlfriend."

"You are my girlfriend." Lissa giggled. "I don't want to overwhelm you. Please tell me if I'm too much at times."

"Oh, Lis, honey." Addison leaned over and gently kissed her.

"Are the long hours over?" Lissa asked.

"It depends. Part of the reason I worked late was because people were out sick or taking vacations. During the holidays we try to let everyone take off when they need to so they can be with family, but it spreads the rest of us a little thin. I may need a favor tomorrow," Addison said, wincing.

"I'm happy to help."

"I may have to be at the hot chocolate stand most of the night. The two other employees who volunteered were out sick today. I want Suzanne and Rachel to enjoy the square and not be stuck with me."

"I don't have to be at our hot chocolate stand. Ben and the boys are supposed to be there to help. I can work your stand or take Suzanne and Rachel around."

"Thanks, babe. I knew you'd help if you could." Addison smiled and liked the way Lissa's face lit up. "Oh, we can walk around the square and shop a little before the parade."

"That will be fun. I'll try not to grab your hand or put my arm around you," Lissa said with a wink. "But it'll be hard."

Addison chuckled. "I don't want to talk about tomorrow. I'd rather do this." Once again she pressed her lips to Lissa's and let all the emotions and pleasure surround her.

Addison was staring at the ceiling as the moonlight shone through her bedroom window. Her head rested on her hands and a smile played at the corners of her mouth. She took a deep breath and sighed. The thoughts of that first kiss were in the front of her mind along with the kisses that followed.

"You are one amazing woman, Calista Morgan, but I already knew that," she said softly. "You know that, too, don't you, Dart." She reached out to where Dart slept on the bed and softly ran her hand along his side.

Something tugged at the back of her mind. The same questions she'd asked herself weeks ago were still there. *Am I gay? Does it even matter?* If the kisses she shared with Lissa tonight were any indication then it didn't matter.

But for all her adult life she had been on one path: to the top. Whether it was being the best in her class, in whatever sport she was playing, or dean's list in graduate school, she was an over-achiever and thrived on attaining goals.

How could this relationship with Lissa affect her goals? She had never had to ask herself this question before. Sure, she'd dated and thought she was in love once, but none of that felt like this thing with Lissa. Yes, it was just beginning, yet somehow Addison knew this was different. She'd never felt so close, so understood, and so cared for—dare she say loved—by anyone else.

Her eyelids were heavy, just as those thoughts were. She had a wonderful day planned with Lissa and her friends tomorrow, so she let the thoughts go and looked forward to the fun.

* * *

All Lissa could think about when she got up the next morning was Addison and, more specifically, kissing Addison. She had to agree that their kiss by the falls was the best first kiss ever. Her chuckle made Callie roll over.

"Oh, Callie," Lissa said to the cat. "I am smitten. Addison said I made her swoon last night, but she made me weak the entire time."

Lissa was trying not to get too far ahead of herself, but she couldn't help it. Addison had shown no apprehension or tentativeness, but Lissa knew she had concerns. Small towns could be great places to live, but they could also be gossipy. People liked to talk about other people. They didn't necessarily care if it hurt the people they were talking about, either. Lissa could never understand how some folks seemed to enjoy other people's misfortunes.

She wasn't kidding herself. Tongues would be wagging when it came out she and Addison were dating. She just hoped prominent citizens, like Sidney, would speak on their behalf, making the gossip mongers move on to other topics.

That was ahead of them, though. Today, she got to spend the afternoon and evening with Addison, Suzanne, and Rachel. She liked Suzanne and Rachel and was sure Suzanne would have plenty to say about her and Addison. It was going to be a wonderful day, she just knew it!

23

"So, are you two still doing yoga?" Suzanne asked playfully, looking over at Addison and Lissa where they sat on the couch.

"Yes," Addison said, drawing the word out. "We only got to once this week because I worked late several nights."

"Is it different doing yoga now?" Suzanne asked in a low voice.

Lissa chuckled. "Not really. Addison still checks me out when she thinks I'm not looking."

Addison playfully slapped Lissa on the arm. "As if!" she exclaimed, putting her arm around Lissa and playing with the hair at the nape of her neck.

"Who, me?" Lissa said innocently.

"You're not as stealth as you think you are." Addison chuckled.

"How can I help it!" Lissa grinned and held up her hands.

"Aw, that's so cute," Suzanne said sweetly.

"Were you working late because of the parade today? We

saw several roads blocked off when we came through town earlier," Rachel said.

"Part of it had to do with the parade," Addison replied.

"Do y'all go all out for Christmas?" Lissa asked.

"We don't," Addison said. "My sister and her family live near my folks so they celebrate together, but my brother and I don't always get home for Christmas. We take a week during the summer to all meet up at home when the weather is nicer. We catch up then."

"We go visit both of our families before Christmas, but we always spend Christmas day at our little house," Suzanne said, reaching for Rachel's hand.

"What do you do?" Rachel asked Lissa.

"We take turns hosting a brunch on Christmas morning. Everyone shows up in their pajamas. The kids tell me all about their presents and we eat. It's very casual and laid back. It's a lot of fun," Lissa explained. "It's my turn to have everyone over this year." She reached over and took Addison's hand. "You know, I could use some help."

"Oh you could," Addison said with a smile.

"Yeah," Lissa grinned. She looked over at Suzanne and Rachel and said, "You are welcome to join us."

"Aw, that's nice of you to invite us," Rachel said.

"It would be your chance to experience a small-town Christmas," Lissa commented.

"Do you do anything else special around here after the parade?" Suzanne asked.

Lissa chuckled. "No, we do the parade and that's it. After that all the Christmas parties begin."

"Oh." Suzanne nodded. "I hear the bank is having quite a party this year."

"It is." Addison chuckled. "There will be gossip flying

after that party. Won't there, babe," Addison said, looking at Lissa. "I hope we're ready for it."

"What do you mean?" Suzanne asked.

"That's how it is in a small town," Lissa replied. "People will be talking about it."

"Weren't they already talking about you anyway?" Rachel commented.

"Yep. I told Lis, if they're going to be talking about me, why wouldn't I want it to be with her? Everyone loves Lissa." Addison smiled at her.

Lissa gave her a sad smile. "Not necessarily. I wish it didn't have to be that way." She looked at her watch and then squeezed Addison's hand. "Let's go do a little shopping before you have to be at the bank."

"That's what I'm here for." Suzanne chuckled.

As they walked around the square going in and out of the shops, Lissa and Addison stole several knowing glances here and there and no one was the wiser.

Lissa noticed Addison having quite the conversation with one of the store owners while she looked at bracelets.

"These are nice," Suzanne said, standing next to Lissa.

"Yeah, I was thinking the same thing. Maybe they'd make a nice Christmas present," Lissa suggested.

"Maybe." Suzanne winked.

"Just look at her," Lissa murmured. "Isn't she amazing?"

Suzanne smiled. "Yeah, she is." She leaned a little closer to Lissa. "I've heard her say the same thing about you."

Lissa took a deep breath and smiled.

Addison walked over and looked at Lissa. "What's that smile?"

"Shh, it's for you," Lissa whispered.

Addison laughed. "It'd better be," she said with a wink.

Suzanne and Rachel both laughed. "Oh, this is fun," Suzanne said.

"Come on, kids. I've got to get back to the bank," Addison said.

They followed her out the door and Lissa walked next to her. Addison reached over and put her hand in the crook of Lissa's elbow. "One of these days we'll walk down this street holding hands and not give a shit who sees or what they say."

Lissa smiled at her and hoped it was true.

"Why don't y'all walk over to Lissa's hot chocolate stand and try it out? Then come back over here and try mine," Addison said.

"That's a good idea," Rachel replied.

"Are you sure you two aren't competing?" Suzanne asked.

Addison chuckled. "I'm sure. Unless..." She leaned in closer so only they could hear.

"Unless?" Suzanne prompted.

"The loser pays in kisses." Addison grinned at Lissa.

"I'm happy to lose that bet."

Suzanne and Rachel laughed. "Sounds like you'd both be winners."

Lissa wanted to lean down and kiss Addison right then, but thought better of it. She chose to reach over and squeeze her hand instead. "We'll see you in a little while."

They walked over to the other side of the square where the hot chocolate stand sponsored by the mill was located. Ben, Leo, and Joe were all there helping the middle schoolers get everything ready.

Suzanne and Rachel were the first customers and

laughed at how Leo and Joe were instructing the kids on how to really sell their hot chocolate.

"According to Joe, this is the best cup of hot chocolate ever made," Suzanne said, blowing on the steamy liquid.

"And how do you know it's not?" Joe replied.

"Oh, he's good," Rachel said with a laugh. "Did he get that from you, Lissa?"

"Of course he did. You have to be confident in your product, don't you, buddy?" Lissa said to her nephew.

"That's right. Confidence is charming," Joe stated.

"Oh my God!" Suzanne exclaimed. "You are too much."

"Let the product speak for itself," Leo added.

Suzanne looked at Lissa and chuckled.

"Taste it," Lissa encouraged them.

They both took a sip and nodded. "This is delicious," Suzanne said, sounding surprised.

Joe held up his hands. "I told you."

Suzanne and Rachel finished their cups while they visited with Ben and the boys. Lissa looked on and wished Addison was here with them. She looked forward to the day when they all could hang out together like one big happy family.

"Okay," Lissa said, "we've got to go try the bank's hot chocolate."

"Addison may be my best friend and all, but it'll be hard to beat this cup of hot chocolate," Suzanne told Joe, Leo, and the kids.

"I have to agree. Well done," Rachel said. She slipped a twenty-dollar bill into the jar on the counter which was for votes and was also a donation to the local civic club that made sure struggling families had a merry Christmas.

On the walk back across the square to the bank,

Suzanne said, "That's a clever way to get donations for a good cause."

"The club does a lot to make kids happy year round," Lissa commented.

"Hey, speaking of happy," Suzanne said, glancing over at Lissa. "I don't think I've ever seen Addison this happy. I'm pretty sure it's because of you."

Lissa smiled. "Really?"

"Yeah. You know how single-minded she can be about her career," Suzanne began.

Lissa nodded.

"I've seen her date a couple of different times and it never lasted long because of her job," Suzanne said.

"That's not altogether true. It's not her job, it's how she *feels* about her job," Rachel added.

"I know she has a plan for the next fifteen years and she'll stick to it," Lissa said.

"I don't doubt that, but I've never seen her like this," Suzanne said.

Lissa looked over at both of them as they neared the bank. "I've never been with anyone like Addison. It's hard to explain. I know we're just beginning..."

"I get it. It's how I felt when I met Rachel. Everything seemed to fall into place. You found the person you wanted to be with and everything is great," Suzanne said with a smile.

Lissa sighed. "It's like that but...I'm also afraid. I don't want Addison to go through the things that will happen because of where we live."

"Do you mean being in a small town and the way people talk?" Rachel asked.

"Yes. It's hard enough coming to terms with the fact that

you're gay and then on top of that, people in town are talking about you because of it."

"Is that how it was for you when you came out?" Suzanne asked.

"My family was supportive, but before I came out I was afraid to disappoint them. And I was afraid my friends wouldn't have anything to do with me when they found out. You know how it is," Lissa said. "People talk about you and there's nothing wrong with you. I don't want Addison to have to go through that and I'm afraid she will because of this small fucking town."

"She's a strong woman. Look at all she's accomplished in such a short time in her career," Suzanne stated.

"That's just it. She has to consider how this will affect the bank and her career. I know she's thought about it," Lissa said.

"Hmm, well that sucks," Suzanne said. "Once again, who you love shouldn't have anything to do with your ability to perform your job."

"I know, babe," Rachel said, putting her arm around Suzanne. "Unfortunately, it does in some idiot's minds."

"I'm so glad she's found you, Lissa. It's nice to see her happy about something other than finance," Suzanne said.

"She's made me very happy, too."

"Who has?" Addison said, walking up behind them.

"Hey, where did you come from?" Lissa said, turning around.

"Y'all were in such a discussion you didn't see me. Who has made you very happy?" Addison asked, raising one brow.

Lissa tilted her head and put her hands on her hips. "You know who has." She leaned in a little closer and quietly said, "I'd show you if we weren't standing in front of your bank."

Addison giggled. "It's not my bank," she said.

"You can say that, but we all know the truth," Suzanne teased.

Addison looked at her and grinned. She reached over and squeezed Lissa's hand. "How was the hot chocolate?"

"It was delicious," Suzanne said. "But the salesmanship of those kids made it taste better."

Addison chuckled. "Were Leo and Joe there?"

"Yep," Lissa said.

"Those two could sell anything," Addison deadpanned. "Come on, you've got to give my stand a try."

They followed Addison to the hot chocolate stand and listened to the kids' sales pitch.

Addison pulled Lissa away from the others. "Hey, when the parade is over I'd like to go by one of the stores before they close."

"Okay."

"I have an idea for a Christmas present for us," Addison said softly.

Lissa's eyes lit up and a smile grew on her face. "Oh, yeah?"

"Yeah. I'll tell you all about it later."

Lissa could feel the butterflies come to life in her stomach. "Okay."

"Just so you know, I'd really like to kiss you right now," Addison said, smiling up at Lissa.

Lissa stared into Addison's eyes and right then she knew it would be so easy to fall in love with Addison Henry. The butterflies gave way to a sinking feeling because she knew in the back of her mind that controversy awaited them and she wondered if Addison could weather it.

24

"You didn't tell us we'd have the best corner for the parade," Suzanne said as she sat down on the curb.

"Yeah, I love these little chocolate Santas that last float tossed our way," Rachel added.

Addison chuckled. "You knew my bank would be the best. Come on, Suz. How long have you known me?"

Suzanne laughed. "Knowing you, you had them change the parade route so the bank was the best place to view it."

"Don't think I didn't consider it."

"Hey, when do we find out who won for the best hot chocolate?" Rachel asked.

"It'll be in the paper on Wednesday," Lissa said.

"Brazos Falls has a newspaper?" Suzanne asked skeptically.

Lissa chuckled. "It comes out twice a week."

Suzanne looked up to where Addison stood behind her. "How many times have you been in the paper already?"

"A few," Addison replied nonchalantly. When Suzanne

raised her eyebrows and widened her eyes Addison continued, "A new bank president is big news and I'm involved in the community."

"Okay, I get it," Suzanne replied.

"Look!" Rachel said, pointing to the next float which was sponsored by a veterinarian clinic. "Is that the vet you use for Dart?"

"I'm not sure you want to use them." The women turned to see a man standing a few feet away from them.

"Why not?" Rachel asked.

"They're lesbians," he replied.

Suzanne scoffed. "What does that matter?"

The man looked at Suzanne and shrugged. "They'd probably treat you okay because you're a woman."

"Oh stop, Jim," a woman standing next to him said. "I hear they are good with small animals, like cats and dogs."

"I don't see how being a lesbian would have anything to do with how good of a vet they would be," Rachel said.

"It doesn't." The woman looked at the man. "You shouldn't say things like that."

The couple walked away and Suzanne looked at Lissa. "Is that part of the small-town charm?"

"Oh, dickheads like that are everywhere, not just in small towns. Unfortunately, that is how some people refer to that particular clinic. They happen to be very good veterinarians."

Lissa noticed Addison had had a stern look on her face as she observed the entire conversation, and she still looked mad. "Forget about him. Look at the lights on this next float," she said, trying to lighten the mood.

Addison smiled at her and discreetly squeezed her hand. As the parade continued Addison leaned over to where

Suzanne and Rachel sat. "Lissa and I have to run back to one of the stores before they close. We'll meet you here when the parade is over."

"Okay," Suzanne replied with a grin.

Addison stepped in front of where Lissa sat on the curb. She offered her hands and helped her up.

"Thanks."

Addison winked at her and said, "I'm not going to say anything about how old you are because I know how much yoga you've been doing. You could've easily gotten up by yourself."

Suzanne and Rachel both gasped then laughed.

"Do you see how she treats me?" Lissa said, shaking her head with a big grin on her face.

"Like the princess of Brazos Falls," Addison said, grabbing her arm and pulling her onto the sidewalk. They could easily walk along the sidewalk while the crowd watched the parade.

They stepped into the store where Lissa had been looking at the bracelets.

"Hi, Emily," Addison said, walking to the sales counter.

"Hey, you made it. Hi Lissa. Let's get you fixed up." Emily walked over to a display advertising bracelets and necklaces.

"Do you know about these?" Addison asked Lissa.

"No. I saw them when we were here earlier, but I didn't understand the part about welding them on," Lissa replied.

"Well, you get to choose the chain style you want and I'll measure it on your wrist to be sure it isn't too tight or too loose," Emily explained. "Then you choose the way you want it welded together. There are colored beads, solid beads, little shapes, and other things."

"You don't take them off?" Lissa asked.

"Nope." Emily chuckled. "If you need to take it off you can cut the chain with regular scissors. But look how dainty they are. I don't even realize I have mine on half the time."

"What do you think?" Addison asked.

Lissa would have said yes to anything after seeing the way Addison's eyes sparkled when she asked.

"Do we get the same one?" Lissa asked.

Addison nodded. "If we can agree."

Emily chuckled. "I'm sure there's something you'd both like. I'll give you a minute."

When Emily walked away, Addison grabbed Lissa's hand and held it where no one could see. "We have been connected since the moment we met. These bracelets will be a reminder of that connection when we're apart."

"I love it," Lissa exclaimed quietly.

They looked at the different styles of chains and laid them on their wrists to get an idea of what they would look like.

"What do you think of this one?" Lissa asked, placing the chain over Addison's wrist.

"Oh, I like it. There are tiny links, then a solid bar and then more links, then more bars. I like the silver better than the gold," Addison said.

"I do, too," Lissa agreed.

"Okay. Now what do you want to join them with?" Emily asked, walking back to the display.

"Hmm, how does that part work?" Lissa asked.

"Well, let's say you want a bead. It has a little metal bar on each side. I'll weld that bar to the chain on each side. Then it's done."

"Is it okay to do everything while wearing them, like taking a shower?" Lissa asked.

"Yep." Emily smiled. "Here, let me show you." She measured the chain around Lissa's wrist. "Is that too tight?"

"No."

Emily cut the chain and let it hang on Lissa's wrist. "See? You can barely feel it."

Lissa held the ends of the chain and smiled up at Addison. "I can feel it." She meant the connection between them and was sure Addison understood by the way she was looking at her.

"Let's connect them with a colored bead," Addison suggested. "What color?"

Lissa looked over the different colors. "Oh, I like this red one."

"Heck yeah," Emily said. "Red is hot, just like the two of you."

Lissa laughed. "Oh yeah, that's me."

"You are, Lissa. Get the red," Emily said, encouraging her.

"What do you think?" Lissa asked Addison.

Addison gave her a big smile. "What about this blue one?"

"Oh, I like that one, too. Let's do blue."

"Okay." Emily smiled at them both and began making their bracelets.

"Who's first?"

"I'll go," Lissa said.

Lissa rested her forearm on the padded part of the table and Emily put the bracelet together on her wrist. "Look away while I weld it because it can hurt your eyes. Don't worry, you won't feel it."

Lissa could hear the machine zap the bracelet twice, but true to Emily's word she didn't feel a thing. "All done."

Lissa held her wrist up and ran her fingers over the delicate chain and blue bead. "I love it," she said, looking up into Addison's eyes.

"I do, too," Addison said softly. "Merry Christmas."

Lissa could feel the joy all over her face and watched as Emily welded Addison's bracelet on her wrist.

"This is the coolest idea," Lissa said. "I'd never heard of anything like it."

"I know. It's fun," Emily said, walking to the cash register.

"When we were in here earlier I was looking at these bracelets for you," Lissa told Addison as they followed Emily.

"Really?"

Lissa nodded. "We seem to like the same things."

Addison grinned and winked at her.

"Let me see, let me see!" Suzanne said, walking into the store with Rachel right behind her.

"You knew?" Lissa asked.

"Addison may have mentioned it when we left the store." Suzanne grinned.

"That's why you were talking so seriously with Emily," Lissa said.

"Yep, I wanted to do them tonight." Addison smiled and squeezed Lissa's hand. "Let's get out of here so Emily can enjoy the end of the parade. Thanks again."

"My pleasure," Emily replied.

"Did she think it was weird that you two got the same bracelet?" Rachel asked.

"Not at all. I explained I wanted this for my friend," Addison said, bumping her shoulder into Lissa's.

. . .

Once the parade was over and they were back at Addison's, she pulled Lissa into the kitchen and wrapped her arms around Lissa's neck. "I wanted to get the bracelets because tonight is special."

"Oh it is?" Lissa said, putting her hands on Addison's hips.

"Yeah, it is. When I look at or feel this bracelet on my wrist I'll always remember our first kiss under the Brazos Falls."

"That's why you liked the blue bead," Lissa said.

"Well, Emily was right. You are hot and red suits you, but—"

"I love the blue. It will remind us of the water and our first kiss." Lissa leaned in and pressed her lips to Addison's. "Mmm, I love kissing you," she mumbled.

"Then keep doing it," Addison said against Lissa's lips.

Lissa was about to deepen the kiss when she heard Suzanne from the doorway. "Aw, look at them. They're so cute."

Addison pressed her forehead to Lissa's and grinned. "Whose idea was it for them to come visit?" she teased.

Lissa laughed. "They're your friends."

"Oh no," Rachel said, standing behind Suzanne. "We're your friends now, too. We're part of the package."

Addison chuckled. "Stop! You'll scare her away!"

"No way," Lissa said.

Addison grabbed her hand and they all went into the living room.

"Hey, Lissa, did you know that man at the parade?" Rachel asked.

"Do you mean the dickhead?" Suzanne clarified.

"He's come to the mill a few times," Lissa replied.

"If he knew about you, would he not buy your products?" Suzanne asked.

Lissa shrugged.

"If someone asked him where he got his dog food, would he say at the mill where that gay girl works?"

"I don't know. I doubt we have lost money because I'm gay, if that's what you're asking," Lissa said.

"That would suck if you have," Rachel said. "I'm beginning to see some not so nice aspects of small towns."

"Our family business has been around a long time. There is only one other place to buy feed in town. That doesn't mean we don't have competition from bigger feed mills in the area, but I don't think me being gay has lost us business."

"But could it if you're in another business, like maybe banking?" Suzanne asked carefully.

"Okay," Addison said. "Can we go back to happier topics of discussion?"

"You don't want to talk about the bank? I can't believe it," Suzanne said.

"You gave that bank most of your time this week," Lissa commented.

"I did and they don't get any more of it when I'm with my girlfriend and my friends," Addison stated.

"Your girlfriend! I love it!" Suzanne exclaimed.

Addison squeezed Lissa's hand and smiled at her.

Lissa hoped the earlier comments weren't giving Addison reservations about them being together. There would be talk and Lissa guessed it could affect the bank, but Addison was smart and would know how to deal with it. Lissa put her arm around Addison's shoulders and pulled her close.

"Hey, one more thing about the bank," Suzanne said.

"What?" Addison said, sounding exasperated.

"When is the big Christmas party?"

"Oh that." Addison smiled at Lissa. "Our big date is next Thursday night."

"I expect to hear all about it on Friday. You don't have to call in the morning because I'm sure you'll still be on the date," Suzanne said suggestively.

Lissa could feel her cheeks turning red and watched Addison give Suzanne a stern look. "That's none of your business. It's our first date!"

"Yeah, come on, babe. Don't be like that," Rachel chided her.

"Sorry, sorry. I was just kidding. I'm happy you two are together," Suzanne said.

"I'll forgive you this time, but watch it!" Addison pointed her finger at her friend.

The rest of the night was spent in laughter and happy conversation.

Later, Addison walked Lissa to her car; they held hands and bumped shoulders.

"Hey," Lissa said, putting her arms on Addison's shoulders. "Thank you for my Christmas gift. I love it."

"Thank you for mine," Addison replied with a chuckle. "Are you sure they're okay? I mean, I kind of forced you."

"No you didn't. I told you, I'd already been looking at them. I just didn't know about the welding part of it. That makes them even more special." Lissa leaned in and brought their lips together in a tender kiss.

"Mmm, I do love kissing you," Addison said against Lissa's lips. They shared another soft kiss and Addison gently pushed Lissa away. "Go, before I don't let you leave."

"Okay, okay. I'll see you in the morning." With that, Lissa

got in her car and as she pulled away she could see Addison's silhouette in the shadows from the light on the porch.

"Oh, Addison. You are diving deeper and deeper into my heart every minute," Lissa said as she glanced one more time in the rearview mirror.

25

Addison looked up from the report she was working on and gazed out at the lobby. The bank was doing well under her leadership. They had attracted new customers and were better able to serve their farmers and ranchers. Addison smiled because Lissa had helped her understand that industry better and she was able to do some things to offer them money at better rates. So much depended on the weather which affected not only what grains could be grown to feed livestock, but also what crops they sold later.

Every bank had a variety of people and businesses that needed money. If they could offer better rates and payment plans then their customer base grew. Addison was continually looking for creative means to not only help her customers, but also make the bank prosper.

She saw a friendly face walk into the bank and waved from her desk.

"Come sit for a minute," Addison said from the doorway of her office.

"Hi!" Marielle smiled as she walked into Addison's office.

"How are you?"

"I'm fine. I took the day off to go shopping with my sister," Marielle stated, with a delighted grin.

"Shopping? That's one of my favorite things." As long as Addison had known Lissa, she rarely took a day off, much less to go shopping.

Marielle chuckled. "Mine, too. My sister has been invited to a Christmas party with someone she likes very much and wanted something new to wear," Marielle said with a sly smile.

"I see," Addison said. She could feel her cheeks begin to warm and pinken at the thought that Lissa had bought something special to wear on their date.

"We drove to the city this morning and met Blythe. We had lunch and found something we all liked for Lissa."

"Oh, so it was a joint effort," Addison replied. "I ran by her house at lunch and now I know why she wasn't there."

"I haven't seen her this excited for something in a while."

"I'm really excited about it, too, but I wonder about the chatter afterward," Addison said honestly.

Marielle gave her a kind smile. "I'm sure there will be talk, but who cares. It's a date with someone you like. Don't let these small-town hicks ruin that for you."

"Or for Lissa," Addison added.

"Oh, believe me, she's thinking about it, especially for you."

Addison sighed. "It shouldn't be that way. I don't know how she and my friends do it."

"It'll be okay. How can two people enjoying time spent together harm anyone? They'll talk, but then move on to something else. That's how gossip works around here," Marielle assured her.

Addison smiled and nodded. She knew Marielle

thought this budding relationship was a good thing and that helped calm the misgivings that had taken up residence in the back of Addison's mind.

"I planned to go by the mill on my way home from work to get cat food. I'll have to ask Lissa about her day," Addison said.

Marielle chuckled. "Her cheeks will get red just like yours did."

Addison reached up and touched her cheek then laughed.

"Just wait until you see Lissa tomorrow night," Marielle said, getting up from the chair.

"She's beautiful every day," Addison said, walking her to the doorway.

Marielle smiled. "Don't say I didn't warn you."

Addison watched Marielle walk away and chuckled. She couldn't wait until tomorrow night.

Addison pulled into the mill parking lot and hurried inside. She knew they were about to close and Dart needed cat food.

She pushed the door open and saw Ben at the counter. "Am I too late to get cat food?"

"Never. Come on in," he said with a grin. "Besides, you know the owner. I'm sure she would've brought Dart cat food if you'd asked."

"Is she here?" Addison asked as she looked over at Lissa's open office door.

"I locked the back door," Lissa said as she came in from the warehouse.

The look on Lissa's face when she saw Addison made

Addison's heart skip a beat. "Hey you," Addison said with a beaming smile.

"Hi! What are you doing here?" Lissa's smile matched Addison's.

"Cat food," Addison stated. "How was your day?" she asked with a lilt to her voice.

"You know I would've brought you cat food if you needed it."

"That's what I said!" Ben exclaimed.

"I appreciate that." Addison tipped her head. "I came by your house at lunch, but you weren't there."

"Uh..." Lissa stammered. She looked at Ben and then at Addison.

"I ran into Marielle at the bank," Addison said.

"Oh. Let's go in here," Lissa said, walking towards her office.

"I'll leave your cat food by the counter," Ben told Addison, then to Lissa he said, "I'm locking the front door. See you tomorrow."

"Thanks," Addison replied as she followed Lissa into her office. Once inside she grabbed Lissa's hand and pulled her towards her. She leaned up and gave Lissa a sweet kiss. She felt Lissa's hands rest on her hips and as she pulled her lips away she smiled.

"That was nice," Lissa said softly.

"As nice as the outfit you got for the party?" Addison teased.

Lissa chuckled. "You can't have a secret in a small town."

"Oh, is it a secret?"

"No." Lissa's face softened. "I want to look nice for our date. As you know, I don't dress up often and..." She shrugged.

"Are we making too much of this?" Addison asked quietly, suddenly feeling a prickle of doubt.

"No. It's a party, but I'd still want to look nice. I'm going out with Addison Henry. She's a big deal; haven't you heard?"

Addison chuckled, her doubts disappearing. "Oh she is?"

Lissa's eyes widened and she nodded.

Addison reached up and cupped Lissa's face with her hand. "You're so beautiful." She brought their lips together and quickly deepened the kiss. With her other arm around Lissa's shoulder, Addison pulled Lissa closer. Both of them moaned softly and sank into the kiss, letting it become its own entity. God, Addison loved this. She could kiss this woman all day long.

When they pulled apart, both breathing hard, Lissa stared into Addison's eyes. "I wanted to ask you something."

"Okay." Addison started to let Lissa go, but Lissa kept her close.

"The other day when Suzanne mentioned us spending the night together, I hope you didn't feel...pressured. Because that's the last thing I want," Lissa said earnestly.

Addison tilted her head. "What's the last thing you want? To sleep with me or—"

"No! Oh, that may have not come out right," Lissa stammered, starting to pull away.

Addison wrapped her arms around her shoulders and didn't let go. "I know what you mean, babe."

"Babe?"

"Yeah, that felt pretty good. Is it okay if I call you babe?"

Lissa smiled. "You know it is."

Addison chuckled. "I won't let Suzanne or anyone else pressure us into anything we're not ready for or don't want to do. But...this is our first date. I'll tell you right now that it's been a long time since I've had sex with anyone." Addison could feel Lissa relax in her arms.

"It's been a long time for me, too. But that doesn't mean I don't want to," Lissa said, "when we're both ready...babe."

Addison grinned then bit her lower lip. "I'm your babe?"

Lissa nodded.

"Then kiss me again, baby."

Addison felt Lissa's lips hungrily claim hers. She kissed her back with just as much fervor and knew it wouldn't be long for the next step in their relationship, but for now she wanted to sink into these luscious kisses they were so good at creating.

Addison gave herself one more look in the mirror. She was wearing one of her favorite dresses that she saved for special occasions and doubted she would have chosen it if she wasn't taking Lissa to the party with her.

"Lissa," she whispered and sighed. Addison couldn't wait to see her and sometimes she couldn't believe what was happening. She'd come to this small town to take over the bank and make improvements on her way to the top of the corporation. So far, the changes she'd made were working. What she didn't expect was to find such a good friend at this stop in her career.

Who was she kidding—Lissa had become more than a friend and that surprised her as well. She had never been attracted to women, but she'd never really been crazy about men either, come to think of it. Her career had always come first. Now here she was, about to go on a date in public. With a woman. She stared into the mirror, wondering, *Am I the next scandal in this town?*

Addison shook that thought out of her head and took a deep breath. When she released it she thought of Lissa. That made her smile and all the doubts once again flew away.

Addison drove over to Lissa's house then smoothed her dress down as she walked up to the front door. When Lissa opened the door, Addison's mouth dropped open and she stared.

"Come in," Lissa said nervously.

Addison pulled herself together, walked into the living room, and reached for one of Lissa's hands. "You look stunning."

Lissa wore a knee length black dress with a v-neck. The sleeves were a see-through gauzy material with little beads stitched in the mesh that caught the light, giving a shimmering glitter effect. The gray streaks in her short hair shone and sparkled along with her earrings that complemented the dress completing the look.

Addison took all this in and was speechless for a moment, then the words became a flood. "You are so beautiful. Good God, those earrings. It makes me want to nibble your ear. Oh shit, I said that out loud. Lissa, you look amazing, but you *are* amazing and I know that!"

"Addy," Lissa said, trying to get a word in, "you look beautiful, too. I haven't seen you wear that dress and I see you dressed up nearly every day."

"Oh, this old thing," Addison teased. She chuckled. "Sorry for all that, but you are so beautiful, Lis, and I'll probably keep saying it all night long."

Lissa smiled shyly. "Thank you. It's been a long time

since I've dressed up for anything special and my heart is about to beat out of my chest."

"Mine, too. I have a question for you."

Lissa raised her eyebrows and waited.

"Do you have more lipstick?" Addison asked.

"I do," Lissa replied, clearly confused.

"Good, because I'm about to kiss you and you'll need more."

The sweetest grin spread over Lissa's face.

Addison reached up and ran her thumb below Lissa's bottom lip as her fingers gently rested on Lissa's cheek. She looked into Lissa's eyes and then to her lips. Addison gently placed her lips on Lissa's and felt an immediate calm. The nerves were gone. Her heart was still pounding, but this kiss was all she needed and wanted in this moment.

26

"Calista Morgan, don't you look lovely," Karen said from behind where Lissa stood.

Lissa turned around and smiled. "Hi, Karen. How are you?"

Addison saw Karen look from her to Lissa and smile. "I'm happy to be here. Our boss," she said, nodding at Addison, "found a way to give us a nice Christmas bonus and have this party."

"I hear she's good at what she does," Lissa replied, glancing at Addison with a smile.

"Our employees can always use a little extra cash at Christmas. I knew we didn't have to have a lavish party, but I did want us to have something."

"I think this is great," Maise said, joining them. "It's like the best of both worlds. Thank you, Addison."

"You're welcome." Addison smiled. "I'm going to get us both a drink," Addison said to Lissa. "I'll be right back."

"I can go—" Lissa started.

"No," Addison touched Lissa's forearm. "You stay and visit."

Lissa nodded as Addison took a couple of steps to the bar. She wasn't far away and because Karen never talked quietly, Addison heard every word of their conversation.

"I'm not surprised you came with her," Karen said. "But is this a date?"

"And what if it is?" Lissa said, meeting Karen's gaze.

"It's wonderful, that's what it is," Maise interjected.

"I didn't know our president was, how should I say..." Karen trailed off.

"Brilliant," Lissa said, "by finding a way to give you a party as well as a Christmas bonus."

"Uh huh. Yeah, that's what I meant," Karen said with a smirk.

"Why do you have to be such a bitch, Karen?" Maise said, speaking up. "There's not a thing wrong with Addison and Lissa dating. They're adults, unlike some of the folks around here."

"I didn't say there was anything wrong with it, Maise. I was just looking out for my old friend here," Karen replied.

"Looking out for me?" Lissa exclaimed.

"Well, yeah. I don't want you to get your heart broken or anything. Isn't that what happens when straight women give being gay a fling?" Karen said, taking a sip of her drink.

Addison walked back to the group, trying not to make it obvious that she'd overheard everything. *Could other people be thinking the same thing?* She'd never play with Lissa's heart like that. *This is our first date,* she kept reminding herself.

"Here you go, Lis," Addison said, handing Lissa a glass of wine.

"Thank you," Lissa replied with a smile.

"Oh, I see my husband over there boring two of the directors. I'd better go stop him," Karen said. "You two really do look pretty. Have fun."

They watched her walk away and Maise shook her head. "That woman should really learn to keep her mouth shut."

"Why? She's been like that since kindergarten, Maise. I don't see her changing now," Lissa said.

Maise chuckled. "Thanks again for all of this, Addison. I'm going to get something to eat."

Addison nodded and sipped her wine. Once Maise was out of earshot, she turned to Lissa. "I heard what Karen said."

"You know how Karen is, Addy. She doesn't know what she's talking about."

Addison looked up into Lissa's eyes. "I'd never do something like that to you, Lis. Play with your feelings that way. You know that, right?" Addison had a bad feeling and the doubts were creeping back in.

"I know that, babe," Lissa said softly, giving her an earnest look.

Addison smiled and sighed. Lissa could drive the doubts away with a look and a word or two. "Let's go mingle and really get the rumor mill going."

Lissa chuckled.

"You are the most beautiful woman in the room, and I know how lucky I am that you're my date." Addison gave her a wink and they began to work the room.

Several different times during the night, Addison noticed people looking at them and whispering. She wondered if they would be doing that no matter who was with Addison, but still, it was unnerving at times. Lissa seemed to know when Addison's anxiety began to rise and would appear at her side with a disarming smile, a sweet word, or a discreet touch.

Addison was impressed with how relaxed Lissa was and how effortlessly she mingled with the employees and their guests. Yes, she knew most of the people there, but she had a kind word for each person she talked to and listened as if they were the most important person in the room. *She really is amazing*, Addison kept thinking.

As the party began to wind down, Addison gave away several door prizes and said a few words to those gathered. She talked about how she was still learning the charms of small-town living and thanked everyone for their patience with her and making her transition easier.

She could see the respect and was that pride in Lissa's eyes? Whatever it was made Addison's heart swell with emotion. This had turned out to be a good night. The party was fun and even though she knew folks were talking about her and Lissa, it occurred to her they could be saying good things.

"Why are you chuckling?" Lissa said, walking up beside her.

Addison turned and gave her a big smile. "What if the whispers about us tonight were positive things and not all negative?"

"We do look lovely," Lissa said.

"That we do."

"I suppose you could be right, but I don't really care at this moment. I've had such a good time with you, Addy. Thank you for inviting me."

"How could I do a party like this without you! But, you're welcome. What do you say we get out of here? The best part of the date is ahead of us."

"I'm with you," Lissa said, wiggling her eyebrows.

Addison laughed, put her arm through Lissa's, and headed for the door. On the way out, she thanked the women who had planned the party and promised to see them tomorrow.

On the way to Lissa's, Addison reached over and held her hand. "What did you think?"

Lissa smiled over at her. "I thought it was really nice. All your employees seemed to have a good time and I could tell how much they like you."

"I want them to like me, but I also want them to respect me. So far, they have been open to the changes I've made and I haven't heard too many grumblings," Addison said, pulling into Lissa's driveway.

As they walked to the front door, they reached for one another's hand. Lissa turned to Addison and rested her hands on her upper arms. "You're coming in, aren't you?"

Addison chuckled. "I'm going to need more than one goodnight kiss, so yeah. Although, we could add to the scandal if someone saw us making out on your front porch."

Lissa laughed and opened the front door. Once they were inside Lissa said, "Would you like something to drink?"

"No thanks," Addison said, sitting down on the couch.

"I'm going to get some water."

As Lissa walked into the kitchen, Addison asked, "Did you know *everyone* at the party?"

Lissa walked back into the living room as she took a sip from her glass. "No," she chuckled, "but I did know most of them."

"You sure are good at making conversation and putting people at ease," Addison said, reaching for Lissa's hand as she sat down next to her.

"Am I?"

Addison dropped her hand and put her arm around Lissa, moving closer. "Yeah, you are."

"You make that sound like a good thing."

"It is a good thing. Especially when everyone seemed to be charmed by the president's date."

"Oh." Lissa grinned. "I see. So maybe if I'm an asset to the president she'll keep me around."

"I didn't mean it like that," Addison scoffed.

"But are you saying it was a good date?"

"It was a good date." Addison grinned. "Was it for you?"

"Hmm, let me see." Lissa leaned in and kissed Addison softly.

"Oh, so a good kiss makes it a good date."

"That was just a good kiss? Let me see if I can do better." Lissa brought their lips together again softly, but then deepened the kiss. Addison felt Lissa's fingers run through her hair and she sank a little deeper. Her heart began to pound and she pulled Lissa even closer.

"*That* was a kiss," Addison said breathlessly.

"Yeah it was," Lissa said as she stared into Addison's eyes. "A good date for me is spending time with someone I care about, but we've been doing that. There is something..."

"What?"

"Spend Christmas with me," Lissa blurted out.

"Okay?"

"No, I mean..."

Addison could see Lissa swallow and take a deep breath. "You mean what?"

"Spend Christmas Eve with me and stay the night. Wake up with me on Christmas morning." Lissa's eyes sparkled and her face was full of hope.

Addison smiled. "I'd love to."

"I'm not trying to rush—"

Addison grabbed Lissa's face and firmly pressed her lips to Lissa's. She hoped this kiss showed Lissa she wasn't rushing anything. When they pulled away, they were both breathing hard.

"I'd stay tonight if we didn't have to work in the morning. Because, you see, I'm pretty sure we wouldn't be sleeping much." Addison grinned and watched Lissa's eyebrows raise higher on her forehead. "I know it won't always be like that, but it will be my first time and our first time."

Lissa's eyes widened. "No pressure."

Addison chuckled. "There isn't any. You know, Suzanne is always telling me there's more to life than work. I'm beginning to understand what she meant by that."

"Well, I don't have nearly as much time as I used to have to read and you know what?"

Addy looked at her. "You mean spend time with your other friends."

Lissa laughed. "I haven't missed it one bit."

"Since coming to Brazos Falls my whole life has been different," Addison said.

"I hope it's better."

"I don't work long hours and when I make changes I can see the effects of those changes almost immediately. I've found my love of being outdoors again. And..." Addison ran her thumb along Lissa's cheek. "I'm falling for the most amazing person."

Lissa softly smiled. "Falling?"

Addison nodded and brought their lips together in a tender kiss. "I could kiss you all night," she mumbled against Lissa's lips then pressed them firmly to hers. She put both arms around Lissa's shoulders and pulled her in even closer. Her lips trailed over Lissa's cheek until they stopped just below Lissa's ear. She nibbled gently and whispered, "I can't wait until Christmas Eve."

Addison pulled away and could see Lissa's now dark brown eyes sparkling with—was that love? If it wasn't then it was a whole lot of like.

"This is going to be the best Christmas ever," Lissa said softly.

Addison smiled. "I'd better go before I change my mind."

Lissa walked Addison to the front door and they shared another searing kiss. "Thank you for a wonderful time tonight," Lissa said.

"Thank you for going with me."

"Promise me one thing," Lissa said seriously.

"Okay?"

"No matter how bad the scandal is in the morning, you won't give up on us."

Addison tilted her head. "I won't. I promise."

Lissa sighed and kissed Addison again sweetly.

"However, if the rumors include anything about you being pregnant with my baby, what now?" Addison said, raising her hands, palms up.

Lissa laughed. "Oh, Addy!"

Addison laughed, too, as Lissa threw her arms around her and hugged her tightly.

27

As Addison packed her overnight bag, she was happy Christmas Eve was finally here. She thought back over the week since she and Lissa had gone to her Christmas party together. There had been looks and she knew people were talking about them that night, but no one at the bank seemed to treat her any differently. They had gone out to dinner one night last weekend and she noticed several stares when they walked in, but Lissa smiled and waved to the gawkers or went by their table to say hello. Lissa knew how to stop the rumors before they could swirl.

Addison smiled as she thought about how Lissa eased her anxiety and doubts. Living in a small town, starting a relationship—with a woman no less—and being the president of the bank were all new to her. She was confident in her job and learning the nuances of small-town living. But she hadn't been in a real relationship in forever.

She wasn't unsure about her feelings for Lissa, but she was uneasy about how their relationship could affect her career goals. In her imaginings of the future she could picture herself running the company, but they had never included a partner and she'd certainly never seen herself with a woman.

Of course that had changed when she met Calista Morgan. Sometimes she let her thoughts wander to what life would look like with Lissa. She could imagine them spending weekends at the lake, having family dinners with Lissa's siblings and their kids, or going to visit Suzanne and Rachel. But what would happen when the holding company brought her back to Dallas?

That's what worried her most.

"Stop!" she said to herself out loud. "You are getting way ahead of yourself."

Addison took a deep breath and checked her bag one more time. It was Christmas and she couldn't wait to see Lissa.

The mill was open until noon on Christmas Eve, but Lissa hadn't planned on working. When Ben called with a computer problem she went in to help. She figured if it was something simple she could fix it right away and wouldn't have an even bigger mess after the holiday.

She was in her office rebooting the system when she heard a man talking to Ben.

"Hey, I heard Lissa turned that bank president into a queer," the man said.

"What!" Ben exclaimed.

"Yeah, I heard they were at that fancy bank Christmas party together holding hands. And then someone saw them kissing at the Mexican food place!"

Lissa looked out her door and could see Ben's anger all over his face and in his body language.

"Your feed has been loaded, Ed. You'd better go," Ben said angrily.

"Why, I didn't mean to offend anybody. I was just asking."

"You weren't asking anything, Ed. You were doing what you're always doing when you come in here and that's spreading gossip. Now, get the hell out of here before I change my mind and send you off with a black eye!" Ben stood rigid with his hands in fists at his side.

Lissa saw Ed quickly exit out the front door. She didn't know when she'd seen Ben that mad.

Ben looked over and saw Lissa standing in her office doorway. "I'm sorry you had to hear that. Ed's an asshole."

"I know that. My brother, on the other hand, is awesome."

Ben smiled and shrugged. "I should've decked him. He's always coming in here talking about someone."

"Has that happened a lot lately?"

"What? Me wanting to punch Ed Thetford?"

"No." Lissa smirked. "Have people been talking about me and Addison?"

Ben shook his head. "A couple of people mentioned how nice you looked at the party." He smiled. "We sure would've liked to have seen you and Addison all dressed up."

"I'm sure there are pictures floating around somewhere," Lissa said.

"Do you think there are any of y'all kissing?" Ben teased.

"We didn't even hold hands at the party. I love how gossip can take on a life of its own," Lissa commented, shaking her head.

"Holding hands is nothing compared to what they'll be talking about next," Ben said.

"I know." Lissa sighed. "Please don't say anything about this to Addison tomorrow at brunch. She says it doesn't matter, but I know it does."

"It bothers you too, doesn't it?"

"Yeah, but I know there's nothing I can do about it."

"They'll be talking about someone else before you know it," Ben assured her.

Lissa nodded. "I hope so. Hey, I got the computer system fixed. So I'm out of here."

"Thanks for coming in, sis. See you in the morning."

Lissa opened the door to leave then turned back to Ben. "Thanks for defending us."

"You've done the same for me."

She chuckled. "That's true, but I'm sorry you have to defend us over something like this."

Ben shrugged. "Some people are assholes."

"And you'll keep putting them in their place?"

"I will when they're in our store!" Ben grinned.

Lissa nodded and went to her car. On the drive home she tried to let all the negativity from the mill go and looked forward to her day and night with Addison. She rubbed her finger along the bracelet that matched the one on Addison's wrist and sighed.

When Lissa pulled into her driveway, Addison was getting out of her car.

"Perfect timing," Lissa said with a big smile.

"I didn't think you were working today," Addison said,

opening the back door of her car. Dart came jumping out of the car and ran onto Lissa's front porch.

"I still can't believe he likes to ride in a car," Lissa said, shaking her head. "Here, let me help you with that." Lissa reached for Addison's bag. "I had to help Ben with a computer issue."

"I'm a little early, but I didn't think you would mind," Addison said, following Lissa into the house.

Lissa dropped Addison's bag on a chair and closed the front door. She pulled Addison into her arms and held her tightly. "You're right. I'm so glad you're here." She nuzzled Addison's neck and felt Addison's hands run up and down her back, taking the last bit of nastiness from Ed Thetford's comments with them. She sighed and let Addison hold her.

After a moment Addison raised her head from Lissa's shoulder and looked into her eyes. "Are you okay?"

"I'm glad to see you," Lissa said, leaning in for a kiss.

Addison put her finger over Lissa's lips and stopped her. "Are you sure that's all? Did something happen at the mill?"

Lissa smiled and stared into the blue eyes she was falling in love with.

"Come on, was someone talking about us?"

"I don't want to start our holiday on a negative note," Lissa said.

Addison smiled. "We're not. What did we get caught doing now?"

"What?" Lissa scoffed.

"Maise told me yesterday that she heard we were kissing at the Mexican food restaurant," Addison stated.

Lissa searched Addison's face and she seemed to be amused. "That didn't upset you?"

"Well, it means I missed out on a few kisses. If they're

going to be talking about us we could at least be doing what we're accused of, don't you think?"

Lissa could see the humor in Addison's eyes as she raised her brows. "Unfortunately, that isn't how it works. They have to make up scandalous things that we're doing to keep it interesting."

Addison narrowed her gaze and looked into Lissa's eyes. Her arms were still around Lissa's shoulders and she grinned. "I have to admit, I've never even thought about kissing you in that restaurant, but I will now!"

Lissa laughed. "Oh, Addy. I was afraid you'd be upset."

"It's okay. Just tell me. You don't have to protect me, Lis."

Lissa nodded and once again leaned in for a kiss and Addison once again stopped her.

"Wait, you didn't tell me what we did this time," Addison stated.

"It's the same rumor. At least they're consistent." Lissa shrugged.

Addison chuckled. "If they knew how wonderful our kisses are they wouldn't blame us."

Addison pulled Lissa down into the most luscious kiss.

Lissa moaned and tightened her hands around Addison's waist as she deepened the kiss. "Mmm, I could do this all afternoon," Lissa said, bringing their lips together again.

"I thought the kids were coming by," Addison said, rubbing her thumb along Lissa's chin.

"They are bringing us Christmas gifts. I wouldn't be surprised if there is a new video game for us to play."

"That'll be fun," Addison said with a grin.

Lissa loved how Addison fit right in her life. The kids had loved her instantly and Addison seemed to like spending time with them. It was almost like Addison was the piece that had not only been missing in Lissa's life, but also the piece Lissa's family had been waiting for.

"I know what else is fun," Lissa said, bringing their lips together in another luxurious kiss.

When the kiss ended, Addison grabbed Lissa's hand and led them to the couch. She plopped down and pulled Lissa down beside her. "I have a confession to make."

"Oh?" Lissa said, putting her arm on the back of the couch.

"You know how I always question the kiss at the end of all those Hallmark movies we watch?"

"Yes," Lissa said, dragging the word out.

"I don't think they are so far-fetched after all."

"Oh really. And what led you to this conclusion?"

"Our first kiss that night at the waterfall still makes me weak when I think about it. I guess there was a lot leading up to it, as you like to claim in each movie. But...you have to admit, that was some kiss," Addison said with a soft smile.

Lissa nodded. "It was some kiss, but so are the ones that have come after."

"You have very kissable lips," Addison said, leaning in and softly touching hers to Lissa's.

"Mmm, and so are yours," Lissa said, nipping at Addison's bottom lip.

Addison groaned and pushed Lissa down on the couch. She looked into Lissa's eyes and earnestly said, "You know I don't know what I'm doing."

"You said that to me before and look how things are working out." Lissa smiled and curled a lock of Addison's dark brown hair behind her ear. "You don't have to do anything you don't want to do, Addy."

"You'll tell me if I'm not doing something right?"

Addison asked shyly. "Because Lissa, I want to show you how you make me feel inside."

"If you're showing me how you feel, it'll be right. I trust you, Addy." Lissa smiled. "But that goes both ways. If I'm doing something you don't like, you'll tell me, right?"

The most beautiful smile crossed Addison's face. "I think we'll know, won't we?"

Lissa nodded and gently pulled Addison's lips to hers. This was going to be a life-changing night. She just knew it.

28

"I win again!" Max shouted.

"Fuck me!" Leo exclaimed.

"Uh, hello, language!" Blythe chastised her cousin.

"Oh, sorry Aunt Lissa, sorry Addison," Leo said. "That little punk is so frigging lucky!"

Addison laughed. "I have to agree with you, Leo. I think he's played this game before."

"I may have seen it a time or two over at a friend's house."

"I knew it!" Leo yelled.

"It's okay, bro," Joe said. "I might have seen the same game in a bag that Mom quickly hid when I got in from school one day last week. We'll practice and take you on again, Max."

Max threw his head back with a sinister laugh. "Practice all you want, cuz. I'll still kick your ass."

"Oh my God! So much testosterone in one room!" Blythe exclaimed.

Lissa laughed. "This has been fun, but you've gotta go!"

"What?" The young people all turned and looked at their aunt.

"Yeah, you can't hang out here all day. Addison and I have stuff to do," Lissa explained.

"What is she making you do, Addison? We're bringing everything over tomorrow," Blythe said with a steely gaze.

"It could be a Christmas surprise, you know," Lissa said, giving her niece and nephews a menacing look.

"Oh! Look at the time! Come on, Joe. We've got to get going," Leo said, hopping up from the floor and putting his controller on the coffee table.

Addison laughed. "Wow, you know how to clear a room, Aunt Lissa."

"Nah," Blythe said, putting her arm around Addison's shoulders. "We want y'all to have a merry Christmas, too. After all, it's your first Christmas together."

"Oh, easy there," Lissa said. "We don't want to scare Addison away."

Max got up and smiled at Addison. "She's not scared. She fits in with us perfectly."

"Maybe it's y'all that fit in with me," Addison said, raising one eyebrow.

"See there! Perfect!" Max laughed and they all followed him out the door.

"We'll see you tomorrow at brunch," Lissa said as she and Addison waved to them from the porch.

Addison put her arm around Lissa as they walked back into the house. "That was so much fun."

"They are a lot!" Lissa chuckled.

"What's this surprise you have for me, Calista?"

Lissa smiled at Addison and put her arms around her. She loved to hear Addison say her full name. It was almost like a melody the way she said it. "Let's make some hot chocolate and then you'll see." She gave her a quick kiss and they went into the kitchen.

* * *

Addison looked over at Lissa as she ran her fingers over the bracelet on her wrist. "We made a thermos of hot chocolate and brought several blankets. I thought you invited me to spend the night with you at your house."

"I love my bracelet, too," Lissa said, glancing at Addison and holding out her hand.

Addison intertwined their fingers and smiled. "Are you going to tell me where we're going?"

"Do you trust me?"

Addison stared at Lissa's profile. She had a few fine lines around her eyes, but Lissa was beautiful. "I understand why your dad wanted to name you Calista. You are beautiful."

Lissa cut her eyes over at Addison and smiled. "Thank you," she said softly.

"Of course I trust you, babe. With a name that means beautiful and eyes that sparkle every time they look at me, how can I not trust you."

"Oh Addy, you are stealing my heart."

"I'm not stealing, I'm walking right into it and making you mine."

"Are you letting me in yours?" Lissa asked as she turned down the road to her friend's lake house.

"It's kind of dark in there because I don't let too many people in," Addison said as Lissa stopped the car.

"No it's not. You are one of the most giving people I know," Lissa said.

Addison looked out the windshield and smiled. The water sparkled in the waning sunlight and she felt such a sense of gratitude. "Now I know why we have blankets and hot chocolate." She turned to Lissa. "Can we continue this discussion as we watch the sunset?"

"That's why we're here." Lissa got out and grabbed the blankets while Addison got the thermos.

They spread one blanket to sit on. Lissa poured them each a cup of hot chocolate and handed one to Addison. "Are you cold? This blanket is to wrap around us."

"You're not going to keep me warm?"

"The idea of cuddling with you makes me hot!" Lissa replied. She put the blanket over their shoulders and gazed out at the water. "This is your Christmas gift from me and nature."

"A sunset at the lake is the perfect gift."

"You've already given me my gift by spending the night with me." Lissa put her arm around Addison and pulled the blanket a little tighter. "I can't think of anything merrier than waking up with you on Christmas morning."

Addison could feel her heart open and fill with love for Calista Morgan. She didn't let any of the hesitancy or, if she was being honest, fear that usually accompanied the idea of loving Lissa stop her this time. Her heart was full and she knew Lissa loved her even though she hadn't said the words yet.

With a sip of hot chocolate Addison lay her head on Lissa's shoulder. She watched the sun slowly fall towards the water. This was turning out to be a magical Christmas. Holidays hadn't meant much to her since she'd graduated college, but this one was different. Addison looked up at Lissa and knew the reason why.

"Do you have other plans for us when we get back to your place, my romantic girlfriend?" Addison asked. She watched as the golden brown of Lissa's eyes turned a little darker.

"Not really, just dinner," Lissa said softly.

Addison reached up and gently placed her hand behind Lissa's neck, pulling her in for a soft kiss. Their faces were cold in the chilly evening air, but Addison felt nothing but warmth flowing through her as she deepened the kiss. A quiet moan escaped Lissa's throat as Addison's tongue sought to touch and tantalize.

She begrudgingly pulled away as a blast of dark red rays lit up the horizon for just a moment. "I don't want to miss this sunset you planned just for me, but I don't want to stop kissing you either," Addison said, taking a breath.

"If you keep kissing me like that I'm not sure we're going to make it home before we lose these clothes."

They held each other close and gazed over the water as the sun disappeared along with the light and the tiny bit of warmth it provided.

"Thank you, Lis. That was lovely."

"It sure is." Lissa said.

Addison could feel Lissa staring and got up, reaching out her hands to help Lissa up. "Come on."

Lissa took her hands and gathered the blankets and quickly put them in the back of the car. "Are you always helping me up because I'm an old lady?"

Addison refilled their hot chocolate cups and handed one to Lissa as she started the car. "You're not old. Do you think of me as young?"

"Hmm, I think of you as my smart, accomplished, incredibly beautiful, smoking hot girlfriend."

Addison threw her head back and laughed. "Smoking hot, yeah that's me. I never think about our ages. I think of you and smile. I've been doing that since the day I met you."

"Since the day you met me?" Lissa said, steering the car onto the highway.

"Yeah. I will admit, at first, when I thought of you I did smile and now, when I think of you, I smile and my heart starts to beat fast and I get all gooey inside." Addison giggled.

Lissa chuckled. "That may be the nicest thing anyone has said to me."

Addison reached for Lissa's hand and sipped what was left of her hot chocolate.

When Lissa finally pulled into her driveway, Addison kissed the back of her hand and waited until Lissa looked at her. She hoped Lissa could tell what she was trying to say.

"We can get the stuff out of the car later," Lissa said, staring back at Addison.

Addison grinned and hurried out of the car. Lissa understood.

They raced up the porch steps and once inside Addison pushed Lissa against the closed door. "Do you remember when we came back from the waterfall after our first kiss?"

"Yes," Lissa said breathlessly.

"I didn't want to stop that night, but knew I should. Not tonight, Lissa. I want more. I want it all." Addison claimed Lissa's lips with her own. She left no doubts about what they were going to do. She had Lissa's hands pinned against the door. She pressed her body against Lissa's with her leg pushed between Lissa's.

A low groan rumbled from Lissa's throat and Addison felt her hands pulled to her sides. Lissa pushed against Addison's body and their lips parted. "I want you, Addy. I want to make you feel everything. I want you to feel every touch, every look, every breath, every heartbeat."

Lissa led them to her bedroom and left the light off. It

wasn't totally dark as the soft light from outside found its way through the creases in the blinds.

Addison let her coat fall to the floor and stood in front of Lissa. "I'm a little nervous."

"I am, too," Lissa said softly. "I want our first time to be as wonderful for you as it is for me."

"But I don't know what I'm doing," Addison admitted.

Lissa smiled. "Yes you do," she whispered and began to kiss Addison's neck.

"You are making me weak," Addison mumbled.

Lissa reached for the hem of Addison's sweater and pulled it over her head.

Addison saw Lissa pause and mirrored her movement.

"You are so beautiful," Lissa said softly as she brought their lips together again and ran her hands up Addison's arm.

Addison could feel goosebumps on her upper arms and was finding it hard to breathe. Without thinking, she reached for the front of Lissa's jeans and unbuttoned them, then pulled the zipper down. Lissa slid the jeans over her hips and kicked them away.

A smile played at the corners of Addison's mouth as she held her arms back so Lissa could undo her jeans. Addison shimmied out of them and reached for Lissa's shoulders. She ran her hands down Lissa's chest and looked up into her eyes. Addison watched as Lissa closed her eyes briefly when Addison cupped her breasts through her bra. She could feel Lissa's nipples tighten through the fabric.

"That feels so good," Lissa whispered as she reached around behind Addison's back, unclasping her bra.

Addison ran her hands around and under Lissa's arms and unhooked her bra as well. She gently pulled the bra away and let it slide to the floor. Addison let her own bra fall on top of Lissa's and then gazed at Lissa's body.

"Oh Calista, my beauty," she said softly. Lissa had the most beautiful breasts. They weren't huge, but they were in no way small. To Addison, they were perfect. She let her hands cup them again and ran her thumbs over Lissa's rock hard nipples. They were so soft and firm at the same time.

Addison couldn't wait to discover all the hidden wonders of Lissa's body. She'd imagined this for a while and now that her hands were actually touching Lissa there was no doubt, no hesitation. It was as if her heart was leading her and showing her what to do and it all felt so wonderful and natural.

Lissa began to back Addison to the bed until her legs were against it. Addison looked up into her eyes then gently sat down on the bed.

29

Lissa cupped Addison's face in her hands then ran her fingers through her hair. The look in Lissa's eyes made Addison feel beautiful. She pushed herself further onto the bed and Lissa reached over and rested her hands on Addison's thighs. She smiled at Addison and hooked her fingers into her undies, pulling them down her legs.

Addison thought she'd feel exposed or even shy, but not the way Lissa was looking at her. She felt adored. Lissa quickly removed her own panties and eased down on the bed with Addison.

Their lips met in lush kisses then quickly deepened into a kiss full of intention and promise. Addison could feel Lissa's soft skin under her fingers as they roamed over Lissa's back and around her side. Lissa's leg was between Addison's and she knew Lissa could feel her wetness. Wherever their skin touched was magical to Addison. All the sensations, the sounds and the kisses, were like a luxurious blanket of desire surrounding them.

"Oh, Addy," Lissa whispered in her ear.

"Mmm," Addison moaned.

Lissa's hand was roaming across Addison's stomach creating even more goosebumps, but when she cupped Addison's breast Addison thought her heart would stop. Electricity surged through her body and she gripped the back of Lissa's neck, holding their lips together. Lissa pinched Addison's nipple, eliciting a groan from deep inside her.

It was Lissa's turn to moan as she tore her lips from Addison's and began to kiss down her neck. She nipped, licked, and kissed over Addison's chest until she circled her hardened nipple with her tongue.

"Oh, God," Addison whispered. She buried her fingers in Lissa's hair and watched as Lissa's tongue circled and circled until she finally took Addison's nipple into her mouth. "Oh, Lis," she said breathlessly.

Lissa sucked Addison in and Addison thought she might come right then. "Slow down," Addison murmured.

"What?" Lissa asked as she raised her head.

"I didn't mean you, I meant me."

"Close your eyes and feel, Addy. Let everything go. There's only you and me, right here, right now."

There she goes again, Addison thought, *saying exactly the right thing.* But the thought was gone because the way Lissa was touching her made her do what Lissa said. Just feel. It was just them.

Lissa kissed her way over to Addison's other breast as her hand lowered to stroke along her outer thigh.

"Mmm," Addison moaned. "So good." She raked her fingers through Lissa's hair then pulled her up for a heated kiss. As much as Addison loved what Lissa was doing with her magical tongue, she needed those lips on hers.

Lissa ran her hand over Addison's leg and she bent her

knee. She opened her legs a little wider, inviting Lissa to touch her. As Lissa's finger barely touched Addison's wetness she hissed, "Oh, God, baby."

"Just feel," Lissa whispered. She circled around and around Addison's rigid clit and ran her fingers through Addison's wetness. Then she gently pushed one finger, then another, inside Addison's velvety center.

Addison gasped with pleasure and Lissa moaned, "Oh, God, Addy."

Neither of them had to think. Their bodies knew what to do. They found the perfect rhythm with Addison's hips meeting Lissa's deft fingers. Their breaths were coming quickly, floating moans and groans throughout the room.

"Yes, yes," Addison groaned. She tightened one arm around Lissa's shoulders and grasped the sheet with her other hand.

Addison felt Lissa push a little deeper and curl her fingers. She opened her eyes and grabbed Lissa's face, kissing her firmly. Then she stared into those dark brown orbs and let the orgasm take her. She hoped Lissa could see how she'd made her come undone and then put her back together.

Addison rode wave after wave of pleasure and release. She'd never felt anything like this. Sure, she'd had an orgasm before, but this was so much better. This was Lissa.

"Good God, Lis," she said softly, opening her eyes. "That was...too good for any words I can attempt to speak at this moment."

Lissa smiled. "That's how you make me feel."

"I've barely touched you," Addison scoffed.

"You make me feel like that with a look or when you hold my hand, or sometimes just when I think of you. I wanted you to feel it, too." Lissa smiled and brought their lips together in a sweet kiss.

"I'm not nervous anymore," Addison said, suddenly feeling bold. She pushed Lissa onto her back and stared down into her eyes. "You make me feel beautiful. Every touch means something. I want to know every inch of you."

Lissa smiled. "I'm all yours."

Addison straddled Lissa and pinned her hands on either side of her head. She swept her head back to get the hair out of her eyes and Lissa watched her every move.

"You like me on top, don't you?" The look in Lissa's eyes lit an even hotter fire inside Addison.

"You have the power, Addy. You've had it all along." A sexy smile crossed Lissa's face.

Addison tilted her head. "Then why do I feel helpless when you look at me that way?"

"Helpless?"

"Yeah, I can't resist you," Addison replied.

"Then don't," Lissa stated.

Addison stared at this beautiful woman who she wanted more than she'd ever wanted anything.

"Show me how I make you feel," Lissa whispered.

Addison leaned down until their lips almost touched. "You make me feel things I've never felt before," she said softly.

"God, I hope so," Lissa breathed against her lips. Then she reached up, trying to capture Addison's lips in a kiss.

Addison pulled back just far enough. "You have to tell me, Lis."

"I will. My body will tell you."

Addison smiled as she kissed along Lissa's neck to her ear. She nibbled on Lissa's lobe then ran her tongue along the edge of her ear.

"Oh," Lissa gasped and squeezed Addison's hands.

Addison raised back up and gave Lissa the kiss she'd wanted earlier. Their hands were still clasped and Addison could feel Lissa move beneath her. Lissa's hips were asking for Addison's touch, but Addison knew where she wanted to kiss next.

She trailed kisses down Lissa's neck and across her collarbone. Her tongue found a sensitive spot on its way back to Lissa's chest and Addison couldn't wait to discover Lissa's other delicate areas.

"You are gorgeous," Addison said softly between the kisses she peppered across Lissa's chest. She could see Lissa's chest rise and fall more quickly now. Mirroring Lissa's earlier movements, Addison licked a circle around Lissa's hardened nipple then sucked it into her mouth.

She heard Lissa gasp, but she was busy discovering how wonderful it was to have Lissa in her mouth. The hardened nipple begged for Addison's teeth to clamp down, so she did. Gently at first, but when she heard Lissa hiss, she bit a little harder.

"Fuck, Addy. That feels so good." Lissa let Addison's hands go and Addison immediately felt Lissa's fingers in her hair.

Lissa's body is talking to me! Addison held the pebbled nipple between her teeth and let her tongue tickle it with pleasure. Lissa's response was a deep groan and Addison could feel her fingers tighten in her hair.

Addison decided to see if Lissa's other breast would garner the same response and could feel the heat rushing through her own body as Lissa moaned and arched her back. Their bodies were getting to know one another, and Addison wanted to continue this discovery until she knew everything about this glorious woman beneath her.

Emboldened by her desire to give Lissa all that she'd given her, Addison kissed lower and lower, amazed at the soft skin and goosebumps her kisses caused. She kissed lower still until she swirled her tongue around Lissa's belly button. She glanced up to look into Lissa's eyes for just a moment because she couldn't wait to taste her. If this was anything like Lissa's luscious breasts, Addison thought she might come again at the first taste.

Lissa smiled down at her. "Are you sure?"

"Oh, yeah," Addison said breathlessly. She raised up and quickly kissed Lissa on the lips then went back to her quest.

Addison could smell the scent she would from now on associate with their love. She could see just how wet Lissa was and knew it was all for her. That did make her feel powerful, but also adoring and passionate. Addison wanted Lissa to know she cherished her, valued her, and treasured her.

Addison tentatively stroked Lissa with her tongue up and over her hardened clit. *OH. MY. GOD. This is amazing.* Addison ran her tongue through Lissa's folds and around her clit over and over. It was like a rhythmic dance with Lissa's moans providing the music. Lissa's hips joined in when Addison sucked her tender clit into her mouth. As wonderful as Lissa felt in Addison's mouth it must have been even better for Lissa because she sat up and Addison had to hold onto Lissa's legs to steady herself.

She thought Lissa was close, but there was one other place she wanted to taste. Addison circled around Lissa's entrance then stuck her tongue inside. Lissa fell back on the bed and thrust her hips higher. Addison held on and took Lissa in her mouth again and let her tongue flutter over the most sensitive spot as Lissa arched her back and fisted Addison's hair.

Addison felt Lissa tense then she began to tremble as her body rose then fell back on the bed. She could hear Lissa panting and feel her fingers in her hair. Addison slowly raised up and looked at the bliss on Lissa's face. She'd put that there. It was such a new feeling for her. It was more than making someone happy. Lissa had trusted Addison with her body and for a moment she'd felt like she was inside Lissa's heart.

Addison began to kiss back up Lissa's body. She wanted to do that again, but this time she wanted to look in Lissa's eyes when the orgasm raced through her. Addison's fingers trailed up the inside of Lissa's thigh as she gazed into that beatific look on Lissa's face.

Lissa's eyes popped open when she felt Addison's finger begin to wander through her wetness. "What...what," she said breathlessly.

"There's more for me to discover," Addison said softly, with a sexy smile.

"Now?" Lissa replied.

Addison nodded and brought their lips together in a long, deep kiss. Their bodies were pressed together and Addison could feel how they fit perfectly. She couldn't wait any longer and pushed a finger inside Lissa. The velvety softness easily welcomed her so she added another finger.

"Oh, Addy," Lissa groaned.

Addison could feel Lissa's arms around her shoulders now. It was time for their bodies to find that sweet rhythm once again. They began to move, tense then relax, push and pull, in and out.

"Lissa," Addison whispered. "Let me see your eyes."

Lissa opened her eyes and smiled up at Addison. They shared another soulful kiss then picked up their pace. Moans, grunts, breaths, and sighs all came in rhythm.

Addison pushed inside Lissa one more time and curled her fingers as she'd felt Lissa do earlier. She looked into Lissa's eyes and could see them shine in the darkness, thanks to the dull light peeking through the blinds from the street lights outside.

Then Lissa's eyes glazed over and Addison swore she could see colors explode in them or maybe it was in her own eyes because it felt like the orgasm ran through both of them, wave after incredible wave.

If she was in Lissa's heart before then Lissa was definitely in hers now. Addison rested her head on Lissa's chest and let the feeling envelop her, hoping it could beat back the fear she was sure would set in next.

Addison listened to the staccato beats of Lissa's heart. It was telling her not to be afraid; everything would be all right. She could feel Lissa's hand rubbing up and down her back. *What was there to be afraid of?*

30

"Are you all right?" Lissa asked softly as her fingers trailed up and down Addison's back. She wished they could stay like this forever, just the two of them. Being together would eventually cause issues, but right now none of that mattered. They were falling in love and it should be joyful.

Addison chuckled and raised her head from where it rested on Lissa's chest. "Are *you* all right? Your heart is still beating fast, or is it purring like a satisfied kitty?"

Lissa smoothed Addison's tangled hair. She had caused those tangles when she'd grabbed Addison in the midst of passion. "You are so beautiful."

Addison scoffed. "Oh, I'm sure I am right now. My hair is wild."

"Take away the suits and glamorous dresses; even in your workout clothes or hanging out watching a movie, you are beautiful." Lissa paused and gazed into Addison's eyes. "It's on the inside and makes whatever you're wearing or however you've styled your hair look beautiful. Your beauty comes through."

"Or what I'm *not* wearing," Addison commented, glancing down at their nakedness.

"You're wearing a very pleased smile at the moment," Lissa said.

"All because of you." Addison leaned down and pressed their lips together in a sweet kiss. She stared into Lissa's eyes. "That was amazing," she said softly. "You know I've never done that and I hope..."

Lissa smiled. "You keep saying you don't know what you're doing, but obviously you do."

"I listened to your body and your heart." Addison smiled.

"My heart has never felt quite like that," Lissa said earnestly.

"I seem to understand what it's saying and I may have just found a new favorite thing with you."

Lissa raised her brows. "Oh? And what was your favorite thing before?"

"Kissing, of course."

"Of course." Lissa pulled Addison down for a kiss that quickly became heated. She knew the issues they faced would be running through Addison's head because the success of the bank and her career were always foremost in her thoughts.

Addison moved on top of Lissa and paused. "What's wrong?"

"Why do you think something is wrong?"

"I can feel it. Your body talks to me."

"I don't want the gossip and problems to be running around your head right now. I want it to be just us in our happy little world that we created right here."

"We'll think about that tomorrow, baby. All I'm thinking about is where I'm going to kiss and touch you next."

With Addison's words Lissa rolled them over and began to kiss down Addison's body. It was her turn to taste.

Lissa could feel the rhythmic rise and fall of Addison's chest from where her head comfortably rested. She could smell the faint hints of sweat and sex, but also the sweet smell of Addison's skin under her nose. They had made love most of the night and she'd fallen asleep in Addison's arms. She could feel them still around her as well as one of Addison's legs that was looped over hers.

Lissa smiled as she thought back over their evening and night. What had started at the lake with a scorching kiss as the sun went down had landed them in Lissa's bed as soon as they hurried through the door. From there it was a night of discovery. Addison may have been tentative at first, but she quickly made Lissa feel things she'd never felt before.

This was so much more than sex to Lissa and she was concerned it could be overwhelming for Addison because it almost was for her. The feelings swirling around them were intense and at times squeezed Lissa's heart. She'd almost blurted out "I love you" several times, but thought better of it.

She remembered the husky sound Addison made deep in her throat when Lissa touched her just so and it did something to Lissa's heart. She wanted to hear it over and over. Then there were the smiles and whispers in Lissa's ear when Addison knew she was about to push Lissa over the edge.

There was a joy in Addison's eyes from knowing she could make Lissa feel that way. She'd told Lissa as much when she'd come back down after another intense orgasm. They'd finally gotten up and had something to eat, but were back in bed devouring each other before long.

This was one of those nights she'd never forget and hoped there'd be many more like it. Lissa could feel Addison take a deep breath and she smiled against her chest.

"Mmm, is that smile for me?" Addison mumbled as her arms tightened around Lissa.

She raised her head and looked into Addison's sleepy face. Lissa leaned up and gave her a peck on the lips.

"My breath may be lethal," Addison said as her eyes popped open.

Lissa smiled down at her. "What a way to go."

Addison slowly smiled and pulled Lissa down for a kiss. "Good morning," she said softly.

"Mmm, it is," Lissa replied just as softly.

"You're beautiful," Addison said as she ran her fingers through Lissa's hair.

Lissa scoffed.

"Un huh, don't do that. If my beauty comes from within, then yours radiates from your heart. And I am in your heart now, so I know."

"Now?" Lissa asked. "You've been in my heart for a while."

"Mmm, let me see if I'm still in there," Addison said, wiggling her eyebrows and rolling on top of Lissa.

"You do like to be on top of me," Lissa said.

"I do." Addison gave her a sexy smile.

"I think I like it too," Lissa said, sliding her hand between them.

Addison's eyes widened. "Oh!"

Lissa's finger found Addison's center that was already wet.

"Can you feel what you do to me?" Addison stared into Lissa's eyes.

Good God, she makes me melt. "Kiss me," Lissa said.

Addison gave her the sexiest smile and leaned down until their lips met in what turned into a blazing kiss.

Lissa slipped a finger inside Addison and heard that deep rasp she loved. "Let's go, babe," Lissa urged her.

Addison held herself up with her hands on either side of Lissa and her hips began to move. Lissa matched her rhythm and added another finger. She looked up to see Addison's eyes were closed and she was biting her bottom lip. Lissa sat up slightly and was able to take Addison's breast into her mouth.

A very pleased moan echoed around the room as Lissa bit down and then sucked Addison's nipple deeper into her mouth.

"Yes, baby, yes," Addison exclaimed breathlessly.

Lissa's other hand was splayed across Addison's back as she pushed her fingers in deeper and held them there. She could feel Addison clamp down on them. "Let go, babe."

Addison threw her head back and let out the sweetest groan. "Lissa!"

"I've got you," Lissa assured her.

She felt Addison's muscles start to ease then she fell down on top of Lissa and Lissa's arms immediately encircled her. They were both panting and neither said anything for several moments.

Addison finally raised her head and smiled down at Lissa. "Merry fucking Christmas."

Lissa laughed and her eyes lit up with delight.

"Yeah, I like being on top of you," Addison said as she rolled off Lissa and propped her head on her hand. "You," she began, "do things to me and make me feel things I never thought I would."

"Addy." Lissa suddenly had a bad feeling in her stomach. "I just want to make you happy."

Addison smiled. "You do make me happy. I never expected another person to make me feel this way."

Lissa furrowed her brow. "Why?"

"Because I won't let them."

Realization dawned in Lissa's brain. Addison wouldn't let anyone in her heart because that could jeopardize her carefully laid out career path. "But you let me?"

"I'm not sure I had a say in it." Addison smiled as she ran her fingers between Lissa's breasts. "You're sneaky, Cailsta. You make me want to know everything about you. You make me want to touch you everywhere. You make me dream of kisses and now this," Addison said, raising her eyes to meet Lissa's.

"You don't have to be afraid, Addy. It's okay to feel all of this," Lissa said.

Addison smiled. "What I feel like I need to do is make love to you one more time before we have to get ready for your family. Touching you, making you move with me, hearing those scrumptious little moans and groans you make is what I need in our little world right now."

Lissa swallowed and her mouth went dry. She didn't know what to say and it didn't matter because Addison was through talking. She brought her lips to Lissa's and stoked a fire inside her that became so hot Lissa didn't think it would ever burn out.

* * *

After they'd showered, Addison helped Lissa get ready for the family brunch. They cleared the table and had it ready for Marielle and Ben's families to set their dishes down. The TV was ready for whichever game the kids wanted to play first. Lissa had glasses on the counter ready to pour mimosas and the coffee was brewing as well.

When Lissa's family arrived, they all ate, shared their Christmas gifts, and afterwards, the kids played video games.

Lissa looked over to where Addison was telling Marielle, Ben, and Kara the latest antics of their cats. When Addison noticed Lissa watching, she winked and smiled. That eased the butterflies in Lissa's stomach.

They weren't the good kind of butterflies. There had been times this morning when Addison hadn't seemed quite herself. Lissa was afraid the doubts and questions were beginning to creep in. Addison may say it didn't matter they were in the sights of the town's gossip mongers, but Lissa knew it did. She wanted to ease the doubts and reassure Addison that everything would be okay. The bank wouldn't suffer just because she was dating a woman; they might be a hot topic for a while, but the gossipers would eventually move on.

"Come on, Addison!" Max yelled from the living room. "It's your turn."

Lissa watched as Addison's eyes lit up. "Prepare to lose," Addison said, getting up from the table. She squeezed Lissa's hand as she walked by. "Are you going to come help me?"

"Always," Lissa replied with a smile. She needed to let this go for now and enjoy the time with Addison and her family. Once again Addison fit right in as if she was meant to be with them.

Addison took the controller from Leo and looked over at Max. "Let's see what you've got," she taunted him.

He started the game and the others watched.

"Wow, you catch on fast, Addison," Joe said.

"Hey, Aunt Lissa, did you know that Uncle Peter gave us the games? He gave each family one so we'd all know how to play, then when we have family dinners we can play each other," Blythe explained.

"Uncle Peter would've liked you, Addison," Leo said.

"You think so?" Addison said. She was focused on her player as she went through the obstacles on the screen.

"Yeah, he loved to watch us play video games, but he never would try them himself. He said he was too slow." Joe chuckled as the other kids laughed with him.

"He'd love it because you play with us, but especially because you beat us. He loved it when Aunt Lissa occasionally beat us," Blythe said.

"Occasionally!" Lissa protested.

"Come on, Aunt Lis, you know you didn't win very often, but you tried," Max said, tapping on his controller.

As Addison continued to maneuver her player she said, "He would've loved Thanksgiving when I beat Aunt Lissa then."

The kids laughed and Addison stole a look at Lissa and winked. Lissa felt her heart melt a little. She was in love with Addison Henry and there was no use fighting it. Over the months since she'd met Addison she'd fought those feelings, but she could embrace them now and let them fill her heart.

Addison wasn't able to beat Max, but she did manage to defeat Joe. Lissa could hear Marielle and Kara putting things away in the kitchen so she got up to help.

"What are you two doing the rest of the day?" Kara asked Lissa.

"I don't know. I'm sure we'll find something to do," Lissa said, gazing over at Addison.

It wasn't long until the games ended and everyone went home. Lissa and Addison waved from the porch then went back inside.

"Is everything put away?" Addison asked.

"Yep," Lissa said, sitting down on the couch.

Addison sat down next to her and sighed. "I think I'm going to go home."

Once again, Lissa had an unsettled feeling in her stomach.

"Maybe to rest for a while," Addison continued. "If I stay here I know what will happen."

"Is that a bad thing?" Lissa asked hesitantly.

Addison chuckled. "No. I just need a minute to myself. You know I usually spend holidays alone."

"Oh." Lissa nodded. "My family can be a bit much."

"No, they're not. I loved spending Thanksgiving with you and your family and I loved today. I need to go home and call my parents. I'll come back later."

Addison got up and went to the bedroom to get her bag while Lissa waited in the living room.

"I'm so glad you spent the night with me," Lissa said when Addison walked back into the living room.

"I am too." Addison dropped her bag and put her arms around Lissa's shoulders.

Lissa felt her anxiety wane somewhat when Addison rested her head on Lissa's shoulder. She pulled Addison close and nuzzled her hair.

Addison pulled back and looked into Lissa's eyes. "I don't know when I've enjoyed Christmas this much. Thank you."

Lissa leaned down and brought their lips together in a tender kiss. "I'll see you soon," she said, pulling slowly away.

"You will," Addison said softly.

31

A ddison got home and Dart immediately jumped on her bed and found a patch of sunlight.

"Are you tired, too?" Addison said to him as she threw her bag on a chair. She sat down on the bed, trying not to disturb his sun bath, and eased back on the pillows.

Thoughts of Lissa ran through her head. She felt like they were in another world last night. It was just the two of them: no work problems, no gossip, no worries. She smiled and then it hit her. This wasn't who she was. She must have succumbed to the whole small-town charm aura. It was pushing her off her path and she needed to get back in her lane.

"What the..." she whispered. "I'm not gay. I shouldn't be the subject of gossip unless it has to do with how great the bank is. What have I done!"

Addison's head swirled with the rumors about her and Lissa. Then she had visions of being passed over for her next promotion. She'd be stuck in this small town doing mundane bank reports.

LISSA! What about Lissa? "Oh, Lissa. I've fallen in love with you and couldn't see what was coming!" she exclaimed. Her voice echoed around the room. Tears pooled in her eyes as a plan began to form in her head.

She jumped up and got her suitcase out of the closet and began to pack. The next two days were bank holidays and she had days and days of vacation saved up. The bank would be fine without her for a few days.

It didn't take long to pack and make the arrangements, but she had one stop to make before she could leave.

Addison could feel the dread physically weighing her down as she got into her car, but she knew what she had to do. Her life path led straight into the CEO's office, no detours allowed. She'd been living in a dream world since moving to Brazos Falls and it was time to be the person she truly was.

The last thing she wanted to do was hurt Lissa. She hadn't meant for this to happen. It was her hope they could somehow remain friends because she was sure Lissa was the best person she'd ever known. But... Addison couldn't live this way *and* attain her goals.

She took a deep breath as she parked and got out of her car.

"Hey," Lissa said with a bright smile as she answered the door.

"Hey," Addison replied as her heart thumped out a dirge of doom in her chest.

"What's wrong?"

Addison sat down on the couch and Callie jumped into her lap. "I've got to leave, Lissa. I'm going home for a few days."

"Did something happen?"

Addison tried to smile at her. "Yeah." She nodded. "I can't do this."

"This?"

"I've got my life planned out and I'll just break your heart. The longer we stay together the harder it will be."

"Addy," Lissa said desperately.

"I don't want to hurt you, Lissa, but I can't do this. This isn't me. I'm not a small town banker who's in love with a woman. I'm not the next scandal in this town. I'm a financial professional on the path to run the entire network of banks. I'm so sorry, Lissa. I never wanted to hurt you."

"You're in love with me?"

"I don't know. I'm not gay." The words tumbled out of Addison's mouth and picked up steam. "I'm supposed to manage the bank, implement a few things and go back to Dallas. None of this was supposed to happen. The small-town charm must have gotten to me. I'm being gossiped about! That's not me! I've lost sight of my goals and I have to get back on the path." She got up and walked towards the door.

"Addison, wait!"

"No, Lissa. I've got to get to the airport. I'm going to my parents' for the rest of the holidays. I'll call Max and ask him to look after Dart."

"I'll do it. Addison, please. Can't we talk about this?"

"No, Lissa. My focus is my career and always has been. I don't know how I got away from that. Anyway, I've got to go. I'm so, so sorry. I never wanted to hurt you."

"You keep saying that, Addy, but what about you?" Lissa called after her as Addison hurried to the car.

She got in the car and drove away as tears streamed down her cheeks. "What about me?" she muttered to herself. "Is this rock in my chest what a broken heart feels like? Is that why I can't breathe?" Addison swiped at the tears and took a deep breath. "Breathe, Addy. All you have to do is breathe."

Lissa didn't know how long she'd been sitting on the couch. It must have been dark outside because it was dark in her living room. She looked at the pile of tissues on her couch, but couldn't stop thinking about Addison and the things she'd said. Lissa was afraid something like this would happen. She knew Addison's focus was on her career, but Lissa didn't get the chance to tell her they could make it work. She was afraid it was too soon for that conversation and she didn't want to scare Addison away.

She kept going back to what Addison had said: She was in love with a woman, but she was not gay. Lissa shook her head. This revelation burned deep inside her. She knew the turmoil of discovering you're different and the confusion over what to do with those feelings. It broke her heart that Addison was going through that and she couldn't help her.

Tears began to trickle down her face once again. Why did this hurt so much?

Her phone rang and she jumped to answer it.

"Addy?"

"Hey, Lissa. It's Suzanne."

"Oh, hi Suzanne," Lissa said, swiping at the trail of tears on her cheek.

"I talked to Addison."

"Is she there?"

"No, she called me from the airport. She didn't dare come by here because she knew we would try to reason with her. I've never seen her like this, Lissa. Did something happen?"

Lissa took a deep breath and slowly let it out. "Yeah, we had the most wonderful day and night then my family came over for Christmas brunch this morning." Lissa sighed. "We…" she trailed off.

"Oh," Suzanne said.

"Yeah, there were a lot of intense feelings."

"She's in love with you," Suzanne stated. "She's trying to deny it and stop the feelings."

"I'm in love with her, too."

"I've never known her to run home," Suzanne said.

"Run?"

"Yeah, I think she's running away. She said she needed some distance from you and Brazos Falls."

"Why wouldn't she come to you then?" Lissa asked.

"Probably because I know you and I know how you make her feel and I would keep reminding her of that."

"I don't know what to do," Lissa said hopelessly.

"Don't give up on her, Lissa. She will figure this out. I believe your love is strong and it won't be easy for her to get over it."

"Get over it? We've just begun and I already can't imagine not loving her."

"She'll be back and she'll have to talk to you. It's a small town. You have that going for you."

"Yeah, I think the small town part has a lot to do with why she left."

"That's part of it, but I think the real problem is that she may be questioning this life path that she's so carefully orchestrated all these years. No one has ever given her a reason to doubt it. I think you may have given her the idea that there's more to life than being the bank boss."

"I don't want to change her path. I want to travel it with her," Lissa said.

"I know you do and hopefully you'll get the chance to tell her just that."

Lissa sighed.

"I'll let you know if I hear from her. She's my best friend, and I don't want her screwing up the best thing that's ever happened to her. She'll figure it out, Lissa. Give it time."

"I hope you're right. Thanks for calling."

* * *

Addison woke up in her childhood bedroom. She rolled over and looked out the window, hoping the clarity that had so far eluded her would appear.

There was a soft knock on the door. "Hey," Rhonda Henry said, partially opening the door. "Are you up?"

"Good morning, Mom," Addison replied.

Rhonda walked in and sat down on the bed. "It's been a long time since you've been home at Christmas. Don't get me wrong, I'm happy you're here. But..."

Addison's forehead creased. "But?"

"I'm ready to listen when you're ready to tell me what's really going on."

"Oh, Mom." Tears began to pool in Addison's eyes.

Rhonda opened her arms and Addison fell into them. She let her mother's comforting arms surround her with love for several moments.

"Your dad has gone to the donut shop for us. How about a cup of coffee until he brings us our favorites?"

Addison nodded.

They went into the kitchen and Addison sat at the table while her mother poured them a cup of coffee. "Your dad and I raised you and your brother and sister to be independent and follow your hearts, but I'm not sure we thought you'd go so far away. We're proud of you, but we also miss seeing you more than a couple of times a year."

"I know, Mom. I miss y'all, too."

"Oh, listen to that little Texas drawl you've picked up." Rhonda chuckled and set a steaming mug of coffee in front of her daughter.

"I feel like I've lost my way a little bit and I'm hoping this trip home will help me refocus," Addison began.

"Lost your way? I thought things were going well at the bank and your superiors were pleased," Rhonda said, taking a sip of her coffee.

"They are, but some things have happened. Things I let happen," Addison clarified.

Rhonda gave her an encouraging smile and waited.

"I've made a good friend that's turned into much more and it's caused the small town to gossip about us."

"Uh huh. And what about you and this friend are gossip worthy? I know you, honey. You are a good person."

Addison smiled. It felt good to hear her mother's kind words. "My friend is a woman, Mom, and I brought her to the bank Christmas party as my date."

Rhonda nodded and smiled. "Does this small town have a problem with gay people or a problem with their bank president dating a woman?"

Addison shrugged. "I'm not sure." She took a deep breath. "Her name is Lissa and she's one of the most beloved people in the town. You're not surprised or upset that she's a woman?"

"I'm not surprised, but I'm getting the idea you are. You mention Lissa every time we talk on the phone, sweetie," Rhonda commented.

"I'm not gay, Mom. I talk about Lissa because...well, she's Lissa. She's amazing. And she's gay." Just speaking Lissa's name made Addison's heart happy and hurt at the same time.

"Then what's the problem? If that town doesn't already love you, I know they will. And you just said they love Lissa. The gossipers will move on to something else. That's how it usually works."

Addison sighed. "I'm not going to be there that long and I don't want to break Lissa's heart, but I think I already have."

"What do you mean?"

"I may be in love with her and I'm pretty sure she's in love with me," Addison said quietly. "That can't happen. I'm going back to Dallas. I have my career path all planned out!"

"I see." Rhonda reached over and squeezed Addison's hand.

"If I don't end it now then imagine how it will hurt when I leave," Addison added.

"Or," Rhonda raised her brows, "imagine how wonderful it will be until you go back to Dallas. And who's to say Lissa won't go with you?"

Addison heaved out a loud sigh. "I've thought of that. What kind of life would that be for her? Do you realize how much I work when I'm at the main office? That's all I do."

"You're not doing that now?"

"No. My hours aren't nearly as long at the Brazos Falls bank. I have all this time to work on special projects and still manage the bank."

"Shouldn't Lissa be part of this decision, or have you two already discussed it?"

"No."

Rhonda studied her daughter. "Have you imagined what it would be like if Lissa was with you in Dallas?"

Addison nodded and looked at her hands.

"You know, all your dad and I want is for you to be happy. All these years, you've worked so hard, but we understood it was what you wanted. You've been doing this since you were in high school."

"Doing what?" Addison said, looking up at her mother.

"Do you remember Kate Lane from high school?"

"Of course I do, Mom. She was my best friend."

"She was your best friend who cheated off your English exam. It hurt your feelings that she went to a party instead of studying with you. When she turned around and looked at your paper you couldn't say no and then she even made a better grade."

"I remember." Addison shrugged.

"You pulled away from your friends and all you did was study. That continued in college."

"I had friends in college," Addison said defensively.

Rhonda smiled. "Yes, you had friends, but I'm talking about boyfriends."

"I dated."

"You always broke up with them when you had a major project or exams," Rhonda stated.

"I had to focus, Mom."

Rhonda nodded. "Since then you have only dated men who work with you."

"That's because they understood the long hours," Addison said.

"What's different with Lissa? Are you afraid work won't be your focus if she's with you?"

Addison shook her head. "I don't know how this

happened. I've dated other people and still maintained my career path."

"Lissa has connected with your heart and, honey, that's one thing you can't control," Rhonda said compassionately.

"I'm always in control," Addison stated.

"Then why are you here?"

Addison met her mom's stare. "I needed distance from Lissa and the situation."

"The situation? Do you mean your relationship?"

"I have been on this path since I graduated from college. I'm not about to abandon it now."

"Who says you have to abandon it? You've been presented with an alternative."

Addison shook her head. "It won't work. I broke up with her. I need distance. I'm going back and making that bank the best it can be, then I'm going to Dallas and moving up the ladder, just as I planned. I don't want to talk about it any longer."

"Okay," Rhonda said. "But you can't deny your heart, Addison. It's stronger than you think."

"I've been in control of my heart for thirty-five years, so why should that change now?"

Rhonda smiled. "Because you're in love with Lissa."

"Who wants donuts?" Addison's father said, walking in the back door.

"I do," Addison said, staring at her mom.

32

L issa sat at her desk, staring at her computer screen. She was trying to work, but it was still hard to keep her mind on business. It had been over a month since Addison had come back from her impromptu visit to her parents.

She came to Lissa's the day she got back and Lissa remembered their conversation like it was yesterday:

The last thing I want to do is hurt you, Lissa, but this isn't sustainable.

Isn't sustainable? We're not some project with a deadline or steps to implement, Addy.

Lissa had begged her to slow down and discuss it. They had time and Lissa assured her she would not get in her way, but wanted to help her achieve her goals.

But Addison wouldn't budge. She kept saying over and over that she was sorry. That's when Lissa told her she would never be sorry for the kiss at the falls, the sunsets, or their walks. She would especially never be sorry for loving her.

Lissa took a shuddering breath as those memories

replayed in her head again. Why did this hurt so much? She'd lost her parents, her brother, and broken up with girl-friends before, but none of those hurt like this.

Her head fell into her hands as the tears began to flow once again. Suzanne kept telling her not to give up, that Addison would figure it out, but Lissa wasn't so sure. The idea of 'giving up' was ludicrous anyway. She was in love with Addison Henry. Her heart was shattered, but the love for Addison was still there and always would be.

"Aww, sis," Ben said, walking into her office and closing the door.

She looked up at him and swiped at the tears. "I'm sorry, Ben."

"Come here." He held his arms open and wrapped them around Lissa. "I should go to that bank," he muttered.

"You can't be upset with her," Lissa mumbled against his chest. "She didn't mean for this to happen. I knew better."

"What?" Ben said, pulling away and sitting in the chair opposite her.

"I tried to stop these feelings or at least slow them down." Lissa sat behind her desk and sighed.

"Oh, Lissa. We don't choose who we fall in love with. Our hearts do," Ben said with a compassionate smile.

Lissa nodded. "I hope Addison's heart doesn't hurt as much as mine does."

"I wouldn't be surprised if hers doesn't hurt more. You are an incredible person, sis. She missed out."

Lissa scoffed. "It feels like we both missed out."

"Have you seen her?"

"I've seen her pulling into her driveway, but that's it. Of course, I haven't been anywhere either."

Ben nodded. "Why don't you go home? I'll finish up here."

* * *

Addison blew out a frustrated breath. "I thought this would get easier as time passed," she said into the phone.

"Why would you think that? You're in love with the woman. Did you think your heart would forget her?"

"I'll never forget her, Suz. I just didn't think it would hurt so much."

"Have you seen her?"

"No. She doesn't come in the bank. I wish we could go back to being friends."

Suzanne laughed sarcastically. "Are you kidding me? You were never just friends. Y'all had a connection from the start. You both fought it, but your hearts won and I'm still betting on them."

"You'll lose. Why in the world would Lissa ever trust me again?"

"Because she's in love with you," Sidney Wray said from Addison's open door.

"I'll call you back, Suzanne." Addison ended the call.

"I wasn't trying to eavesdrop, darling," Sidney said, walking into Addison's office and sitting down.

"What can I help you with?" Addison asked with a curt smile.

"You can tell me why my new favorite couple isn't together," Sidney stated.

Addison closed her eyes briefly and took a breath. "Things didn't work out."

Sidney gave Addison a kind smile. "You could've said it isn't any of my business."

Addison genuinely smiled. "It wouldn't have made any difference, would it?"

Sidney chuckled. "You're right. You know, Addison, I've

known Calista Morgan all her life. I've seen her go off to the big city and come back because her family needed her. I've watched her bide her time yet still believe she'd find her love someday. Do you think there's someone out there for you?"

Yeah, I broke my someone's heart a few weeks ago, Addison thought but didn't say aloud.

"I don't know what is standing in your way, but usually it's not something, it's someone."

"It's me," Addison said softly.

"Then I'm telling you to get out of your own way and afford you and Lissa the happiness I can see waiting on you."

Addison stared at Sidney. "You can see the future?"

"You could too if you'd simply open your eyes. I suspect your heart is trying to show you the way."

Addison swallowed. She didn't know why she believed Sidney Wray when both her mom and Suzanne had been telling her the same thing for weeks, but here she was hanging on her every word.

"I'm quite sure Lissa hasn't lost trust in you."

"I would have." Addison finally found her voice.

Sidney smiled. "No you wouldn't. Use that extremely bright mind of yours and get your girl back." Sidney got up and started for the door. "It was nice to see you, Addison."

What the hell! That was bizarre. Addison rested her chin in her hand as she gazed out her office window. The sun was shining brightly this February afternoon. She ran her fingers across the bracelet on her right wrist then she did something she'd never done.

"Maise, I'll be gone the rest of the afternoon. See you tomorrow," Addison said as she left the bank.

She got in her car and began to drive. The radio was

playing softly in the background and she heard the familiar notes of a song her parents used to listen to. It was "With Your Love" by Jefferson Starship.

She turned it up and listened. The singer crooned, *you've got my heart and I don't know what I'm going to do with your love.*

"Ain't that the truth," she muttered and began to sing along. "Don't know what's happened to me since I met you. I feel like I'm falling in love since I met you. I got to know what you're doing, doing to me with your love," Addison sang. "Oh yuck! That's enough of that sappy shit," she mumbled and changed the station. The words rang true though. She didn't know what to do with this love.

"Oh, yeah. I love Dua Lipa. Sing to me," Addison said as "Be the One" began to play. She focused on the road and listened to the words of the song. The singer was asking for another chance with her love. She said she was wrong, please come back. "Whoa, that hits a little too close to home."

Addison turned on the lake road and headed in the direction of the cabin that belonged to Lissa's friend. She thought back to the first time Lissa had taken her there and played James Taylor's "The Secret O' Life" for her. What did he say in the song? *The secret of love is in opening up your heart. It's okay to feel afraid, but don't let that stand in your way.*

What was going on? A tear rolled down Addison's cheek. "It's okay to be afraid?" she whispered. Sidney had just told her to get out of her own way. "Are my fears really holding me back? Fuck! I need an upbeat song!"

She changed the radio station again and landed on Maren Morris' "Make You Say." The beat was lively but then she heard the words. A sarcastic laugh barked from her lips.

I'm one in a million, maybe a billion. Go ahead, walk away, you're gonna miss the way I used to make you say, oh my God.

"That's what you should be singing to me, Lis, because you are definitely one in a billion. I can't tell you how much I miss you."

Before the words of the song could sink in, "Never Be Sorry" by Old Dominion began to play. What station was this?

"Wait a minute," Addison said softly. When she got back from her parents' and went by Lissa's to tell her she was sorry, Lissa had told her she would never be sorry for loving her. Those words had been roaming around her head and heart since Lissa said them.

"Oh, I fucked up!" she yelled as she hit the steering wheel with both hands. Her heart slammed in her chest and she felt sick to her stomach as the song went on. *I'll never be sorry, I'll never be sorry for loving you.* Tears stung her eyes.

The next song came on and Addison knew Avril Lavigne was singing to her. "I'm a Mess" began to play through the speakers. *I'm a mess, I'm a mess, when we're not together. Such a wreck, such a wreck.* The tears began to fall again.

"This is me," she muttered. *I wish it was me and you till the end. I wish it was me and you till the end.* She pulled over and sang along until the song ended.

Addison sniffed, took a deep breath and wiped away her tears. She pulled up her contacts and connected the call. "I need your help."

* * *

Lissa's heart nervously pounded in her chest as she opened the door. She'd gotten a text from Addison asking to meet her at the library. It was strange and she was trying to tamp down the hope blossoming in her heart.

As she went through the main entrance she saw Addison sitting at a table facing the door. She was playing with the bracelet on her right wrist, the one that matched Lissa's. Her stomach flip-flopped at the sight of the woman she was still in love with. It had been nearly two months since Lissa had been this close to Addison and her body was humming with electricity.

Addison gave her a tentative smile. "Thanks for meeting me."

Lissa returned her smile and looked around the room.

"We're the only ones here," Addison said.

Lissa nodded and sat down across from Addison.

"Have you ever made a life-changing mistake? One that made you look deep inside yourself and question your own truths? Then when you realize it, you hope to get the opportunity to make things right?"

Addison didn't give Lissa a chance to respond.

"Do you remember when we walked through the cemetery for the first time then ordered from the food truck near your work?"

Lissa felt her expression soften. "I remember."

"You tickled me and won the race back to our cars. I asked you how you knew I was ticklish—"

"And I said I took a chance," Lissa said, finishing Addison's statement.

"That's right." Addison nodded. "I'm going to ask you to take a chance again, Lis, but I want to tell you some things first."

Lissa could see tears glistening in Addison's eyes. That made her throat tighten and she willed herself not to cry. "Okay," she said softly.

"Your friendship has meant more to me than anything in my life. I know the lines blurred rather quickly and it evolved into love even though we both fought it. But when we admitted our feelings, what started as a sweet exploration turned into a hot, sexy love affair. I know that may be a bit dramatic, but I think it fits."

Lissa nodded in agreement.

"Those were the best days of my life, but being the intelligent, sensible, level-headed person that I am, what did I do? I ran away." Addison paused.

Lissa watched as Addison took a deep breath and shuddered.

"I didn't let you in, the one person who could help me understand all the feelings, good and bad, that were bombarding my heart and mind. I held fast to the one thing I was sure of: my life plan. But you see, Lis, that plan is no longer sustainable."

Lissa's mouth fell open. "I've heard that somewhere before."

Addison smirked. "You remember."

"Of course I remember."

"I'd like to show you something," Addison said, getting up and waiting for Lissa to follow her.

They stopped at the first section of shelves. Lissa looked up and saw it was the romance section. She began to read the titles and the authors and gasped.

33

"These are all sapphic romance and sapphic fiction! There must be over a hundred books here!" Confused, Lissa looked at Addison. "I don't understand."

"This is the new expanded LGBTQ section of the library. They'll be adding more titles, but the librarian wanted your input."

"How?" Lissa looked at Addison and shook her head.

Addison shrugged. "Money talks and I asked a few friends for help."

Lissa stared at Addison and waited.

"Suzanne helped me order the books and Sidney convinced the librarian this was in the town's best interests."

"I can't believe it," Lissa said, gazing at the books.

"I did this as a way to be close to you and I also thought if people were considering moving here and saw this part of the library, they would know we're gay friendly."

"Aren't you leaving someday?"

"Not without you," Addison firmly stated.

Lissa grabbed both of Addison's hands. "I don't want you

to give up your dreams, Addy. I want to help you live them," Lissa said, almost pleading.

Addison tilted her head and smiled. "I know that, but what if my dreams have changed?"

"I don't want you to change. You are who I fell in love with."

"The uber-focused, success minded bitch that I am." Addison shrugged.

Lissa smiled. "That and the big-hearted, extremely sexy woman who has my heart."

"What better way to show we're gay friendly than to have a prominent gay couple in town?"

"A prominent gay couple?"

"You are the sweetheart of Brazos Falls and I happen to run the bank. Will you take a chance on us?"

"That depends. The next time you are confused or over-whelmed, are you going to run away?"

Addison shook her head. "I'm going to run to you."

"Do you remember the first time Suzanne and Rachel were here and you said they only had eyes for each other?" Lissa asked.

"Yes, and you said that's the way it should be," Addison replied.

"I said when I'm with someone, I'm all in." Lissa put her hands on Addison's shoulders. "I've been all in with you from the beginning."

Addison put her hands on Lissa's hips. "You are more important to me than any bank or any job. I never dreamed love could be like this. That's why I didn't understand, but I do now."

"I don't want you to give up your dreams. I thought we were moving to Dallas in a couple of years."

Addison grinned. "I'm all in, Calista. As long as I'm with

you, I don't care where we live."

"But I do," Lissa said earnestly.

"What?"

"I want to be the CEO's girlfriend. Ben and I have found a way for me to work remotely."

"If I'm the CEO, you don't have to work, babe. But you're more than just my girlfriend." Addison paused. "You're my partner."

"Slow down, Addy. That's what got us in trouble."

"Slow down? I'm not going to waste another second being away from you, Lissa. I tried to control my heart and I learned that's not possible." Addison raised her hands to cup Lissa's face. "I'm in love with you, Calista. My heart has never been this happy."

"Oh Addy, I love you, too!" Lissa couldn't wait any longer. She crushed her lips to Addison's and an overwhelming sense of joy and happiness surrounded her.

Tears flowed down both of their cheeks and mingled together to wash away the hurt in their hearts.

"I love you so much." Addison peppered kisses all over Lissa's face.

Lissa chuckled. "I love you, too, baby."

"Thank God!"

They both turned to the front of the library and there stood Sidney Wray.

"I was prepared to sit you both down until you came to your senses." She walked towards them with a big smile on her face.

"What are you doing here?" Lissa asked, not letting Addison go.

"The librarian didn't trust me with the key, but she does trust Sidney." Addison laughed then shrugged.

"Love can be hard, if you let it. Don't let it. Get out of

your own way and make each other happy," Sidney said, pointing a finger at both of them. "I'll take care of the gossipers if you'll take care of each other."

Addison looked into Lissa's eyes. "I don't care about the gossipers." She reached up and kissed Lissa softly. "The gossip didn't bother me as much as my carefully crafted plan crumbling around me. I couldn't understand what was happening, but I do now. Calista Morgan has taken my heart; however... it's okay, because I have hers. And I'm going to cherish it, adore it, nurture it, and love it for all time."

"Oh, Addy. Let's go home," Lissa said, resting her forehead against Addison's.

They walked out of the library and stopped while Sidney locked the front door.

"I love the books," Lissa said, reaching for Addison's hand. "But I want to live our story. I want to live our happily-ever-after."

"You've made it through the break-up," Sidney said.

"What now?" Lissa asked using one of Addison's favorite phrases.

"I start making up for my life-changing mistake," Addison said, opening her passenger door for Lissa. "I'm never letting you go."

"I hope you're naked within the hour," Sidney said with a sly grin.

"Sidney!" Lissa exclaimed, getting into Addison's car.

"Thanks for your help," Addison said, hurrying around the car to the driver's side.

"I'm a sucker for a happy ending." Sidney waved as they drove away.

* * *

Addison drove them to her house, grabbed Lissa's hand, and pulled her through the front door. "We need these clothes off. Now!" Addison stated.

"She can't control her heart, but she is in control of everything else," Lissa said, taking off her coat.

"It's your fault."

"Me?"

"I can't help it if I love the way your body feels under my hands and lips." Addison grabbed the front of Lissa's shirt and pulled her close. "Do you have any idea what it does to me when you gasp as I touch you? Do you know how my heart feels when you quiver as my lips kiss down your stomach? When you look at me and let me see into your soul, I come undone," Addison said, her voice lowering to a whisper.

"Fuck," Lissa said breathlessly. "Get me out of these clothes."

Addison smiled then pressed her lips to Lissa's. They left a trail of clothes as they kissed their way down the hall to Addison's bedroom.

"Oh, my beautiful Calista," Addison said softly when they stood next to the bed. She cupped Lissa's face with both hands and brought their lips together in a soft, luscious kiss. Her hands trailed over Lissa's shoulders and across to cup her breasts. "I'll slow down now."

Lissa stared at her in anticipation.

"I'm going to love you all over," Addison said. She gazed at Lissa's breasts as her nipples began to harden. Addison lowered to her knees and wrapped her arms around Lissa. She pulled her tight and rested her cheek against Lissa's stomach. Addison could feel Lissa's fingers thread through her hair.

"I love you so much, Lis. I'm sorry I hurt you."

Lissa reached down and pulled Addison up. "Love me, Addy. Love me."

Addison crawled onto the bed on her knees. She reached out her hand for Lissa to join her. They faced one another and Addison softly said, "Together?"

Lissa nodded and looked at Addison with such love. "Follow me," she whispered.

With one finger Lissa traced the outline of Addison's lips then slowly ran her finger over Addison's chin, down her neck, pausing briefly at the hollow of Addison's throat before stopping between her breasts.

Addison could feel her heart pounding and let her finger follow the same path on Lissa's body. She was rewarded with Lissa's sharp intake of breath as Addison's finger grazed the sensitive spot at the front of Lissa's neck.

With the same hand, Lissa cupped Addison's breast and ran her thumb over her already rock hard nipple. Addison mirrored her movement and smiled as Lissa's nipple pebbled under her touch.

"God, you are amazing," Addison whispered then looked up into Lissa's eyes. The soft brown had become so dark Addison could see her reflection in them.

"Kiss me, Addy," Lissa whispered.

Addison leaned in and gently ran her tongue over Lissa's lips before touching them with her own. Lissa reached up and put her other hand behind Addison's neck, holding their lips together, and moaned. Addison felt Lissa's mouth devour hers and matched her moan.

Lissa slid her hand down Addison's stomach until it rested between her legs. Addison quickly followed Lissa's movement and couldn't wait to feel her wetness. Suddenly she felt Lissa's palm on the back of her hand. Lissa guided Addison's hand until she pushed two fingers inside.

"Oh, God, yes, baby," Lissa groaned.

Addison felt Lissa let her hand go and then she was filled with Lissa's expert fingers. "Ohhhh," she moaned. Addison leaned forward and put her other hand on Lissa's back, holding them steady.

She looked into Lissa's eyes and could see the love and the passion. Then, as they began to slowly move together, Addison saw something else. She could see them together, could see their happily-ever-after. She could see forever.

"I've got you," Lissa whispered. "Do you have me?"

Addison nodded. "Forever," she said breathlessly. They leaned in and their lips met just as the orgasms began to roll through them. It washed away the pain of uncertainty and the doubts that tried to break them apart. All that remained was love and possibility.

When Lissa shuddered one more time, Addison wrapped both her arms around her and eased them down on the bed. She held Lissa to her chest. "I love you, I love you, I love you," she whispered over and over.

Lissa started to pull away but Addison wouldn't let her move. "Just a moment longer. I can't let you go."

"Mmm, I need to see your eyes," Lissa muttered against Addison's chest.

Addison relaxed her hold and Lissa raised her head. She looked into Addison's eyes.

"This is my favorite shade of blue," she said softly. "They are so dark and around the edges they are a lighter blue." Lissa smiled and ran her thumb along Addison's cheek. "I've only seen them like this when we make love."

"Then they're going to look like this the rest of the night."

Lissa chuckled then her face turned serious. "I love you, Addison. I will always be here with you."

"Thank God." Addison sighed.

"I know you were hurting, too. I'm sorry it's so hard to love me and that it makes people talk about you."

"No, no, no. Loving you is the best thing, Calista. And I'm going to do it forever."

Lissa sighed contentedly and rested her head on Addison's chest. "By the way, you know what you're doing."

Addison chuckled. "I'm learning from the best."

It was Lissa's turn to laugh. "Do you remember Thanksgiving?"

"Like it was yesterday. That's the day I let everything go," Addison said, stroking Lissa's hair.

"You did?"

"Yes. I'd been wrestling with these feelings for you and I decided to not worry about it and enjoy the day."

"That was a wonderful day. You have fit in with my family from the beginning."

"I love your family. They may not love me at the moment, but I'll win them back. That was the day you almost kissed me."

Lissa gasped and looked at Addison. "When we were back at your house and I grabbed you? You knew?"

"I was there. I almost kissed you!" Addison exclaimed.

"Oh, I wanted to kiss you." Lissa grinned.

"I wanted you to kiss me!" Addison smiled. "I wasn't afraid or apprehensive. Speaking of kisses," Addison said.

"Yes?"

"I now realize that you were right about the kisses at the end of all those movies we watched."

"What?"

"I would've never believed it if it hadn't happened to me," Addison declared.

"Please, go on."

"Come on." Addison chuckled. "You know as well as I do that our kiss at Brazos Falls was one of the best kisses of all time."

"I couldn't agree with you more; however, I plan to keep trying to top it. How about you?"

Addison giggled.

"God, I love when you giggle like that," Lissa said, squeezing Addison.

"I feel like we were living in a Hallmark movie. Everything that led up to that kiss and then when our lips met, just wow!"

"It was completely spontaneous too. I simply wanted you to hear the water to ease your stress."

Addison looked lovingly into Lissa's eyes. "You're always doing nice things for me."

"You do nice things for me, too," Lissa said softly. "You came back to me. You didn't let your fears or your doubts win."

"Sorry it took so long," Addison said, stroking Lissa's cheek. "Suzanne was talking to me nearly every day. My mom kept assuring me that I could have both you and the career I envisioned. Thank you for waiting on me."

Lissa scoffed. "I didn't have a choice, babe. You have my heart."

Addison pulled Lissa down for a passionate kiss then she flipped them.

As she looked down at Lissa, she shook her head. "God, I do love being on top of you!"

Lissa giggled.

"Remind me to tell you about Sidney coming to the bank and my playlist in the car." She leaned in to kiss Lissa, but Lissa stopped her.

"Wait, what?"

Addison sighed. "Sidney came by the bank and told me to get my girl back. I went for a drive—"

"Wait! You left early?" Lissa asked, astonished.

Addison chuckled. "Yes, I couldn't work. I ended up driving around the lake and all these songs came on the radio about love. I kept changing the station, but it didn't matter, another love song would play. I wanted you then, just like I want you now."

This time Lissa didn't stop her. Their lips met in a searing kiss. The time for talking was over.

34

"Are you going to take me to get my car this morning?" Lissa asked as her fingers played with Addison's hair.

"Hmm, how about this. You get ready for work here with me." Addison rubbed her hand softly over Lissa's stomach.

"I don't have any clothes here," Lissa said. "We could shower—"

"Together." Addison raised her head, looked into Lissa's eyes, and smiled.

"Obviously." Lissa grinned. "While you're getting ready I'll make breakfast."

"I'll take you by your house to change and get your car."

"Perfect plan," Lissa said.

"On one condition." Addison raised her brows.

"What's that?"

"You have to have lunch with me today. There's something I want us to do."

"I would love to have lunch with you, babe." Lissa smiled.

"You'll come by the bank?"

Lissa nodded and smiled. "Last night may have been the best night of my life."

"Christmas Eve may rival it."

"Last night was better. On Christmas Eve, I knew the doubts were there and would hit you eventually. They weren't there last night."

"It was all love, baby. There was no room for anything but love," Addison said with a smile.

"I love you, Addy."

"I love you, too, Calista," Addison happily replied. "Come on."

They got up and put their plan in motion.

* * *

Lissa walked into the bank and the look on Addison's face when she saw her made Lissa's heart melt. There was such love in her eyes.

"Hi!" Addison came around her desk and kissed Lissa on the lips. She paused for a moment and kissed her again.

Lissa tried to mask the surprise on her face, but couldn't stop the smile that grew.

"Everyone needs to get used to it," Addison said with a grin. "I love you and I'm going to show it."

"Okay."

"Tastefully and respectively, that is."

"But of course." Lissa nodded. "Where do you want to have lunch?"

"Let's walk across the square to the pizza place we love; it's not too cold today," Addison said, getting her coat.

"The strangest thing happened this morning when I got to work," Lissa said.

"What's that?"

"Ben met me at the door with a huge smile and hugged me. It seems he could tell by looking at me that we were back together, or maybe he already knew," Lissa said suspiciously. "And then Marielle and Kara both called me."

Addison chuckled. "I had a contingency plan in case you didn't want to meet me."

"Marielle and Kara were part of that plan?"

"They were," Addison admitted. "But it all worked out." She reached up and kissed Lissa again then wiped a smudge of lipstick below her lip.

"Oh, I could get used to this." Lissa pleasantly sighed.

Addison reached for Lissa's hand as they walked into the lobby of the bank.

"Hey," Karen said, walking towards them.

Lissa braced herself for Karen's snide comments. There was no way she could dampen the happiness surrounding her and Addison.

Karen looked down at their joined hands. "It's so good to see those smiles on both your faces. This is just what this town needs. Enjoy your lunch." With that Karen walked away.

Addison and Lissa looked at each other surprised.

"How about that?" Addison remarked.

"Karen would never say anything like that if she didn't like you, babe," Lissa said as they left the bank.

"Me?"

"Yeah. She's been my friend for a long time, but to say something nice like that... she likes you."

"Maybe she likes us together."

Lissa shrugged. "You mentioned wanting to do something at lunch."

Addison swung their hands up and down. "This is it." She looked over at Lissa and smiled. "Do you remember at the parade I told you we'd walk down this street holding hands someday? Today's the day!"

"I can see the headline in the paper," Lissa began. "'Prominent gay couple seen holding hands on the downtown square.'"

"I'm going to be holding your hand for a very long time." Addison winked and held the door to the restaurant open for Lissa.

* * *

"Hey, can you leave work early today? There's something I want to show you," Addison said to Lissa on the phone.

"Sure. It's such a beautiful day. Would you want to drive out to the lake after?"

"Do you think it's too cold to get in the water?" Addison asked.

"It's May, babe. The water will still be chilly," Lissa said.

"Okay. Maybe I'll just stick my toes in. See you soon. Love you."

"Love you, too."

Addison ended the call and felt a little flutter in her stomach. She left the bank and drove to the mill to get Lissa. It had been three months since Lissa had agreed to meet Addison at the library. With Lissa's help the librarian had expanded the LGBTQ section further with non-fiction books and memoirs. Addison could tell it made Lissa proud.

They hadn't spent one night apart since then, trading out staying at Lissa's house a few nights then at Addison's. It wasn't a problem, but an opportunity had presented itself at the bank today and Addison wanted Lissa to see it.

When Addison pulled into the mill parking lot, Lissa came bounding down the steps.

"Hi, honey," Lissa said, getting into the car. She leaned over and kissed Addison then reached for her seat belt.

"Hold it." Addison grabbed the front of Lissa's shirt. "I need another kiss."

Lissa chuckled and pressed her lips to Addison's.

"Mmm, thank you." Addison grinned.

Lissa looked around the car and sniffed. "Do I smell pizza?"

"How about a picnic for supper?" Addison said, driving out of the parking lot. She turned on the lake road and smiled at Lissa.

"Are we going to the lake first?"

"What I want to show you just happens to be at the lake."

Lissa sat back and reached over for Addison's hand. "You know, sometimes I feel a little spoiled."

"Spoiled?"

"Yes, you're always opening doors for me, you drive us places, hold my hand, put your arm around me."

Addison chuckled. "That's not spoiled. It's me cherishing you. I've never been like this before and I like it."

"I like it, too!"

"Your girlfriends didn't do that in your other relationships?"

"No, I was the one who did things like that."

"You do those things for me, too."

"I guess it's showing our love instead of saying it," Lissa explained.

"See! You're not spoiled. You're loved."

"I certainly am."

Addison slowed the car and turned into a driveway that meandered down to the lake.

"Wow, this is a nice place. Who lives here?" Lissa asked.

Addison stopped the car between the water and the house. "No one does right now. Let's look around."

They walked down to the water and stepped onto the covered dock. There was a slot to park a boat and also a larger area for sunning.

"Do you think it's deep enough here to jump off the dock and swim?" Addison asked.

"Oh yeah." Lissa nodded. "You could swim from the end of the dock back to this little beach. It's a great set-up. Is it the bank's?"

"Let's go look inside," Addison said, taking Lissa's hand and ignoring her question for the moment.

"You have a key?"

Addison grinned and held up the key as they walked across the lush lawn. "I love this big back porch. Well, I guess it's actually the front porch since the house faces the lake."

"I'm sure you could enjoy some killer sunsets from here," Lissa said, glancing at Addison and then back over the water.

"It's two bedrooms and two baths," Addison said, opening the front door. "This open living-kitchen area is huge."

"That's the way it should be. You want to be able to enjoy the view from anywhere in the house. I love these big trees on either side of the yard. It's like they frame the view of the lake," Lissa said, spreading her arms wide while looking out the large windows next to the door.

"Wow! Look in here, babe," Addison said from one of the bedrooms. "Isn't this gorgeous? Can you imagine waking up to this view?"

"Oh, babe!" Lissa exclaimed. She turned to Addison and stared. "What are we doing here?"

35

A ddison smiled. "Let's sit out on this little private porch."

They sat on the small loveseat that looked out over the lake.

"The bank is about to foreclose on this property." Addison turned to Lissa and took her hands. "What would you think about us living here—together?"

Lissa's eyes widened. "Really?"

"We've already talked about how dumb it is having two houses. We could sell both our places and make this our home," Addison said hopefully.

"I've always wanted to live at the lake, but couldn't afford it," Lissa said.

"You can now, babe. I'm loaded. When all you do is work there is no time to spend money." Addison laughed. "I can't imagine a better investment, can you?"

"An investment in our future? Aren't we leaving in a year or so?" Lissa asked.

"Yes, that's the plan. We could come out on weekends. You'll be working remotely, but you'll still have to come in once a month and be in the office. I'm not going to work forever. This would be the perfect place to retire, wouldn't it?"

"You want to retire in Brazos Falls?"

"Don't you? It's your home, you have family here."

"You have family, too."

Addison smiled. "But you're my home. This is where we fell in love."

"Can we afford to keep this place when we move back to Dallas?"

"God, I love it when you say *we*!" Addison beamed.

"You told me you were never letting me go. I am holding you to that." Lissa reached up and cradled Addison's face with her hands. She brought their lips together in a sweet kiss.

Addison felt her heart swell. She didn't know how, but every day she loved Lissa even more.

"We can make it work, babe. I would've never brought you out here if I didn't think we could make it ours. Do you like it?"

Lissa scoffed. "What's not to like? Honestly, Addy, I don't care where we live as long as I'm with you."

"Oh, Lis. I don't care either, but..." Addison looked around the property and back at Lissa. "This is fucking perfect for us."

"Yeah, it is." Lissa chuckled and kissed Addison again.

"We'll get a good price on it and keep the bank from losing money. I'll get things started tomorrow. What do you say we have our first picnic on our beach?"

"Oh, Addy. I love you so much."

"Consider this another way we show our love," Addison said.

"I am the luckiest woman in the world!" Lissa exclaimed.

"After me!" Addison jumped up and went to the car to get the pizza.

Lissa spread a blanket out on the grass at the edge of the beach. The water slowly lapped onto the sand as the sun started its fall to the water.

"To our first sunset in our home," Addison said, handing Lissa a beer.

"You came prepared." Lissa grinned.

"I was hopeful, but I knew you'd love this place, too."

"To our first of many sunsets together in our home." Lissa clinked her beer to Addison's.

"Oh, wait," Addison said, setting her beer down and grabbing her phone. "One more thing." She clicked a couple of buttons and a song began to play.

Lissa gasped. "Is that the 'Secret O' Life?'"

"Yep. *The secret o' life is enjoying the passage of time*," Addison sang. "I want my time to be spent with you." Tears sprang to Addison's eyes.

"*The secret of love is in opening up your heart. It's okay to feel afraid, but don't let that stand in your way,*" Lissa sang in reply. "You didn't let fear stop us. My time is all yours."

Addison half leapt and half fell into Lissa's arms. Their lips crashed together in the sweetest, most heartfelt kiss. They fell over onto the grass and Addison deepened the kiss. She could feel the love in how tightly Lissa held her.

When they pulled away, Lissa was breathing heavily. "This is our *what now*." Then she rolled on top of Addison. "And this is our love."

Addison felt this kiss through her entire being. She forgot about pizza, the house, the lake, the sunset. There was simply her and Lissa and their love.

* * *

Fourteen Months Later

"I'm so glad y'all live at the lake. It's the perfect place to celebrate the 4th of July weekend," Ben said.

"Our neighbors across the lake love fireworks. Just wait until tonight," Addison said.

"Aunt Lis, when are we eating?" Max asked.

"Soon. There's something else we have to do first," Lissa said, grinning at Addison.

"What are you two up to?" Suzanne asked. "I see that twinkle in both your eyes."

"Well." Addison walked over and put her arm around Lissa's waist. "My bosses have seen the brilliance of my work and have called me back to Dallas."

The group collectively gasped.

"Wait, there's more," Lissa said. "Tell them."

"I thought they would put me over the banks in this area, but—"

"They've given her the entire Southwest region!" Lissa blurted proudly.

"Congrats!" Marielle exclaimed.

"I'm not surprised! You are one badass businesswoman," Rachel said.

"Do you have to move?" Kara asked.

Addison nodded. "Yes, but we have a little time to find a place."

"I'm so frigging proud of you!" Lissa squeezed Addison to her side.

"We're ready for you to work remotely," Ben said. "That won't be a problem."

"There's just one thing we want to do before we leave

and decided today would be the perfect day," Addison said, grinning up at Lissa.

"Yeah, you're all here," Lissa said, looking around the porch where her niece, nephews, and siblings sat. Next to them were Suzanne and Rachel.

"Our immediate family," Addison added.

"Right." Lissa nodded. "We're going to get married down on the beach."

"What!" Kara yelled.

"Right now?" Ben asked.

"Right now," Addison and Lissa said together, laughing.

"Who gets married in swimsuits?" Leo said.

"We do!"

"I love it. My aunts are so badass," Joe said, punching his fist in the air.

"But wait, who's going to marry you?" Marielle asked.

"I am!" In all the excitement, no one had seen Sidney Wray walk up from the side of the house.

"We wanted something simple," Lissa said.

"And we wanted to do it now before the major life change of moving and buying another house," Addison said.

"But what about your family?" Kara asked.

"Rachel is going to live-stream the ceremony to them and they're having a big party for us when we visit at the end of the month," Addison explained.

"Are you ready?" Sidney asked.

"We've been ready since the day we met," Lissa said.

"Almost." Addison smiled. "I had to go through the whole devastating fear and doubt stuff." She put her arms around Lissa's neck. "But you were right there with me. Your heart was pulling me into the light."

"It was love, *our* love," Lissa said earnestly.

They led their family down to the beach and surrounded by love they pledged to spend their lives together with happily-ever-after as the goal.

FIFTEEN YEARS LATER

"Aww, babe. We're home," Addison said, gazing out over the water. Lissa's arms were wrapped around her and Addison leaned back against Lissa's chest.

"Are you sure about this? I'm the one who's at retirement age," Lissa said, resting her chin on Addison's shoulder and following her gaze.

"But you're not retiring. You're still planning to work part time," Addison said.

"Max and Joe are doing amazing things with the mill. Ben is guiding them and I don't have to do much."

"I still can't believe Max came back here after college," Addison commented.

"What! You of all people should understand. The love of a good woman can change everything."

Addison laughed. "That's true and I do know it. But you helped me become CEO and now I'm trading that office on the top floor for the one in my laid back little hometown bank. I couldn't be happier."

"But you were only the CEO for five years," Lissa commented.

"Yes, but I was the youngest CEO and I managed to get everything done that I hoped to do. Now, I want to go back to the bank level and try a few things that I think could be good for all the banks."

Lissa chuckled. "You always have a project."

Addison laughed with her and turned in her arms. "You know, if someone would've told me seventeen years ago that I would end my career in a small town bank, I would've thought they were nuts."

"Seventeen years ago there was a little voice inside me whispering that I was about to begin the best part of my life. I'd waited and my love found me."

Addison draped her arms over Lissa's shoulders. "Oh, honey, I hope it has been the best. You know, I remember not long after we met I asked you why you and your ex broke up."

"My ex?"

"Yes, I remember it vividly. You said that she thought you were the one," Addison made air quotes with her fingers. "But for you there was something missing. You couldn't see yourself living the rest of your life with her."

Lissa pulled Addison close. "That's right and since the day we met, there's been nothing missing between us."

Addison giggled. "Good. That was the goal."

Lissa scoffed. "You and your goals!" She laughed and pulled them inside the house. "Come on, we've got to add this picture to our wall."

When they first moved in, Addison had started a time-line of sorts in the guest bedroom. Pictures were hung depicting different events in their life. It started with a picture of them walking their first 5K together at Fall Fest. There were pictures from the Christmas parades and other events in town. Several vacations were represented as the pictures continued around the room. Family dinners at the lake, Marielle's, and Ben's were sprinkled along the wall. There were visits with Addison's family here, at the lake and in Dallas. And of course there were pictures of Callie and Dart at their old houses and at the lake. One special picture was a little larger than the others and had been taken at their wedding. Everyone had the biggest smiles on their faces as they looked on while Addison and Lissa faced one another.

They were adding a picture of the two of them in Addison's high rise office. Suzanne and Rachel were on each side of them.

Lissa stared at the picture and smiled. "I am so proud of you."

Addison hammered a small nail into the wall. "Thank you, babe."

"No, I mean it, Addy. You set out to become the fucking CEO of your company and didn't let anything stop you. That is amazing!" Lissa hung the picture and made sure it was straight.

"I was ready to give it up because it wouldn't have meant anything without you," Addison said, draping an arm over Lissa's shoulders and staring at the picture.

Lissa glanced sideways at her and smiled. She walked over to one of the first pictures of them on the other side of the room. "This is my favorite picture of us."

Addison followed her over and gazed at the photo. They had been with Suzanne and Rachel at Brazos Falls, playing in the water on a crystal clear day. The sky was a brilliant blue and the water was flowing. Suzanne had captured a moment when they stood in front of the waterfall with their arms around each other and were about to kiss. They were both smiling and their faces were as bright as the day.

"It is?" Addison asked.

"Yes, because we're doing my favorite thing." Lissa looked down at Addison and grinned. "I love kissing you."

Addison smiled. "It's one of my favorite things, too," she said in that low husky voice she knew drove Lissa wild. She reached up and kissed Lissa. It started out sweet, but Lissa deepened the kiss. They weren't sure how long they'd been kissing because time stood still when they had their arms around one another like this.

Addison pulled back and smiled. "Let's do my other favorite thing." She pulled Lissa out of the room and down the hall as their clothes fell away.

Their giggles echoed around them. Lissa chuckled and pulled Addison in for a kiss. She had no doubt that Addison would be on top of her in a matter of minutes as her heart began to pound and electricity flowed through her body at the thought.

What now? We're home.

ABOUT THE AUTHOR

Jamey Moody writes heartwarming sapphic romance. Falling into a sapphic romance is an adventure. Her characters are strong women, living everyday lives with a few bumps in the road, but they get their happily ever afters. You can find her books on Amazon and on her website at jameymoody.com.

Emails are welcome at jameymoodyauthor@gmail.com

As an independent publisher a review is greatly appreciated.

On the next page is a list of my books with links that will take you to their page.

After that I've included the first two chapters of The Woman at the top of the Stairs. Dru Rae gave up everything to get away from her *mafioso* family.

Marina Summitt was an uber successful realtor in a thriving housing market.

On the first day of Dru's new job staging houses, Marina comes by to approve the listing. She wasn't prepared for what happened to her heart when she saw the woman at the top of the stairs.

ALSO BY JAMEY MOODY

Live This Love

The Your Way Series:

* Finding Home

*Finding Family

*Finding Forever

The Lovers Landing Series

*Where Secrets Are Safe

*No More Secrets

*And The Truth Is ...

*Instead Of Happy

*It Takes A Miracle

One Little Yes

The Great Christmas Tree Mystery

Who I Believe

The Woman at the Top of the Stairs

The Woman Who Climbed A Mountain

The Woman I Found In Me

With One Look

*Also available as an audiobook

THE WOMAN AT THE TOP OF THE STAIRS

Prologue

"You've been arrested! Why did you call me?"

"You're a lawyer."

"I'm an assistant district attorney. I keep people *in* jail, I don't get them out, Dru! I'm sure your family has several defense lawyers on retainer."

"They do, but I need your skills. Please, sit."

"I thought you wanted out of the family business."

"I do and you're going to help make that happen. You owe me."

Drucilla Rae Augustino was the youngest child and only daughter of Michael "Mick" Augustino, the man who had grown the empire his grandfather and father had built into one of the most respected organized crime families on the east coast. When her father died, Dru's oldest brother, Michael, had taken over. He ruled the family and the business with a firm hand. What he lacked in polish and finesse he made up for with strict rules and adherence to said rules —or else.

"Owe you?" Rick Russell had met Dru when she was in her first year of college. At the time, he had one year left in law school and they became fast friends.

"You wouldn't be the up and coming star in the DA's office if I hadn't hidden you in my dorm room the night your entire fraternity decided to make all those bad choices. Your arrest would've ended your political aspirations before they even started."

Rick sighed and narrowed his eyes. "This is the last time you get to use that particular instance to get you out of a jam."

"I don't want out of this jam."

"What?"

"I told Michael he was running too much money through that particular location and he didn't have the receipts to back it up. But does he listen to his little sister? His newly graduated little sister with degrees in accounting *and* finance?"

"With honors," Rick added.

"Yeah, with honors!" Dru said angrily. She blew out an exasperated breath and sat back in her chair.

"How did you get arrested?"

"I happened to be at the store along with two of his right-hand men when the feds came in," she began. "But this is my opportunity and I'm taking it."

"What do you mean?"

"Don't tell me you didn't know I was here. Surely you heard about the raid. I mean, come on, Rick. One of the Augustino kids and two of the top tier managers were arrested and you didn't hear about it in your office?"

"I didn't know you were the family member they nabbed. They're saying someone is going to do time, though, Dru. They aren't messing around."

Dru nodded. "That's why I need you. I'll do the time so those guys can go back to their families, but in return, Michael has to let me go."

Dru shifted as Rick studied her. She knew she must look tired—it had been hours since she'd been arrested and brought down to FBI headquarters for processing. She hoped her dark eyes reflected her focus and the hope she felt. "Have you talked to Michael?"

Dru shook her head. "You were my one phone call."

"You want me to let the two guys go and prosecute you?"

"No. I want a deal."

"Oh! You want a deal. I guess you have something in mind?"

"I do," Dru said with a sly grin. "They should have enough evidence to convict me of money laundering. You convince them to let the others go and keep the sister of the Augustino family leader. That sends a message to all the other crime families and to the public. You'll be the hero!"

"What makes you think Michael will let you do this?"

"He needs those other two men more than me. I'll convince him."

Rick sighed and shook his head. "You could get ten years, Dru."

Dru nodded and gave him a small smile. "I know," she said softly.

"What about your mom?"

"Nick and Stefan's wives will take care of her. She loves them," Dru said flatly. Nick and Stefan were her other brothers. They did what Michael told them to so she knew she couldn't count on them to help her.

She looked down at her hands and thought about all that she was leaving. How she would miss her nieces and nephews and especially her mother, but she couldn't disregard or condone how her family made their money. She'd gone to Michael and begged him to let her go, but he wouldn't hear of it. *"You're an Augustino, just like me. This family and this business is your legacy,"* he'd said to her. *"It's in your blood."*

But it wasn't in her blood. For as long as she could remember, the idea of stealing and strong-arming other people made her sick. Her dad tried to tell her that wasn't what they did. He said they simply helped people get the things they wanted. Sometimes it took a little convincing, he'd said.

During her senior year of college she'd gone to him and explained that she wanted her own life. He'd agreed that when she graduated she was free to find her own job. She had six months to prove herself then he'd consider not bringing her into the family business.

When he died near the end of her senior year in college, she'd told Michael about their agreement. He laughed and said things had changed, claiming they needed her "talents" in the family business. She'd left it alone and decided she would try again when it was closer to graduation.

Two months before graduation she was working an internship at one of the major Wall Street banks in New York City. When she was leaving work one evening she'd found Michael waiting for her in the lobby.

He stressed to her not to get any ideas of taking a job with the bank, or any other financial institution for that matter, because he had a job waiting as soon as she gradu-ated. She protested and they argued. With one last attempt she went to her mother and asked her to intervene. Her mother had tried to help, but Michael explained that he ran the business and Dru was part of it.

Dru knew he'd never let her go unless she had something to offer in exchange. And now, sitting across from Rick, she recognized her chance. She took a deep breath, knowing this was it.

Rick reached across the table and took both of Dru's hands in his. "Are you sure this is the only way?" His expression showed the anguish he felt inside.

Dru bowed her head. "I'm sure."

Rick nodded and squeezed her hands.

"I need something else, Rick."

He looked at her and raised his trimmed eyebrows.

"You have to get them to send me to a federal prison. Far away."

"Do you think Michael will hurt you?"

"No, but I think he'll try to keep up with me."

Rick nodded. "I should be able to do that."

"And I want you to drop my last name."

He gave her a puzzled look.

"I don't really want to go to prison and have someone find out I'm part of the Augustino crime family. It could cause even more problems. That will also help when I'm released. I can start a new life."

"Hmm." He contemplated her request. "I could accidentally drop your last name and put you in the system as Drucilla Rae."

Dru smiled. "Thank you, my friend."

Rick gave her a sad smile.

"You know, Rick, you are a pretty man."

"What?"

"Some woman is going to be very lucky to look at you for the rest of her life."

"Just not you, right?"

"No, I'm more inclined to want your wife." Dru shrugged.

Rick chuckled. "Prison might be fun for you after all."

Dru dropped her head and stared at him.

He laughed. "Too soon?"

His laughter died away and they stared at one another.

"You're sure you can convince him?"

"I'm sure."

Their eyes locked then realization washed over Rick's face. "You have something on him!"

Dru arched one eyebrow and the corners of her mouth turned up.

"Be careful, honey. I know he's your brother, but he's also Michael Augustino."

"I can't live like this, Rick. I'll die," she said with tears in her eyes.

Rick got up and came around the table to embrace her. "I'll help you." After a moment he pulled away and put his hands on her shoulders. "You're sure you can start over as Dru Rae?"

Dru nodded. "I have to."

CHAPTER 1

Eight Years Later

Dru Rae walked out of the federal prison in Fort Worth, Texas. She was excited, nervous, relieved, self conscious, and wary. One big inhale and a slow exhale helped calm her hammering heart.

"Need a ride?"

She whipped her head around at the familiar voice and a huge smile split her face. "Rick! What are you doing here?"

"I couldn't let you do this all on your own." He opened his arms and Dru walked into them.

She sank into the hug and enjoyed the feel of his arms around her for a few moments. It was against the rules to have any physical contact in prison. She could count on both hands the number of hugs she'd had in the past eight years.

When he pulled away he said, "Don't worry, no one knows I'm here. I'm sure you have everything planned out, but come on, let me buy you a milkshake."

"A milkshake?" Dru chuckled.

"I figured the food wasn't great and you deserve a treat. What's better than a milkshake?"

Dru laughed. "Let's go."

Rick drove them to the nearest Dairy Queen. They went inside and placed their orders. When they both had their milkshakes in hand, Rick led them to a table in the back by a big window.

He took a pull on his milkshake and his eyes widened. "Hey, this is really good."

"Really good?" Dru said, slurping on her treat. "This is amazing!"

They both laughed and sat back, enjoying their milkshakes.

Rick took an envelope out of his pocket. "Do you plan on staying here?"

"I'm on parole for a few months and it was a hassle to get it transferred, so I'll be here for a while anyway."

"I think they like to keep you on paper so they know where you are in the beginning."

"Yeah, but I can't believe they paroled me. I don't have any family or anywhere to tell them I'm planning to live. My sentence was eight years plus six months, so why not just keep me?"

"They like to have a point of contact upon release."

"Oh, I get it. A place to start looking for me if I do something wrong."

Rick nodded and took another drink. He slid the envelope over to Dru and she took a moment to look inside, finding a driver's license and a passport.

"How did you do this?"

"I may have contacted the parole department here and traded a few favors."

"Rick, what did you do? I'm trying to disappear, remember?"

Rick held up his hands to calm her. "It's okay. I made sure you had a good parole officer. He is aware of the situation and has set some things up for you."

Dru narrowed her eyes at him and her heart sped up. "Rick, the more people that know, the easier it will be for Michael to find me."

"This guy has an ideal place for you to live and the perfect first job for you, Dru. What were you going to do?"

Dru tried to calm herself. "I know it will be hard to get a job at first. My priority was to open a bank account and have the money I saved transferred to it."

"But you need a place to live to do that. I'm just trying to help you." Rick looked at her with compassion.

Dru smiled. "What, are you going to be my big brother now?"

"No, but you were right. Putting a member of the Augustino family behind bars made me a rockstar. I'm now the number one Assistant to the DA."

"You'll have his job by the time you're forty." Dru grinned.

"That's the plan." He grinned back at her. "Look, Dru, you're my friend and I love you. Please let me help you get started. I promise, no one knows I'm here or why. I'll keep you safe."

Dru drank from her straw and eyed Rick. She knew all he wanted to do was help, but the more people that knew who she was made it easier for her to be found.

"How about this," Rick began. "We have a meeting with your parole officer this afternoon."

"This afternoon? I don't have to report for seventy-two hours."

"Let's see what he has to say. If you don't like the job or the living accommodations, we'll do something else. Okay?"

Dru sighed. This wasn't going the way she'd pictured it, but in reality, nothing had since she was in middle school. "Okay." She smiled at him and took another drink. When the slurping sound that signaled she was at the end of her shake echoed in their corner of the near empty restaurant, her eyes widened. "Hey, thanks for being here. It means a lot."

"It means a lot to me, too." Rick sucked on his straw and the same slurping sound made them both chuckle.

They threw their cups away and on the way to her parole officer's office, she gazed over at Rick.

"Go ahead and ask me how your mom is," he said with a quick glance her way.

"Is she all right?"

"Yeah, Dru, she's okay, but after you left there was a noticeable difference in her."

"What do you mean?"

"She's heartbroken and you can see it in her demeanor."

"You've seen her?"

"Not me, but I hear things. She spends time with her grandchildren and that's when she's happiest. But your going to prison has been hard on her."

Dru sighed. "I miss her so much, but I'm telling you, Rick, if I contact her, Michael will find me and I don't think the years have eased his anger."

"Actually, after you were transferred from New York he did try to find you. He even came to my office."

"Oh shit!"

Rick nodded and Dru noticed his hands were tightly gripping the steering wheel. "When he could tell he wasn't going to find you, everything settled down."

"What do you mean?"

"Well, there haven't been any turf wars or other organizations trying to expand without giving notice. Things have been kind of quiet. Don't get me wrong, they're still doing all their illegal activities, but the violence is minimal. The Augustinos have been very quiet."

"Hmm. I'd be wary, Rick. Peace doesn't last forever when you're trying to make money and control thieves."

"Your observation is duly noted. This is the street where we're supposed to meet your PO," Rick said, turning onto a residential avenue with big houses and manicured lawns.

"I thought we were going to his office?"

"No, he said to turn in the driveway and go around back. Look for 1401."

Dru looked on her side of the street then she pointed. "It should be that one."

Rick turned into the driveway and followed it to the back of the house. There was a fork in the driveway. To the left was an attached garage to the house. Straight ahead was a little house with a carport next to it. There was a car in the carport and a man sitting outside in one of two chairs on the small front porch.

He waved at them and Rick stopped his car behind the one in the carport.

They got out of the car and the man said, "You found it. I'm Wilson Dennison."

Rick walked up and extended his hand. "Rick Russell." He looked over at Dru and smiled. "This is Dru Rae."

"Nice to meet you both. I know this is a strange place to meet, but I thought it would be better than my office. Fewer eyes. Y'all come on in."

Dru and Rick followed him into the small house. They

both sat on the couch and Wilson sat across from them in a chair.

Wilson looked into Dru's eyes and smiled. "I imagine you're feeling a bit overwhelmed."

Dru visibly relaxed. "I am." She thought he had kind eyes and hoped she could trust him.

"I want you to succeed," Wilson said. "Most of these parole and probation plans are set up for the people to fail. I don't want that to happen to you. You can trust me and tell me when anything happens to you. Good or bad. Okay?"

Dru nodded.

"It's easy to hear me say that, but you don't know me. Mr Russell—"

"Rick," Rick interrupted.

Wilson smiled at him. "Rick has filled me in on your special circumstances. I'm the only one in my office who knows who you were. You are now Dru Rae, newly released and ready to be a contributing member to society, living a happy, productive life."

"That certainly sounds good," Rick said as he smiled at Dru.

"Even though you are highly educated, your lack of experience won't get you the job you probably want in the beginning. I have you set up with a staging company."

"A staging company? Do they set up houses for realtors or construction companies?"

"That's right. You may not have noticed, but when you turned into the residential area, there was a shopping center on your right. Shelby's Staging and Style is located there."

"I did see it. That's only a couple of blocks from here."

Wilson nodded. "Shelby and I have worked together for several years. She gives people like you, coming out of prison, a second chance. You can trust her and she, too, wants you to succeed."

"So I would be helping set up houses that are for sale?"

"That's right. Unloading furniture, arranging rooms, those kinds of things."

Dru smiled. "That sounds perfect. It will feel good to do physical work."

"When we talked last week you mentioned you have a place for Dru to live?" Rick asked.

Wilson looked around the room. "This was my daughter's place. She recently graduated from college and has moved to start her career. I've paid rent for the month and I thought it would be a good place for you to start. Let me show you around and you can decide."

They got up and followed him a few steps to the area that was the kitchen.

"This island divides the kitchen from the living area. There's a bedroom with a bathroom through there."

Dru walked through the door and looked around the bedroom and peeked into the bathroom. *This would be perfect,* she thought. It was small, but that's all she needed.

When she walked back into the living area she smiled at Rick.

"Oh, there's a washer and dryer in the closet in the bedroom," Wilson said.

"This is exactly what I need. What about the people that live in the big house?" Dru asked.

"They travel and aren't around much. They won't bother you. All they want is for you to pay the rent. That's it. They like having someone on the property because they are gone a lot."

"They don't mind that I just got out of prison? I swear it feels like 'ex-con' is tattooed on my forehead."

"The lease is in my name, so don't worry about that for now. This is a nice, quiet neighborhood. My daughter loved living here. If you like it here and want to stay after your parole is completed, I can put the lease in your name."

Dru nodded as she surveyed the room.

"It's natural to think everyone is staring at you, but they aren't. Do you have a car?"

"Not yet." Dru stared at Wilson. He'd said to trust him and she decided to take a chance. "I saved money while I was in college in hopes of leaving my family someday. I want to open a bank account this afternoon and start the process of transferring the money. Then I can get a car and..." She looked down at herself then back at Wilson and Rick. "I need clothes."

"We're going shopping after we go to the bank," Rick said.

Dru couldn't believe she'd thought she would walk out of prison today and start a new life by herself. But these two men had other ideas and were ready to help. It was unbelievable and she couldn't quite wrap her head around it.

"I know that look," Rick said. "You'll pay me back when your money gets here."

"But what about the paper trail?"

"Do you think your brother is looking for you?" Wilson asked.

Dru sighed. "I don't know. I have to be alert, though, in case he does. I don't want to put other people in danger."

"Dru, he hasn't looked for you. I had a flag set up on your name in the system. It let me know if anyone was searching for your name under Augustino or Rae."

"As I said before, no one in my office knows who you are," Wilson said. "They think you are just another inmate that's been released and put on my caseload. We don't have to meet in the office for our check-ins. I can meet with you at Shelby's or here."

"Why would you do that? Why are you doing all this?" Dru asked, spreading her arms wide. "It's hard to believe."

"You're brave," Wilson said. "You had a good life and chose to leave it. Not many people would do what you did. If most people don't get along with their family, they move or choose not to talk to them. You went to prison to get away from yours. The least I can do is help you start your new life."

"I told you that you got a good parole officer," Rick said.

Wilson shrugged. "There are a few of us still around."

Dru nodded and sighed. "I don't know how to thank you."

"Sure you do. Go to work, do your job, find something to do that makes you happy in your down time. Rinse and repeat. That's it."

"He means something legal," Rick teased.

Dru glared at him. "I can't believe you said that."

Rick chuckled. "Yeah you can."

"Okay then," Wilson cut in. "Do you have any questions?"

"I'm sure I will after all this sinks in."

"Here's my card with my cell number on it. Call or text me when you get a phone. I'll answer all your questions." Wilson handed Dru a card and also gave one to Rick.

"Here's your key. I'll tell Shelby you'll be at work the day after tomorrow. Will that give you enough time to get your shopping done and settle in? I've found the sooner you start work and get a routine, the better. I've written her number on the back of my card."

Dru flipped the card over and saw the number. "Thank you. I'll get a phone this afternoon."

"Okay. Rick, it was nice to meet you," Wilson said as he shook the other man's hand. "I'll check on you tomorrow, Dru. Welcome to your new life." He gave Dru a kind smile.

After he left Dru looked at Rick. "Is this for real?"

Rick laughed. "You can trust him. He was sincere. Besides, I checked him out."

Dru fell down on the couch and shook her head. "I can't believe I'm finally out."

Rick sat down next to her and put his arm around her. "You're going to have a great life."

"I hope so." She leaned her head over on his shoulder as a few tears ran down her cheeks.

Get The Woman at the Top of the Stairs

Made in the USA
Middletown, DE
06 September 2023

38106231R00201